THE KINGDOM OF ETERNAL SORROW

THE GOLDEN MAGE BOOK ONE

C.G. GARCIA

Fantastical Press

http://CGGarciaAuthor.com
Cover Design by C.G. Garcia
Model Stock Photography by Janna Prosvirina

ISBN-10: 0692529144
ISBN-13: 978-0692529140
Second Paperback Edition

Dedicated to all fantasy readers

ALSO BY C.G GARCIA

Fractured Multiverse
The Supreme Moment
Black Crimson (Blood Fire Chronicles Book One)
*coming soon

Old Souls Trilogy
Old Souls
The Ties That Bind the Soul
The Name Within His Soul *coming soon

The Golden Mage Trilogy
The Man Within the Temple
The Last Stone Cast

Dedicated to all fantasy readers

CHAPTER ONE

There it was again, that strange sensation of fingertips brushing against the back of her neck, a feathery touch lasting for only the space of a breath. Allison McNeal instantly jolted out of her troubled thoughts as she sat in the morning traffic with her younger sister waiting for the light to change. She would have absently dismissed it as nothing more than a wayward strand of hair tickling the back of her neck if it had not already happened dozens of times ever since she had woken up that morning.

Then, as if those ghostly fingers weren't enough, she was once again overwhelmed with the disconcerting feeling of being stared at intently from seemingly every direction, as though she had become the center of attention within a stadium full of hidden eyes. Allison knew, without looking, that none of those eyes belonged to her sister, Katherine, no matter how much the teen had been glaring at her earlier.

No—she had the distinct feeling that whoever or *whatever* the presence, it wasn't just staring out of idle curiosity or even just to get under her skin. It was *studying* her, weighing her, considering her for— something, almost as if somebody had whispered the knowledge, unbidden, into her mind.

As had happened the last time she had sensed the staring, the temperature inside her car had dropped noticeably within the last few seconds. Allison could feel the hairs at the nape of her neck start to rise, and she began to shiver from both the unnatural chill and its implications. It took all of her self-control to prevent herself from shouting out to the air to demand to know who was staring at her. Only the fear of worrying her sister kept her lips firmly sealed.

Instead, she gazed around the interior of the car and into the rearview mirror as discreetly as possible, but as she suspected, neither Katherine nor even the cab driver in the lane beside her were even looking in her direction. Kat was staring out her window as if she was seeing the most fascinating sight in the world, presumably sulking from their earlier argument.

Allison clenched her hands around the steering

wheel and tried to will the feeling away. Yet, no matter how much she wished it, how hard she tried to ignore it, the sensation of being watched persisted. She could almost feel the presence of somebody behind her, almost hear it steadily breathing next to her ear.

It *had* to be a ghost, one that had somehow attached itself to her rather than a building or place, because the alternative—that she had finally cracked after everything she had suffered the last few years—was just too scary and depressing to contemplate.

After enduring the scrutiny through block after block, Allison knew that if it continued any longer, she wouldn't be able to stay quiet and pretend as though nothing was wrong. Those unseen eyes made her feel as if she was once again under the disapproving, fanatical eyes of her stepfather. She *had* to make it/them stop looking at her before she really went mad—or worse, had another one of her panic attacks right there in the middle of driving. It had been a year since her last one, a rather embarrassing situation involving several hundred people at her university that she loathed to remember.

Stop it! she mentally shouted to whatever entity was watching her with such fury that she outwardly shook with the effort.

She was shocked when, a moment later, whatever it was that was spying on her did stop. Her skin no longer crawled with the sensation of eyes scrutinizing her. Even the air around her didn't feel as cold.

Allison raised a pale, shaky hand to rub the back of her neck in an attempt to rid herself of that horrible feeling. She waited breathlessly for a few minutes, waiting for the sensation to return, but it didn't. She exhaled slowly and gave a mental sigh of relief.

She glanced over at Katherine and marveled that her little sister hadn't noticed that anything was amiss at all, not even to complain that it was too cold inside the car. Although it was September, it was still pretty hot, and both girls were dressed in short sleeves and shorts.

Or she's too busy sulking and giving me the silent treatment to have noticed.

So shaken by the experience, when they finally reached James Park, Allison's knees nearly buckled when she climbed out of the car because her legs were trembling so badly. Luckily, Kat was still sulking and not looking at her, so she didn't witness Allison's near fall.

To make matters worse, Allison instantly saw that an unusual amount of people littered the park, a family reunion in all probability from the varying ages all wearing the same bright orange t-shirts. They looked like a scene from a bad G-rated movie. Loud voices and the wails and laughter of children reached her ears even from the parking lot.

Allison sighed. *I should have expected this to happen. After everything that's been happening to me this morning— Kat suddenly showing up at the crack of dawn in tears and phantom eyes staring at me from God-only-knows-where—I shouldn't be surprised at all. Oh well, so much for my hopes of a nice, private chat under the shade.*

"It's usually a lot quieter here," Allison said apologetically, breaking the tense silence between them. "Why don't we just take a walk for a while along the jogging trail, instead."

The trail was located on the far side of the park, so the long walk over would give them ample time to talk—if her sister ever decided to talk to her again.

When Kat merely shrugged in indifference, Allison sighed again and began to walk along one of the many paved walkways towards the beginning of the trail as Kat followed silently behind. A light breeze blew over her, bringing with it a faint smell of impending rain. She glanced up at the sky with a frown, but it was almost completely clear.

Shrugging, Allison glanced over at Kat as the younger girl finally quickened her pace to walk beside her. Kat was walking with her head bent low, her hands crammed into the pockets of her shorts. She was the very picture of defeat. Allison suddenly felt ashamed that she had automatically assumed Kat was merely sulking.

Kat probably thinks I'm really angry with her about possibly bringing her dad's wrath down on me if he finds out she's here with me after sneaking out of her house this morning. She hasn't spoken a word to me in over twenty minutes, and that's definitely a record for her!

She suddenly felt like crying.

Yeah. Some big sister I'm turning out to be, Allison thought glumly, *but how can I make her understand the situation from my point of view? God, why does everything always have to be so complicated?*

As they walked in silence across the grass, Allison suddenly noticed in alarm that it was *too* quiet in the park. Allison glanced around and was surprised to see only a handful of people strolling through the park, even less sitting on the benches that had been completely filled only ten minutes earlier, and only a couple of families picnicking under the trees. The reunion group had also conspicuously vanished. It was as though she had only hallucinated the crowded scene earlier.

Even so, the changed scene wasn't the thing that had her nervously wondering if they shouldn't just turn around and head back to the car. Though one of the reasons why she loved this particular park was because of its serenity, never once in the dozens of times she had strolled through it had it been as utterly soundless as it was at the moment.

No birds sang. No insects buzzed. She couldn't even pick out a tendril of conversation. The wind had even stopped blowing. The whole park had succumbed to an unnerving, preternatural stillness that suddenly sent an icy chill down Allison's spine. All of nature seemed to be holding its breath for a reason unknown to only her and Kat.

What the hell—

Then before she could even truly begin to freak out about the abrupt silence, everything fell back to normal. A few sparrows began to sing at the same time a cool breeze began to gently whip through her hair. A few sounds of faint conversation even reached her ears from the surrounding park.

That's odd, Allison thought. She half-expected to feel those invisible eyes focused on her again; they certainly fit in with the strangeness she had just witnessed, but she didn't feel them at all.

A few seconds later, she laughed aloud, to her sister's alarm.

I'm just being silly. This issue with Kat is really doing a number on my wild imagination. I'm starting to see shadows where there aren't any. Just because the birds stopped singing for a moment doesn't mean something strange has happened.

"Allie, what's wrong?" Kat suddenly asked anxiously, her voice jarring Allison from her thoughts. "Why'd you laugh? You look like someone just told you the world's ending, but instead of crying, you're laughing!"

"Nothing," Allison assured her, perhaps a little too quickly. "Nothing at all. I just suddenly had a funny, random thought—but enough about that." She regarded her sister's alarmed expression and smiled apologetically at her. "I was also trying to decide how I'm ever going to manage to make you understand why you can't live here with me just yet. That probably explains my doomsday expression."

Might as well jump back into the argument so we can figure this whole mess out. After all, she mused, *Kat can only risk staying here with me for a day or so, and lord knows when I'll get to see her again. I don't want to waste this rare time together!*

"And here I was hoping you might've changed your mind," Kat said a bit bitterly. "Okay, let's hear it."

"You've only just turned seventeen," Allison explained gently, the bitterness in her sister's voice making her heart clench painfully, "still a minor, and he has sole custody. Your dad could easily accuse me of taking a minor across state lines without his permission and have me arrested for kidnapping or something. You know the old bastard would do it, too. After all, we're blasphemers, unbelievers. He's been dying for the excuse to make Mom and me suffer some more for trying to take you away from him and all his craziness the first time."

Kat opened her mouth to speak, a mulish look on her face, but Allison cut her off.

"I know, that emancipation thing you started to tell me about earlier before my roommate wandered in."

"It could work," Kat insisted. "I've only got eleven more months until I'm eighteen, anyway."

Allison looked at her sadly. "You don't think I haven't considered it before, that it was the first thing I looked into once you turned sixteen and had a better shot of finding a job?"

Kat stopped in her tracks. "You *have?*" she exclaimed incredulously.

Allison stopped and turned to face her. "Of course I did. Don't you think I would have done everything I could to find a loophole around the custody problem that didn't involve actual kidnapping or for us to have a million dollars to spend on legal fees?"

"Then why didn't you ever tell me about it?" she asked bewilderedly.

"Because—while in theory it sounds like the answer to all our problems, becoming an emancipated minor isn't likely to happen. For that to be granted, you need to be able to prove to the court that you have the ability to support yourself, and that doesn't mean living jobless at your sister's tiny apartment with two other starving college students who can barely make the rent. You would have to do everything back in Cedar Ridge, anyway. Plus, you'll still have to go to school and follow the child labor laws. That alone should be reason enough for you, but from the look on your face, I see that you still aren't convinced."

"I can get a job," she said stubbornly.

"Enough to pay for your own apartment?" Allison countered. "Living expenses are steep everywhere, not just California. Why do you think I have to live with two other girls just to make ends meet? If I still lived with Mom, even if she wasn't so sick and could work, we would've still been struggling. The judge will never approve you, even if you were somehow lucky enough to get a different judge other than your dad's old buddy. Please, *please* try to hold on for a few more months."

Allison winced as she saw her sister's face crumble after having the last of her hopes extinguished. *What have I done?*

Before she could even think of a comforting reply, Allison flinched and actually backed up a step as Kat's face suddenly transformed from a look of despair to white-hot fury.

"Don't you *get it*!" Kat exclaimed angrily through clenched teeth. "I didn't risk stealing some of his money and sneaking out in the middle of the night to take a bus halfway across the country because the old bastard's planning on sending me to just any old stupid missionary camp for the year. It's like one of those behavioral wilderness programs rich parents are always sending their kids to "correct" their behavior, only it's a million times worse because it's run by those cultists!"

She fisted her hands at her sides, her entire body shaking, she was so angry. "I'll run away!" she threatened. "If I can't stay here with you, then I'll just run away and live on the streets! I'd rather die in the gutter than be forced to go to that *Village of the Damned* place!"

"Kat! You can't—"

Allison broke off abruptly when her voice sounded way louder than it should have. The sudden silence that had fallen over the park earlier was happening again, even more noticeable now than before because she had been talking this time. It wasn't just her imagination. Something very strange really was happening. Having that same eerie silence fall over the park within minutes of each occurrence was just too much of a coincidence.

She turned to a red-faced Kat and whispered, afraid to disturb the unnatural silence, "Kat, do you notice anything strange about the park right now?"

Looking suspiciously at her, Kat demanded rather loudly, "What the hell are you talking about? And why are you whispering?"

Allison blinked in surprise at the coldness in her sister's voice. She opened her mouth to reply but quickly shut it when she saw the icy glare Kat directed at her.

"You're just trying to change the subject so you don't have to deal with what I said, aren't you?" she accused. "You don't believe that I would really do—"

Her voice broke off abruptly, the pissed off look on her face melting into first, confusion, then alarm. A wave of relief washed through Allison at her sister's reaction. She *noticed*. If Kat was hearing, or rather *not* hearing, the same thing, then Allison couldn't be crazy. What was happening was real and not just in her head.

For a long moment, Kat stood frozen and listened, seemingly not even daring to breathe as if she, too, was scared to disturb that unnatural silence. Her eyes had slowly widened in what could have been fear or wonder, but the tremble in her voice as she spoke pointed towards the former.

"The silence," Kat said nervously, her anger long forgotten. "The silence is what you're talking about isn't it? It's not—*right.*"

"Exactly," Allison confirmed, more to herself than to her sister. "Birds should be singing, people talking and laughing, a breeze blowing, but they all stopped when things got heated between us. That's why I noticed it. My voice suddenly sounded ten times louder than it should have, even raised in panic. It's as if nature is expecting something unnatural or catastrophic to happen, like the animals they say sense earthquakes days before they happen in California. They sudden begin to act strange, and I think we can qualify what's happening right now as strange."

"Are you sure that the reason why the birds stopped singing wasn't because of my shouting?" Kat asked. "That could've scared them into silence, couldn't it?"

"Maybe so," Allison answered without conviction, "but the breeze also stopped. Your shouting wouldn't have affected *that.* This isn't the first time this has happened, either. Several minutes ago, I noticed that everything was *too* quiet, even for this particular park, but I dismissed it as nothing, a coincidence. Now I'm not so sure."

Allison paused for a moment, torn between

wanting to confide her earlier feelings of being watched with her sister, but then afraid of Kat's reaction to something that sounded like no more than a case of paranoia. *But I need to know if she felt the staring, too, or if that part really was me making something out of nothing. If she also felt it, then maybe it has something to do with what's happening now.*

"Kat, I'm going to tell you something that may seem as if I've finally gone off the deep end and am drowning alongside your dad, but just hear me out before you laugh in my face."

Kat eyed her with something akin to fear, shifting her feet uneasily and glancing over her shoulder once as if expecting an attack before she nodded reluctantly.

Feeling somewhat foolish, Allison began, "All morning, ever since your pounding woke me up, I've been feeling as if someone was watching me. I ignored it at first, thinking it was just my imagination, then it kept happening over and over until I could actually feel something like fingertips brushing against the back of my neck. It made me feel like I was under your dad's gaze all those times when he was deciding if I should be punished or not—you know, small and helpless. The last time was in the car. That's why I was so quiet. I'm sorry if it seemed like I was totally ignoring you just to spite you, but I was just trying to figure out what was happening to me. What I want to know is if you've been experiencing something similar to that?"

Kat didn't answer her right away. Her expression was thoughtful, and Allison wasn't sure if it wouldn't have been better if Kat had laughed in her face. Was she remembering something? Allison shifted her weight from foot to foot nervously in the suffocating silence, waiting for her sister to speak with the air of a defendant waiting for a jury's verdict.

"Well, I haven't felt like anyone was watching me," Kat finally replied quietly, "but now that you mention the ride over here, I did notice that it got cold all of a sudden. In fact, I was just about to ask if your air-conditioner was being wonky, but the cold just suddenly went away."

"I noticed that, too," Allison whispered.

"This is getting really creepy, Allie," Kat said uneasily, her eyes flitting around the park. "Let's get out of here. I don't care where we go, as long as it's far away from here!"

"I agree."

Allison turned around and began retracing her steps across the park, Kat walking so close that their hips occasional brushed. However, she only managed to walk a few feet, when without warning, a brilliant light as potent as looking directly into the sun flashed a couple of steps in front of them.

Kat was instantly struck mid-scream with a force so great that it caused her to fly back about twenty feet, landing in a crumbled heap at the foot of a tree, while at the same time, Allison was brutally knocked to her knees as that same force hit her legs, crying out as pain reverberated up her legs from landing hard on both kneecaps and momentarily blinded by the searing light that had seemed to materialize out of thin air.

What the hell...? Allison's mind echoed those words a split-second before she felt a violent tug on her body that jerked her towards the source of that brilliant flash, and half-blinded, she frantically dug her fingers into the moist ground and hung on for dear life.

***

Kat cried out in shock as an unexpected flash of light blinded her, and a tremendous force, like the fist of God, crashed into her body, flinging her back though the air. She squeezed burning, tear-filled eyes shut a split-second before she felt the bone-crushing impact of her body slamming unmercifully to the ground. A blinding pain shot up the length of her arm from her forearm, feeling as though it had been bent in half.

She choked on her scream, her mind instantly filling with a blackness that promised a painless oblivion.

No! Gritting her teeth, Kat fought off the welcoming darkness and the bile rising to her throat. Had a bomb just gone off? Allie—where was Allie? She opened her eyes wide and blinked them rapidly to try to clear the colorful lights of blue, red, green, and yellow that clouded her vision.

Once she had focused her blurry vision enough to see the scene before her, she gasped in horror when she finally spotted her sister. Where the flash of light first appeared now stood a luminous, circular light, undulating like small waves across a lake and reflecting every color of the spectrum that was visible to the human eye and even some that Kat's mind couldn't make sense of, that made her head hurt, and the darkness already threatening her with oblivion expand when she tried to focus on them. The mind-bending phenomenon appeared as though someone or something had torn a hole in the very fabric of the world, allowing the illumination of another world to shine through.

However, the light was not what horrified Kat. What really turned her blood cold was the sight of Allison and the fact that half of her body had already disappeared into that rippling brilliance. She had dug her fingers into the grass and earth in front of her and was clinging with all her might, sobbing in terror, and desperately calling out Kat's name.

"Allie! *No!*" Kat heard herself scream as if she was listening to someone else.

As Allison's body abruptly lurched back, she frantically clawed at the grass, at the earth, *anything* to prevent herself from being sucked into that rip of light, Kat struggled to sit up, trying to unsuccessfully ignore the bleached-white bone that had splintered out through the skin of her arm and now lay exposed in a mixture of gushing blood and torn muscle.

"Katherine! For God's sake, *help me!*" Allison screamed hysterically as she slipped farther back into the rip, clawing desperately for anything to prevent the light from swallowing more of her body than it had already claimed.

Trying to ignore the pain that seemed to grow more unbearable by the second, Kat staggered to her feet and almost immediately nearly collapsed, weakened from both shock and the alarming amount of blood flowing from her compound-fractured arm. She swayed dizzily for a second or two before she regained enough of her balance to keep her feet.

Cradling her mangled arm with the other, the teen stumbled as quickly to the aid of her sister as the threatening blackness and weakness allowed. Time drastically slowed until Kat felt as though she was stumbling against the high-powered current of a rain-swollen river. Allison seemed to be miles away. The world had become as surreal as a dream.

That light could suck me in too! her mind screamed frantically at her, but she ignored it. Her entire being was focused on reaching Allison before that light swallowed her whole.

Then Allison suddenly lost her grip on the moist earth and was drawn, screaming, back into the light and the unknown. In a last frantic attempt to save her sister, Kat dove forward, ignoring her injured limb totally, and reached out her good arm to snatch at Allison's frantically scrabbling fingers.

When Kat hit the ground, a wave of unbearable pain flashed up her arm and through her body simultaneously with the realization that her fingertips had maddeningly only brushed the tips of her doomed sister's. This time she went willingly into the black oblivion that awaited her, taking with her the terrible image of her sister's face twisted with terror as she disappeared into the mysterious rip of light and the distant sound of footsteps pounding towards her. A last fleeting thought comforted her as she lost consciousness, assuring her that all she had just witnessed had to have been a nightmare and not reality.

CHAPTER TWO

Disorientation greeted Allison the moment the blinding light had completely pulled her body into its shimmering chaos by an unexplainable force that had seemed to grab at her body almost hungrily with its greedy, invisible hands. She immediately felt the light, itself, as a presence, a living entity. It surrounded her, penetrated her entire body with a heat that was almost unbearable, a fiery ocean ready to drown her, to devour her. The essence of the light completely saturated her very atoms, forcing them to pull away from each other until she no longer had a physical body and only the separated particles remained.

Although she was merely a seemingly infinite amount of detached atoms, she still felt an essence of herself—her thoughts and emotions—still aware and attached to every one of those microscopic units that had once been her body. It was as if her atoms were the grains of sand that made up the beach and the light, the incoming tide that saturated it.

Terrified, Allison tried to scream, but in her present state, it was impossible. Nor could she hear anything while inside that world of white-hot light she "saw" only through her mind's eye. She could only feel the sole emotion of fear radiating throughout her entire being.

I'm dead, she thought frantically, grasping at anything that sounded even remotely rational to her frightened mind that helped to explain what was happening to her. Death seemed the only logical explanation, though her mind instantly railed at the thought of having her life so abruptly and inexplicable snuffed out.

Then terror became madness.

Without warning, her newly separated atoms rushed forward within that strange realm of light at an impossible speed, weaving in and out of perceived bright showers and pulsing swirls of light that were filled with every color of the spectrum and even a few that weren't ordinarily visible to human eyes.

Reason completely left Allison at that point of her preternatural journey, along with her conscious awareness of everything that she was experiencing. It was as if she had lost her abilities to think, feel, to function at all, while she was in her current state of being. All she had were momentary images of her surroundings and places she had never seen flashing rapidly in her mind like the incoherent dream images of a fevered mind.

Then phantom voices broke through the silence. They seemed to surround her, to penetrate her, feeding information into her being so rapidly that she could not grasp any of it. She was no longer Allison, but only a cluster of cognate particles pulsing with their own radiant life.

Mercifully, the trek ended almost as quickly as it had begun. Her separated atoms violently combined once again in a whirl of glistening chaos to reform her physical body. A blinding, white light illuminated her entire world, and Allison soon found herself once again alert and gasping desperately for breath as if she had abruptly been revived after drowning.

Dizzy and lightheaded, Allison realized with a start that she was standing on firm ground, and her knees were beginning to buckle. With a cry of dismay, she crumbled to the ground.

Lying sprawled out on her stomach in what felt and smelled like grass, her face pressed uncomfortable into the thick growth, Allison finally noticed that a vast darkness embraced her instead of the brilliant light of that strange realm.

Dear God, I'm blind!

Panic threatened to wash over her for a minute or two before she noticed that she had yet to even open her eyes. If circumstances had not been what they were, she would have burst out laughing at her absentmindedness, but she only sighed inwardly with extreme relief that the experience had not blinded her.

Allison cautiously lifted her head, which felt as if it weighed a thousand pounds, and gingerly opened her eyes.

Immediately, she wished that she had just kept them shut. The world spun aimlessly before her in an array of greens, blues, and flashing yellows, causing an insistent pounding to begin in her temples and her stomach to lurch. Allison moaned miserably and squeezed her eyes tightly shut until the drums in her head ceased to beat so strongly.

God, what happened? Did I just experience death? No—that can't be right. I'm still breathing, and my body hurts too damned much for me to be dead. Maybe it was a near-death experience—

Her thoughts froze as the sound of whispering abruptly reached her ears as if a couple dozen people had suddenly surrounded her. Her eyes flew open again at the sound, and she hastily rose. This time the pounding in her head did not resume, and though she still felt a bit dizzy and woozy, the world was no longer spinning in circles before her as though she was riding an out-of-control merry-go-round.

It can't be—

There was no circle of curious onlookers surrounding her, nor was anyone in sight, but that wasn't what had her staring dumbly with rapidly widening eyes at the scene before her. She knew within a heartbeat that she was no longer in the park, or for that matter, in California. What she saw before her— her mind stubbornly refused to believe.

A vast, highly intimidating forest with a species of trees that she had never seen replaced the cypress and pines that had dotted the landscape before that oval light had appeared out of nowhere to claim her.

These trees were enormous—larger even than the familiar redwood trees of California, but their size was not the main characteristic of them that had caught her eye. It was the appearance of the peculiar structure of the limbs and the strangeness of the leaves they sported. Bent at unnatural angles in every possible direction imaginable, the trunk and branches of these trees reminded her immensely of the Okinawan *bonsai* tree one of her roommates kept in their living room.

"It's almost as if someone multiplied the size of

that little tree by a hundred," Allison muttered wondrously under her breath.

That's where the resemblance to the *bonsai* tree ended and the unfamiliarity began. The leaves—if they were in fact leaves—were a shade of green so deep that they were almost black. From where she sat, the leaves appeared to be like the blossoms of a monstrous rose that had mutated to be ten times its normal size. Hundreds of these rose-like leaves littered the many twisted branches of the trees.

On their own accord, her eyes darted from the trees to the ground. She gasped in surprise. What she had believed was grass when she had felt it earlier, was in a sense, *not* grass as she knew. It had three times the width of ordinary crab grass and was a pale green in comparison to the green-black of the leaves above.

It was then that Allison noticed that something in the air was—wrong. It smelled heavily of nature, a scent unfamiliar to her city-bred nose, but that was not the reason for her sense of wrongness. Some essential element was missing, something she could not quite grasp completely. It even tasted different.

This can't be happening! Where in God's name am I?

As Allison glanced wildly around in the vicinity of where she sat, she noticed that she seemed to be in a small clearing within the forest that was no more than fifty yards wide. There were no visible paths emerging from the trees that suggested that anyone had ever visited this particular clearing, and she didn't know whether to feel relieved or distressed.

She squinted up into the sky and instantly cried out in shock at what she saw. Not one, but *two* suns radiated down upon her. One was high in the sky, about twice as small as Earth's sun, but just as blinding. The other was barely rising over what little of the horizon she could see through the gaps in the trees. She noisily released a breath she hadn't realized she was holding and put her hands over her eyes to childishly block out the scene that was right out of a sci-fi movie.

I didn't see that—dear God, I couldn't have seen that—

While she had been observing the alienness of her new surroundings, Allison had completely forgotten about the faint whispers that initially had caused her to open her eyes and sit up in alarm. They now returned to her, a little more audible than before, and also, a little more insistent for her attention.

Allison immediately dropped her hands from her eyes and scrambled to her feet, whirling around from left to right still a bit unsteadily to try to locate their source but spotting no one once again. There was only the forest in every direction as far as the eye could see. The whispers seemed to be coming from the air directly around her.

—or the inside of my head—

She shuddered uneasily and tried to banish that last, unnerving thought from her mind, but it persisted no matter how hard she tried to shake it. It was then, as her mind was frantically trying to find another line of thinking, that she remembered Katherine. Had she been sucked into the light as well? Allison was a bit alarmed that she couldn't remember anything between the time she had first seen Kat running towards her and right after she had been pulled completely into the light.

"Kat!" she shouted urgently. Her voice sounded small and weak against the magnitude of the trees that loomed all around her.

Only the whispers filled her ears.

"Kat! Are you here? Please *answer* me!" she shouted again through a half-choked sob.

Still nothing.

Realizing that she was alone, a blow that was as affective as a fierce kick to her stomach, Allison began to cry earnestly in fear and despair. She didn't know where she was or understand how being sucked into a light had brought her here. All she knew was that this strange forest she now stood sobbing in was completely foreign to her, and the whispering she heard was growing frighteningly louder with every breath she took.

She sucked in several slow, deep breaths in an effort to stop the tears as she stared out into the forest, convinced that the voices she heard originated somewhere far back within the thicket. One minute, two, then she abruptly felt something inside her head shatter as if it was a mirror shattering into a thousand slivers of glass after striking the ground. There was no pain.

Before she could contemplate what the odd sensation could have been, the incoherent babbling of a million voices suddenly swelled up in her mind, filling it with a shrillness and volume that was impossible to bear. It was as though she was wearing headphones and someone had abruptly turned up the volume to an unholy maximum.

Allison screamed in sudden agony and fell to her knees, instinctively throwing her hands over her ears in a vain attempt to silence the infinite amount of voices that seemed to be booming all around her. A warm stickiness began to run through her fingers. Still, the voices came, swelling in volume and frequency with every passing second.

Screaming terribly at the top of her lungs, Allison's mind mercifully shut down a few moments later, no longer capable of bearing the trauma and pain those voices caused. She fell over onto her face for the second time that day, consumed into the darkness of an unfeeling unconsciousness that still harbored the endless amount of voices that continued to swell in her mind.

CHAPTER THREE

W histling the tune of an old ballad he loved, Aidric gazed lazily up at the sky through the tree branches high above. Not a single cloud loomed in sight, which meant that this time there wasn't even a remote chance that he would be caught in an unexpected downpour and drenched as he had been the previous quarter-moon.

He still seethed with the indignation of it. He had been propped up against a tree in his favorite spot along the Lake of Tears, reading a newly discovered spellbook that King Diryan had given him and much like today, greatly enjoying what little free time he had been given away from his ever-demanding duties.

Not even a flash of lightning or a crack of thunder had sought fit to warn him of the incoming storm before the Thrones above decided to let loose a rather nasty downpour that had his robes drenched within beats. He still had not lived down all the jokes that had resulted from his arriving at the palace resembling a drowned snowbird.

If only I was a weather-mage, then I wouldn't have to worry about something as trivial as a little rain, Aidric thought slyly, urging Shadow, his midnight-black steed, to slacken his pace as he trotted along the well-worn path that snaked its way through the thick trees to the banks of the lake.

It was a beautiful day, perfect for relaxing under his tree with the warm, morning suns soothing his tired limbs. All around him, nature also seemed to notice the beauty of the day. The air resonated with the sweet, harmonious voices of the birds, singing their endless melodies until all of them interwove into an enchanting chorus that radiated the happiness of the world. Even the trees seemed to wave their limbs in a cheerful dance in the cool breeze.

Aidius, what I would give to have a maiden accompanying me to my spot right now, he thought wistfully. *The Thrones know that I have been without a lover for far too long.*

Aidric sighed irritably at that lonely thought, wondering, as always, why he insisted on torturing himself with that particular thought over and over again, especially on a day so beautiful that it demanded only cheerful thoughts. He seldom had time for a personal life after his mage duties to Lamia, his beloved kingdom. The irregular hours he kept and all his abrupt departures during emergencies often turned people away from him in frustration.

When Aidric first announced to the kingdom that he had achieved the title of a mage after years of study under Othos, then the Mage-general of Lamia and also King Diryan's personal court mage, women by the dozens flocked around him, competing amongst themselves for his favor. He had enjoyed their attention immensely.

The mystery of his mage powers made him extremely fascinating to them, and he had them immediately enthralled when he began to perform little feats for them with his magic. The fact that he had a handsome face didn't hurt either. He'd had no trouble finding a lover during those first few moons as the new mage at court. His popularity also raised several notches when it became known publically a few moons later that he was King Diryan's choice to succeed Mage-general Othos upon his death.

Nevertheless, Aidric could never keep a lover longer than a few moons. The ladies he courted would realize how much of his time his duties to the kingdom required. Some even went several moons between the times they would see him. It seemed as if he was always being summoned off in the middle of the night to the aid of a neighboring kingdom that was under attack, and the battles sometimes continued on for several moons.

Frustrated and unhappy, they always eventually gave up on him and moved on to other lovers, leaving him alone with his guilt over the fact that his duties would always have to come first over his own life and the life of those he cared about.

Then there had been Alina, a maiden as charming as she was beautiful. She never minded his long tours of duty, making sure that they made the most of the time they *did* have together. She had seemed a gift sent straight from Seni during those difficult times. Aidric had never been as happy as he was during the time Alina and he had shared. Then the world had come crashing down on him. But no—he would not think of those times, would not torment himself. He *refused* to think of them.

As if brooding ever helped anyone, he thought wryly. *Selwyn would hang me from my toenails if he knew I was chasing my own tail again after that magnificent lecture he gave me over how I'll find the right maiden someday. Right maiden, indeed. What utter nonsense! Look what my last "right maiden" did to me! Sel already has Raya, so what does he know of loneliness?*

Aidric instantly felt guilty. He gave himself a

mental kick in the backside for that last whine as he continued down the grassy path with only the trees as his companions.

"I should be relaxing after all," he announced to the trees as if he expected them to reply. Shadow whickered as if in agreement.

However, fate had other plans for him. Almost in the same instant, his mage senses awoke screaming. His mind instinctually began to probe the area before he could even gasp in surprise. What it encountered—Aidius—it was power that hit his mind-probe with all the subtlety of a landslide!

As he hastily wrenched his mind away, Shadow reared violently, causing Aidric's teeth to clamp together painfully. He wrestled with the steed for a few endless moments before he was finally able to settle Shadow down enough to take action.

He banished the spellbook he had been leafing through into his magical storage plane for safekeeping and quickly strengthened the defensive magical shields about his body before turning cautiously towards the south where the origin of the power source was like a beacon of raging fire to his mage senses.

Aidric could neither see anyone, nor sense anything else hidden amongst the trees that the power could have originated from, yet, he knew *something* was out there. He could even feel a faint glimmer of human emotion, but it was too distant, too vague to decipher. Praise Seni that it was not a Summoning at least! The magical energies were not quite right.

Though a great deal of unease began to wash through him, Aidric also felt a familiar rush of excitement at the thought of investigating the alien power source. What manner of creature contained such power as to have the ability to both cross the Lamian border, and to also have successfully kept those powers hidden from the suspicious eyes and senses of the mages assigned to the border station?

Cursing as he realized the implications, Aidric dismounted and hurriedly tethered Shadow to the nearest tree. Then with his heart pounding, he carefully directed another Probe of Inquiry from his mind into the forest to see if he could touch the mind of whoever or whatever was recklessly sending out such radiant vibes of power for any soul with mage powers to perceive.

Several hundred handspans into the forest, his mind-probe suddenly touched the mind of his target, the raw power slamming into his mental shields. He instantly drew his mind back as if burned, but that brief touch had been enough from him to sample the "flavor" of the mind, that the one he sought was a woman.

There had been no sense of startlement, no indication at all that she had even sensed that her mind had just been touched. That was a good sign. If she was not blocking her thoughts from intrusion, then he would be able to easily steal the thoughts directly from her mind with her being none the wiser.

I wonder if she even realizes how stupid it is to leave her mind so completely unguarded. Or— His thoughts darkened. *Could this mindlessness be a trap?*

Aidric cautiously touched her mind again, this time bracing for the onslaught of power, and slowly searched for anomalies along the surface as her power raged against his mental shields. Then without warning, something clicked in her head, a light *thump* against his mental "hand," and a blast of power in the form of a piercing scream crashed into his mind shields, instantly shattering not only them, but his bodily shields as well.

The sheer blast of her power knocked Aidric flat, his back hitting the ground so violently that it drove the air from his lungs. As he lay stunned and gasping, her screams began to fill his head at an intolerable volume.

Aidric half-choked, half-cried out himself, reflexively throwing his hands over his ears in a foolish attempt to block out the sound of her terrible screams that dripped with fear and agony. He knew that the screams were purely mental. He only had to reset the shields to his mind to silence them.

But he couldn't. The concentration he needed to rebuild the shields was utterly impossible as her shrill screams ripped excruciatingly through his mind. Aidric writhed on the ground and moaned, feeling as if his head was going to explode any moment. Then between one beat to the next, the screams within his head swelled to a new, impossible height, and his screams were now a match for the ones in his head.

Panic threatened to overwhelm him. His mind was being ripped to shreds!

Then, just as suddenly as the screams began, they cut off as if someone had abruptly encased his mind within a spell of silence. The silence was as profound and as unnerving as an unexpected clap of thunder on a cloudless day.

Aidric slowly brought his hands away from his ears, his heart pounding to the point of pain and gasping for air. He had completely expected them to be sticky with blood, but they were clean. For a moment, he could only lay where he had fallen in stunned silence. What in Seni's name had happened?

Only after sensing that the immediate danger had passed did he slowly climb to his feet and begin to brush off the soil and dead leaves that clung to his robes. The mundane exercise helped to calm his nerves a bit and to slow his racing heart back to an almost normal pace.

He then immediately rebuilt his mind and bodily shields, still visibly shaken on how the unknown woman's single blast of power had instantly shattered his strongest shields on contact.

No one had ever done that.

By Aidius, what in the six hells was that all about? Aidric thought wildly, his eyes still widened with shock. *That power—*

His head whirled towards the direction he had sensed her. He *had* to find her. If she proved to be an ally, a mage such as she would be an enormous asset to King Diryan's magical defense. It might even be the very thing they needed to tip the scales enough to end their current silent war with Mihr.

Unless that whole episode was actually a deliberate attack, a test of her abilities, and she has already transported herself out of Lamia—

That disturbing thought sent Aidric crashing through the forest like a deer with the hunt at its heels, weaving skillfully between the trees whose lower limbs maddeningly seemed to grab at his clothes with their prickly branches in an attempt to prevent him from going any farther.

A few beats later, he skidded to a halt as he entered a small clearing of thick grass about the diameter of ten strides that he had never seen before. It vibrated strongly with residual magic similar to that of Lamia's Mage-field but on a much smaller scale.

Before he could even puzzle over the strangeness of the place, Aidric's eyes fell on the body of a woman. She lay sprawled face down on the forest floor, her body still and twisted in a painfully unnatural position, appearing to be dead at first glance. Sunlight streamed all around her, enveloping her body in a faint glow that was both disturbing and beautiful to behold. He cautiously invoked his Inner-sight and saw a small cloud of residual Mage-field particles hovering about a finger-span above her body, causing a mystical illusion around her of tiny, shimmering crystals.

Aidric edged over to her cautiously, an incantation ready on his lips for defense should she suddenly awaken and strike out at him, but she didn't so much as twitch a finger. Once he reached her side, he got his first good look at the woman—and cried out in shock, if not a little fear.

Aidius!

Her hair was *gold!* What he had first assumed was a patch of sunlight surrounding her head, was in fact a long mane of golden hair. No mortal of any of the many races of Seni's World possessed hair of that hue. Yet, here lay a maiden before his very eyes that indisputably had hair of gold. The only thing that even suggested that hair that color was possible was an old Lamian legend of a prophecy that many believed—and feared—would one day come to pass.

This cannot be possible—what in the name of Seni could this possibly mean? Has the legendary Golden Mage actually come?

Aidric suddenly felt dizzy as he continued to stare down at the woman as if she was Aidius, himself. She wore very peculiar clothing, a top and bottom piece that appeared to be undergarments of some sort but made of materials he could not name. One cautious touch of the thick, deep blue material that indecently hugged her thighs confirmed their strangeness.

Although alone, he couldn't help feeling embarrassed at having observed the nakedness of her legs. No lady of Lamia ever dared to show as much flesh as was now visible on the lady before him—well, at least no lady of *decent* society.

He knelt down beside her and gently rolled her body over onto her back so he could view her face. Only then did he see her youth. She couldn't have lived more than twenty summers. He frowned as he noted a trickle of blood flowing from both her nose and ears—a telltale sign of magical trauma to the brain. It was a condition common to mages, especially the apprentice-mages. He, himself, had fallen victim to the condition on more occasions than he could count. Rest and a potion or two would easily remedy the damage.

Nevertheless, even in her disarrayed state, she was intoxicatingly beautiful—just as the prophecy claimed, he suddenly remembered, but that was hardly proof, no matter that she was more beautiful than any maiden he had ever laid eyes upon. Aidric wistfully wondered what color her eyes were, resisting the urge to pull her eyelids up for a peek. He imagined them to be a shade that he had never seen on another, just like her golden locks.

Perhaps rose—

A flash of light on her wrist suddenly caught his attention, jarring him out of his ridiculous musings. He gave his head a sharp shake. He must still be in shock.

Aidric cautiously bent over to examine the source of the flash. The light proved to only be a reflection off the glass-like surface of a strange piece of what he thought was a bracelet that she wore loosely on her wrist.

He gingerly lifted her wrist closer to his face so he could get a better look and immediately dropped her arm in alarm when something inside the glass centerpiece moved. He backed away suspiciously from the object and sent a Probe of Inquiry down at the object to try to discern if the source of the movement had anything to do with magic. What his probe encountered left him puzzled.

It isn't magical, Aidric thought in confusion. *There is energy about it, but it isn't Mage-field or life-force energy. What, then, could possibly be the source? Could this object have come from the Thrones themselves?*

Once again, he lifted up her wrist and inspected the strange object. Inside the circular glass against a backdrop of swirling, green waves, a small, pointed bar extending out from the center moved rhythmically around in a circle. Around the outer edges of the circle lay a series of peculiar, evenly-spaced symbols engraved into the background. Two similar bars also emerged from the center of the circle, one shorter than the other, but they did not seem to move.

Baffled, Aidric delicately tugged on the bracelet-like object until he was able to slip it over her hand, and once free, he immediately banished it into his magical storage plane to examine later. At the moment, the young woman was his primary concern.

Her face was locked in a grimace of pain that distorted her beauty, which was far more concerning than the sight of her blood. Normally, magical trauma caused weakness and bleeding but nothing more painful than a prolonged wine headache. Only a severe case would cause unconsciousness.

It isn't magical trauma alone that ails her, then. Could she have foolishly seared her own mind away?

He laid a tentative hand across her dampened forehead, closed his eyes in concentration, and sent out a mind-probe to read her.

Pain!

Aidric recoiled and nearly lost the probe when his mind touched the pain. He drew a sharp breath in and cursed. It was the same—the same pain he had felt when her screams had filled his mind. Even though her screams had ceased, her mind was still experiencing that terrible agony. Had she not fallen unconscious, she would have been writhing in agony and probably half mad.

She was unconsciously reading the minds of every soul within the borders of Lamia. The volume those millions of voices created within her mind had never been meant for mortal ears to hear. Magical trauma and shock would be the least of her problems if she didn't receive the care of a healer, and soon, not if she ever hoped to awaken from her unnatural sleep.

Through his probe, Aidric could also see the raw, untamed magic of that miniature Mage-field that now surrounded them flowing wildly through every particle of her body, causing every nerve ending to be alive with pain. He withdrew his mind-probe with a shudder, unable to imagine the pain she was enduring, but one thing was perfectly clear. She was untrained.

Though Aidric was a powerful mage, luckily for her, he was also a powerful healer. The young woman needed treatment immediately from both types of practitioners, or else the magical energies would consume her.

Gently caressing her troubled face, he eased her pain by placing his own magical shields around her mind, blocking the stream of voices from entering it and also blocking her ability to use her mage powers. He could sense the wild energy pushing against the shields, but he was confident that they would hold until he found the time to strengthen them.

Her face immediately relaxed from her grimace once he had relieved the cause of the chaos within her. She sighed weakly in her unnatural sleep, shifting her head restlessly to the side before she fell silent once again. With the grimace gone, she looked even more beautiful to his eyes than before.

Satisfied that she was no longer in excruciating pain, Aidric shrugged off his cloak and draped it around her body. Then he gathered her into his arms and rose swiftly from the ground. She felt as if she weighed nothing in his arms. She didn't even stir.

Turning towards the direction where he had left

Shadow tethered, Aidric pondered over whether or not he should use the portal spell to transport them to his quarters at the palace at once or to ride. The portal spell required a tremendous amount of channeled power and concentration that usually left him feeling battered and weary for several sand-marks unless accompanied by another mage who added their own channels and strength to the spell.

He needed to begin healing the magical shock she was suffering as soon as possible, but he knew that he would be too drained to tend to her if he performed the portal spell. He could always ask the king's personal healer to tend to her, but the thought of letting another touch her made him feel surprisingly uneasy.

No, it's better for me to heal her since I already know her mind so well, he reasoned. *Besides, the fewer people that know of her, the better.*

He glanced down at the sleeping girl in his arms and said to her, "You're safe now, milady, and when you wake, I'll discover if the old Golden Mage prophecy has any truth to it."

With those final words, he set out into the forest again, retracing his steps back to the Lake of Tears path, resigning himself to an agonizingly long ride back to the palace.

CHAPTER FOUR

The palace grounds swarmed with the usual assortment of servants, mages of every class, apprentices, bards, petitioners, and noblemen hurrying to and from the huge, iron gates of the palace wall to whatever tasks demanded their attention for the day. Aidric watched them from afar, tightly shielded from emotion, hidden from view by a convenient clump of trees. He knew that if he attempted to ride through the palace gates with the young woman in his arms, too many curious eyes would see. Many questions would be asked, questions that he had no answers for at the moment.

Aidric muttered heartfelt curses under his breath. There was no choice. He would have to use magic if he hoped to slip into his rooms unnoticed, something he would have rather avoided while the girl was still so raw and damaged. The shields he had placed around her mind *should* keep her from sensing any magical energy, but with the way the untamed power within her was currently battering against those shields, he feared even the smallest hint of magical energy would get through and trigger another burst of power and shatter them just as she had easily shattered his own shields earlier.

Still, he really couldn't risk anyone learning of his discovery just yet, either. Those in power might see her as a threat to the safety of the kingdom and order her to solitary confinement until they decided what to do with her. He shuddered, knowing all-too-well how miserable the palace dungeons could be. Most of the weaker prisoners never emerged alive again.

I'll not *allow that to happen to her!*

Shadow would have to stay behind. Although the steed was as silent and well-mannered as a horse could be, Aidric could not take the risk of Shadow whickering at an inconvenient moment.

Aidric carefully dismounted and set the girl as gently as he could onto the soft grass. Quickly, he tied Shadow's reigns to one of the trees, giving the horse enough slack to graze as he pleased. He would send one of the stable boys for Shadow later.

He then closed his eyes and carefully began the

spell that would ensure all eyes that tried to look at them would see nothing but what they expected to see, making them for all intents and purposes, invisible. The wave of magic flowed from his hands and settled over the girl's body like a thin film of mist. He did the same to himself and afterwards, gathered her into his arms again.

Luckily, the line of people entering and leaving the palace grounds had thinned somewhat, so the danger of bumping into someone and ruining the effects of the spell was not as great. He kept to the edges, and after a few close calls with children suddenly darting in front of him, Aidric was safely through the gates.

Not one of the two dozen guards on either side of the gate glanced in their direction even once. In fact, they eyed the travelers with a bored indifference. Frowning, he wondered if that indifference was feigned or genuine. The matter definitely deserved further scrutiny, but for the moment, the light weight in his arms reminded him that he had more pressing matters to attend to first.

It seemed to take an eternity for Aidric to cross the seemingly endless lawns surrounding the palace before he safely reached the side entrance of the palace that led to the Mage Hall where his private suite lay. The area was currently empty.

Heaving a huge sigh of relief, he prayed to Seni that the main hallway would also be empty as he awkwardly reached for the door handle, trying not to jostle the girl too much, and cracked open one of the two tall, golden-bordered marble doors. He saw none of his fellow mages as he peered down into the gloom of the main corridor. Just to be extra sure, he sent out a Probe of Inquiry, but it found no one still within the Hall.

Satisfied that they were alone, Aidric stepped into the hallway and dismissed the invisibility spell. He hurried down the corridor to his quarters at the end of the corridor that lay thankfully unlocked. He seldom spell-locked his door since none of the mages ever worried about thieves entering their domain. Most of the common folk believed that a dire spell would strike dead any potential thief if he or she even attempted to enter the Mage Hall without permission. Completely untrue, but the mages allowed the uninformed to continue believing it. If the rumor kept their quarters safe from thievery, then the mages saw no reason to set the record straight, and for once, Aidric totally agreed with them.

He quickly passed through the sitting room, ignoring the enormous spread that a servant had left him on the dining table against the far wall for lunch, even though his stomach began to growl in protest at the delicious aroma. He carried the girl into his bedroom and gently laid her onto his enormous feather bed.

She moaned softly as she sank into the coverlet and her head hit his down pillow but otherwise, showed no signs of reviving. A mercy, really, since she would be spared the misery of consciously feeling the shock-headache.

Aidric pulled his robe from her and replaced it with one of the thick blankets that lay folded at the foot of the bed. There was a cold bite to the air, and he had enough to worry about with her extreme case of magical-shock, let alone the problems a chill could add to the mix. His bedroom, despite being windowless, annoyingly could sometimes be quite glacial, the result of bad architecture.

Satisfied that she was warm enough, Aidric bent over her and lightly laid both hands onto her forehead to begin the healing. He closed his eyes and wove slivers of his own life force through her mind, finding and healing the places most traumatized by what she had done to herself in her apparent ignorance of her mage powers.

He winced at the state of the natural magical "channels," a type of energy ley-line that wound throughout her entire body. It was worse than he had thought. Her channels pulsed in some places with a type of inflammation. In others, the flow of energy was disrupted, redirected, to the point of seeping out beyond the normal flow as though through cracks in a barrier, causing significant damage to the surrounding tissues that were never meant to be touched by the energy of a Mage-field.

Aidric found it hard to believe that anyone would do this to themselves intentionally, even a potential spy testing out her abilities against Lamia's Mage-general. Another sand-mark without treatment, and the damage caused to her brain would have been irreversible, possibly even fatal.

A few moments later, he drew his hands and mental connection away with a shiver of pleasure, her healing complete. The feelings that healing aroused in the healer were very similar to those aroused by lovemaking. Aidric always felt embarrassed after healing a patient because most were well aware of the feelings of pleasure he was experiencing. Some even teased him about it, but with his current patient unconscious, this time he was thankfully spared the awkwardness. He listened closely to her rhythmic breathing without the usual discomfort and determined that her sleep was now natural and not shock-induced.

For a long moment, Aidric stared down at her sleeping face and debated whether or not to wake her or allow her to awaken naturally when she had slept off the exhaustion. No one was expecting him anywhere for a few sand-marks, so sitting by her bedside and keeping watch wouldn't be a problem. However, he wasn't so sure any of them could afford to let the mystery of this powerful maiden go unsolved any longer, even if she did need the rest.

Taking a deep breath, he mentally touched her mind and sent a mind-thought that commanded her to awaken, hoping in the same instant that he was not making a serious mistake.

***

She was dreaming of colorful lights of no distinct shape that danced in a large circle around her, shimmering beings at least twice her height, gleefully laughing at her because of her obvious fear of them. She turned from left to right in a futile attempt to escape them, but they were *everywhere*, slowly closing in on her as if they meant to devour her.

She seemed to be standing in a vacuum of darkness with the only source of light being those dancing lights and the light radiating from herself. She could hear their mocking laughter surrounding her as if it were wisps of fog ready to squeeze the warmth from her body.

It didn't take long for their persistent ridicule to finally anger her enough to banish most of her fear and to rush at the nearest dancing light, the energy emitted by her body glowing more fiercely, her mind focused on one thing—to destroy it. God, she had never felt so *alive*!

However, before she could reach the offending light, the dream suddenly faded, and Allison awakened to the unfamiliar sensation of something incredibly soft enveloping her entire body. Disoriented, she tried to remember where she was. She only knew that the bed she was sleeping in was not her own. It was simply too comfortable.

Then, as sleep gradually left her foggy mind and remnants of her strange dream returned to her, she suddenly recalled the brilliant rip of light that had sucked her into its realm of madness and the strange forest that she had found herself in after her terrifying experience moving through that colorful realm of light. Had that been real?

Her eyes instantly flew open, and what she saw made her heart freeze.

A strange man loomed over her, staring down at her with a mixture of curiosity and wariness evident on his face, but that was not what made her heart begin to race in sudden fear.

He didn't look altogether *human*.

He had a mop of hair as white as newly fallen snow that fell in soft waves to the top of his shoulders, hair that should have belonged to an old man, but this man's face was smooth, young. He was no older than mid-to-late twenties, surely. His eyes were a strange, but beautiful, pale-violet that she had never seen on another human being—not even with colored contacts. His skin was only a shade or two darker than his hair, as pale as any albino's skin. He was not incredibly tall, about six feet, but he still appeared to tower over her like a giant out of myth.

His clothes looked as if he had just stepped out of the pages of a history book describing the fashions of the past. He wore a long, full-sleeved shirt the same color as his hair of a material that resembled silk but cast off a brighter luster. It was laced together in the center with laces that seemed to have been coated in real gold. Small jewels that appeared to be diamonds, sapphires, rubies, and emeralds adorned the cuffs of the shirt, as well as the shoulders and collar.

A cape of silky sapphire edged in gold fell down his back to come to rest a couple of inches above the floor. It fastened around his neck by a gold and sapphire brooch in the shape of a teardrop more beautiful than any piece of jewelry Allison had ever seen.

The breeches he wore were of the same sapphire

THE KINGDOM OF ETERNAL SORROW

blue of his cape, tucked into a pair of brown, leather boots that rose to just below his knees.

All of this, Allison took in with a single sweep of her rapidly widening eyes.

She was suddenly very afraid.

After a moment of tense silence, near tears, she worked up enough courage to ask, "What are you? Where am I?" She nearly choked on the words as she all but whispered, "Am I—dead?"

The man frowned and shook his head. His whole demeanor seemed to become suddenly agitated at her words. She instinctively shrunk back.

Oh God—maybe I insulted him when I asked him what he was, she thought in alarm as the stranger continued to frown, his pale-violet eyes staring intently down at her own as though trying to see down to her very soul.

"*Mei agio nea legera ois ventia. Aut ois legera meis?*" he said with a shrug, looking expectedly down at her.

Allison's heart clenched painfully as a maelstrom of fear and confusion thundered through her entire being, and she recoiled as far away from him as the bed permitted, finally losing the battle to keep the tears at bay. She had never heard the language that he was speaking. She only knew the few phrases and words in French and Spanish she could remember from school, but neither of those languages sounded even remotely like the words he had spoken. His language seemed to consist of mostly vowels with a few harsh consonant sounds.

Where the hell was she?

The man took a hesitant step towards the bed and stopped when Allison whimpered in fear.

I've got to get out of here! she thought frantically, her eyes darting wildly around the room until they settled on the wide-open door across the room. *But—can I make it through before he can stop me?*

***

Aidric looked down at the girl's tears in dismay.

I'm frightening her. Although, I can't say that I really blame her. Waking up in a strange room with a strange man looking down at me—I imagine I would be quite alarmed. He clenched his fists at his side in frustration. *How in the six hells can I make her understand that I mean her no harm when we can't even communicate?*

The language she had spoken was totally foreign to him. It was a tongue that resembled nothing he had ever heard uttered, even in the strangest of dialects, much less was it amongst the dozens of languages that the Master Linguist, Zenas, had magicked into his memory.

Even so, Aidric had hoped that she would at

least understand Lamian. Instead, she had looked at him as though his words had been the snarls of a beast. He couldn't even resort to reading her thoughts since touching a mind so recently traumatized in such an invasive way could cause irreparable damage to her psyche.

I can't stall any longer, he thought gravely. *I don't like it, but I need Zenas's help.*

Unfortunately, the only way the linguist would ever agree to magick the Lamian language into her mind was by receiving King Diryan's approval. The king would undoubtable demand to see her first. Aidric had never spoken about the Golden Mage legend with the king, or anyone for that matter. He had no idea how the king would react to seeing the girl and realizing her probable identity. He had wanted to bring Diryan as much information about her as possible to lessen the chances of her being imprisoned, but without being able to understand each other...

A sudden movement in the corner of his eye interrupted his thoughts, and Aidric turned his attention back to the girl in enough time to see her bolt out of his bed, obviously heading for the open door. In a panic, Aidric raised his arms and threw a paralysis spell at her. With a sinking feeling, he watched her collapse onto her face without so much as a gasp onto the marble floor as the spell overtook her.

Now she will never trust me... he despaired. *What have I done?*

***

A blast of what felt like hot air abruptly hit her from behind, and Allison suddenly found that her limbs no longer obeyed her in mid-stride. The momentum instantly had her diving forward until she fell flat on her face, her forehead hitting the marble floor hard enough to make her see black for a few seconds. She tried to cry out, but her voice didn't seem to be working, either. All she could manage was a strangled gurgle, along with short, shallow breaths. She struggled to rise again, but her body simply would not obey her.

Dear God, I'm paralyzed! she realized with horror. *Somehow*—somehow *that white-haired man did it to me!*

Allison heard footsteps approach her from behind, and the man's strangely cut, brown leather boots came into her field of view. She tried desperately to shrink away from them, to curl into a protective fetal position, terrified that one of those boots would suddenly bury itself into her stomach as punishment for trying to run away, but she couldn't even so much as blink an eyelid. She tried to speak again, ready to lose all dignity and beg for mercy as she stared helplessly at the tip of his boot, but it was as if an invisible hand was squeezing her throat to prevent the words from emerging.

She mentally braced herself for the expected blow, half-suppressed memories trying to push to the forefront of past times she had found herself in this same position as a child, the same terror of the threat of violence. Instead, he squatted down, and a couple of tense seconds later, Allison felt him gather her into his arms, bridal-style. He then carried her back to the bed. It was then that she got a good look at the bed and noticed that the tips of a few large, white feathers peeked out along the edges from beneath the coverlet and the thick top sheet. Was that the *mattress*? A bunch of huge feathers piled high on what appeared to be a regular bed frame? Except this bedframe was as ornate as a king's might be.

The frame was of a dark, almost black wood, constructed from what she suspected was the wood of those strange, monstrous trees she had seen. The headboard rose approximately five feet from the bed. Many different murals of various nature scenes were skillfully carved along it as well as the sides of the frame, some of the animals alien to her. What appeared to be solid gold was also plated along the edges of both the frame and headboard.

Allison was shocked when the strange man carefully laid her down onto the coverlet and draped the thick blanket she had thrown off earlier over her body up to her neck. She lay there enveloped in the warmth of soft feathers and blankets, unable to even blink, helplessly gazing up at his strange, but exotically beautiful, face as he looked down at her with an unreadable expression. She was scared, waiting for blows with the surety of past experiences and confused that they hadn't come. She could feel the tears leaking out of her eyes, but like everything but her breathing, she had no control over them.

Standing over her, looking tall, regal, dangerous, and unearthly beautiful, he was the most intimidating creature she had ever seen.

He looks like an angel of death…

And still, the expected blows didn't come.

Instead, he sighed dramatically, a stricken look on his face, as he pointed his finger at a sheathed dagger that hung from a belt she had not spotted earlier and shook his head firmly.

Her confusion deepened. *What is he trying to tell me?* He hadn't tried to speak to her again after she had bolted, so he must have figured out that she couldn't understand him. She considered the dagger. It being a weapon, was his gesture meant to tell her that he wouldn't hurt her?

—or was it wishful thinking?

Abruptly, he extended a hand over her forehead. Allison eyed it suspiciously, half-expecting him to strike her with it. Had she been capable of it, she would have flinched. However, he merely waved it across her face in a fluid pattern that didn't once touch her.

To her astonishment, she felt her limbs instantly begin to tingle with a strange sensation, and the hair on her arms stood on end. A few seconds later, they came alive again, no longer feeling like dead weights attached to her body. She moved both her arms and legs cautiously, not ready to believe that he had cured her paralysis with literally just a wave of his hand, but they moved freely at her will, showing no signs of resistance. Inexplicably, her overwhelming fear also left with her paralysis, leaving only a deep sense of curiosity.

Allison timidly chanced a look at her strange companion and saw that he wasn't even looking at her. He seemed to be deep in thought, his pale eyes staring out at nothing in particular. As he stood there, motionless, he suddenly reminded her of a statue of a Greek god she had once seen.

God, he really is beautiful...

He seemed to sense that Allison was looking at him because he immediately turned to lock eyes with her until the heat of his gaze was too much for her to bear, and she quickly looked down at the coverlet, her heartbeat speeding up.

In the next second, she felt him place his hand on her forehead. It was warm to the touch and had a surprisingly soothing effect on her. Remarkably, she didn't flinch away. She risked another glance into those searing, pale-violet eyes, and that was the last thing she remembered seeing before a rising darkness came to take her away from all her confusion and fear.

CHAPTER FIVE

After the sleep spell that he had placed on the girl had taken effect, Aidric immediately set out to speak with King Diryan. He didn't want to give himself enough time to back out of his decision. The young woman had too much power at her disposal, power that could easily destroy them all, especially if used untamed. They had to find out where she had come from and why.

If she was indeed the Golden Mage of their prophecy, the fate of Lamia depended on how they handled the situation. One wrong move and they could all perish, squashed like bugs under the sheer force of her power. He knew he would do everything in his power to prevent that tragedy from ever coming to pass. Everything, that is, except destroy her.

That's what I'm really afraid of, Aidric thought as he

concentrated on weaving a shield around the door to his suite that would prevent anyone except himself or a mage more powerful than he from entering. *I guess that's why I'm so reluctant to reveal her presence to anyone. If they believe her to be the Golden Mage as I do, I'm not certain how they would react to the knowledge that the old prophecy is true, how Diryan will decide to act.*

All was still silent as he made his way down a branch corridor of the Mage Hall, and for once, he welcomed the silence. The emptiness of the Hall often reminded him of the loneliness he carried within his soul, so treading down its corridors was not something he enjoyed doing under normal circumstances.

The good luck he had been experiencing thus far expired when he reached for the handle to the door leading to the palace's large, indoor garden and was promptly bowled over onto his rump as it suddenly swung open before he could even touch the handle.

Cursing, he looked up at whoever it was that had knocked him over, ready to give him or her a piece of his mind and suddenly bit back whatever words he had been ready to spat out at the offending person when he saw who it was.

Damn, Aidric thought with a groan. *Just my luck, the one person I needed to avoid most of all.*

"By Aidius, Aidric, I didn't mean to knock you

on your ass like that," Selwyn said apologetically, "but I thought that everyone had left the Hall by now and didn't bother to probe."

He offered his hand to Aidric, who grabbed a hold of it and hoisted himself up onto his feet again.

"No harm done, my friend," Aidric assured him, forcing himself to smile, "except maybe my pride, but I guess everyone needs to be knocked on their ass every once in a while to help keep them grounded. Remember that the next time *you* go to open a door."

"Promises, promises," Selwyn said with a grin. "All joking aside, what are you still doing here? I thought that His Majesty gave you a few sand-marks off today. Don't tell me that you've wasted most of them on sleep!"

"Hardly," Aidric replied dryly. "You know well enough that my name and sleep are never associated with each other. I have been up and about well before you even began to *think* of dragging your lump out of bed, thank you very much. I only returned because—because an urgent problem arose that had to be dealt with immediately."

When that last sentence was out of his mouth, Aidric was instantly sorry. He hadn't meant to reveal so much about what he was doing there, but it had just slipped out as usual. He never had been the type of person who could hold back anything, much less in the presence of his best friend who always seemed to be able to weasel anything out of him before he even knew there *was* something to weasel out of him.

"Oh?" Selwyn said, his eyes immediately lighting up with interest. "What's happened now? Is that where you were off to before I so graciously knocked you on your backside?"

"I—" Aidric began uncomfortably, searching his mind for something to tell Selwyn other than the truth, but when he looked into the honest face of his friend, he knew that he couldn't lie to him. Yet, he couldn't bring himself to tell the truth, either. Inexplicably, the fear that everyone would want to destroy the girl when they learned her likely identity burned strongly within him as if the fear of another.

That gave him pause. Was he still somehow connected to the girl's mind and the fear hers? The thought was unsettling. He had been extremely careful with his mind-probe. If any connection between their minds remained, then it had to be a result of something *she* had done...

"I—cannot tell you—just yet," Aidric said, alarm adding a tinge of impatience to his tone. "This is something that I must discuss with the king first."

Selwyn's eyes suddenly narrowed. "Aidric, what wrong?" he demanded. "I sense fear in you, and don't you dare tell me I'm wrong. What could possibly be so dire that it would frighten *you*?" He folded his arms against his chest stubbornly. "I'll not allow you to leave until you tell me."

Aidric cursed creatively in his mind. Distracted and unsettled as he was, a little of his fear must have managed to leak out through his shields, which of course the strongest empath in Lamia had no trouble sensing, damn his ability. Aidric sighed heavily and glared at the redhead. He knew that it was pointless to argue with Selwyn. Once his friend made up his mind about something, it was almost impossible to change it. What was even more irritating was that he had no one to blame but himself for this one.

"All right," Aidric said reluctantly, "but I insist on telling Diryan along with you. I have come across something today that is so amazing, and yet so frightening as well, that we all must act quickly and wisely. To do that, Diryan must be informed at once."

Selwyn paled a little at the severity of Aidric's words and nodded stiffly, allowing Aidric to lead the way to the Council Room while he silently followed.

Why did I have to run into him? Aidric thought irritably as they walked across the palace's magnificent indoor garden and into the central courtyard. The garden might as well have been a barren wasteland for all the notice he took of its beauty. *The fewer people that know about this, the better. Seni knows that the first thing Selwyn will do is run home and fill Raya in on all the gory details. Aidius, and what a mouth that woman has!*

King Diryan was currently in a meeting with his councilors over the issue of whether to send more troops over to Kemos to aid them in their current troubles with Mihr, the kingdom bordering Kemos to the south. It seemed that Mihr and Kemos was all anyone talked about these days.

For the past two decades, King Roderick of Mihr had been fighting a silent war against Lamia, lusting for the power of their Mage-field. Protected by a magical shield that had proved in the last few centuries to be indestructible, Lamia was well beyond Roderick's reach. Thus, he had begun a long campaign of attacking the kingdoms in which Lamia was sworn to protect with no end to his tyrannies in sight, hoping to force King Diryan into a position Aidric did not like to contemplate.

The last silent war Lamia had endured was with Rathtyen, a kingdom to the northeast of Mihr, and it had occurred during Diryan's great-grandfather, King Palles's reign. It had ended with the death of the Rathtyen monarch. Now, nearly two centuries later, it was happening again, but this time with Mihr. It was also beginning to look as though this silent war would not end until Roderick was condemned to the same fate as the Rathtyen king.

Aidric hated to interrupt, but he felt that his current dilemma was more important to the safety of Lamia than the Kemosian-Mihran border squabbles.

"I must speak to the king," he demanded firmly to the guards posted outside the Council Room door.

Without blinking, the guard on the left replied, "Milord, Mage-general, the king has ordered that he is not to be disturbed for any—"

"I understand," Aidric interrupted sharply, "but I must insist. The matter I wish to discuss is urgent, else I wouldn't wish to interrupt their discussion."

"But I have my orders—" the guard insisted uncomfortably.

"—which I'll take full responsibility for making you disobey them," Aidric assured him firmly. "You must understand that the matter I wish to speak of is far more important than the skirmishes they are now discussing."

"Very well," the guard said reluctantly. "Wait here, and I'll see what I can do."

"Thank you, sir," Aidric said politely, sympathizing with the guard's unhappiness of being forced to disobey direct orders from the king.

He knew that this abrupt interruption would not anger Diryan too much, if at all. The king knew that

Aidric would not insist on interrupting an important meeting unless what he had to say was equally, if not more, important. The others, however…

Through the closed door, Aidric could hear Lord Ion, the king's Seneschal, angrily demanding to know the reason behind the guard's interruption.

Poor man. I must remember to apologize to him again later.

A few moments later, the king appeared, lines of worry etched across his forehead that told Aidric that the meeting had not been going well. Not surprising, really. His councilors never seemed capable of agreeing on anything.

The king took one look at the seriousness in Aidric's eyes and said, "Come. We shall speak in my study. I have a feeling that what you are about to tell me warrants that level of privacy."

Aidric nodded and he and Selwyn followed their king through the palace to the royal suite in silence. Diryan's stiff gait told him that the king expected nothing short of a disaster. Everything from his shoulders to the blankness of his expression radiated tension, and he kept rubbing his left temple as if he had a headache coming on, which Aidric suspected he probably did. As of late, not a day passed that Diryan did not suffer a headache.

Not for the first time, Aidric wished that he

dared to probe the king's mind to see what he was thinking, but stealing one's thoughts without their consent was a crime punishable by death in Lamia unless it was done to an enemy or a person behaving suspiciously such as the girl that now lay in his bed.

Once they reached the royal suite, Diryan ushered them into his study after threatening the guards with being relieved of their duties if they allowed anything to disturb them.

"It's good that there aren't two of me or else I would feel very sorry for the poor soul who had to disobey your orders at my request with that threat hanging over his head," Aidric joked to relieve some of the tension while he turned to cast a spell of silence over the room.

Diryan smiled thinly. "There could only be one of you, my dear lad, and thank the lord, Seni, for that."

It took Aidric only a few moments to spell-silence the room. He called upon and directed a bit of the energy particles from the Mage-field into his bodily channels, silently chanting the proper incantation, bending the energy to his will as it flowed from his hands. He placed the invisible force almost effortlessly across every wall and the ceiling of the study to form a seamless barrier to the outside rooms. No sound, no matter how loud, would escape the room until he willed it so.

"Now, tell me what it is that has you so worried, Aidric," Diryan commanded once Aidric had turned to face him again.

Aidric sighed and said, "It's that obvious, huh? Well, there's no sense in prettying it up with jewels is there, but I do think the both of you had better sit down, first."

The king merely raised an eyebrow but said nothing as he took a seat in the large, thickly-cushioned chair behind his cluttered desk. Documents, several maps, and personal letters littered the top in a carefree fashion, giving the room a lived-in appearance instead of the impersonal formality of all the other rooms in the king's chamber.

This was one room that the king had forbidden the servants to enter unless specifically instructed. Diryan had once told Aidric that it was the only room that made him feel as if he was just a normal man and not a man that carried the lives of thousands of subjects on his shoulders.

Selwyn followed the king's example by taking a seat in one of the chairs next to the desk, looking as giddy as a young child waiting for a promised surprise to be revealed to him. Aidric had to smile despite himself. It seemed as though anything could arouse excitement in his friend, and Aidric was envious of that particular trait, though he would never admit it to Selwyn.

Once both were situated and gazed back at him expectantly, he became nervous. A thousand "what ifs" ran through his mind about what could possibly result in his revelation, and unfortunately, none of them were good. Typical, since Sel often joked that Aidric could make even the worst pessimist seem like an optimist. More than a life of a maiden was at stake here. He could *not* screw this up.

Aidric looked into the smoky-blue of Diryan's eyes and was comforted by the kindness and promise of understanding in them. He swallowed with some difficulty and banished all the dire thoughts from his mind.

He then looked sharply at his friend. "Sel, what is said in this room *must* be kept strictly confidential until His Majesty deems otherwise. What I am about to reveal has the potential to create great chaos within the kingdom if mishandled."

Selwyn merely stared back at him innocently, his eyes asking "who me?"

"I don't want you to run home and tell Raya," Aidric elaborated. "She will know in good time, I'm sure."

Selwyn opened his mouth as if to protest but quickly held his peace when he saw the glare Aidric was directing at him.

"All right," he grumbled. "I give you my word that I'll keep whatever you say in this room behind my teeth, even under the most horrible torture."

Aidric didn't even crack a smile, which he was sure had been Selwyn's intention. "Good," was all he said, making Selwyn blink in surprise.

As he locked his eyes with Diryan's again, he felt that same wave of strong reluctance wash over him, the one that he was not altogether certain came completely from him.

What are you thinking? Aidric scolded himself with disgust. *Diryan would never hurt her, you fool! You know that! Sure, he might fear what she symbolizes. Hellsfire, I fear it, but you know perfectly well that he would never order the execution of an innocent woman!*

"*Aidric?*" Selwyn inquired with worry via thought-speech.

That jolted Aidric out of his troubling thoughts, and he turned his eyes from Diryan's to Selwyn's. Worry etched itself across his friend's usually passive face, and he no longer fidgeted with impatience in his chair.

"*Sorry,*" Aidric sent back with forced cheer. "*I guess I was just woolgathering.*"

"Your Majesty," Aidric voiced suddenly, breaking the uncomfortable silence in the room and startling the king, though he was trying very hard not to show it, "you are familiar with all the prophecies of Lamia, are you not?"

"Yes…" Diryan replied slowly.

"So you know the Prophecy of the Golden Mage very well, I presume?"

"I do," he answered, then demanded, "What are you hinting at, lad?"

Aidric hesitated for a moment, grasping for words on how to reveal his find to the king as delicately as possible but then deciding that there really was no sense beating around the bush about it.

"I believe that I have found her, that very Golden Mage, and she is now, as we speak, lying unconscious in my bed by the sleep spell I cast over her," he stated bluntly.

Silence.

Aidric shifted uneasily on his feet. This was *not* the reaction he had expected from them. He half-expected Selwyn to burst out laughing and call him a daydreaming fool, but instead, Sel looked completely dumbfounded, his mouth actually dropping in shock.

As for the king, he had expected immediate questions, even skepticism, but Diryan expressed neither. The shock and fear that now reflected in the eyes of the king was enough to almost make him lose his composure.

"Are you certain, Aidric?" Diryan finally managed to ask after a prolonged silence.

"Almost completely positive, Your Majesty," Aidric confirmed grimly. "I would not have pulled you out of an important Council session to tell you of her unless I was that certain. Diryan, she has hair of gold and more power at her disposal than all the mages of Lamia put together!"

"Golden hair..." Selwyn muttered under his breath in wonder. "But I thought the Golden Mage was only a myth, a tale told to frighten children into good behavior. It certainly frightened me! Now you are actually telling me that such a person exists?"

"At least *I* am mostly convinced," Aidric said. "She flattened me with a single thought, and I had all of my shields up at full strength!"

Rubbing his temples, King Diryan said, "I think you had better start at the beginning."

Aidric nodded and began to pace. "I was heading for the Lake of Tears when my mage senses suddenly alerted me to the presence of a person with more power than I had ever felt before. I could feel it radiating all around me without even having to probe to see it.

"It was rather alarming. This was more power than I had ever confronted, and I didn't know whether the person behind the power had ill-intent or not. I sent out a Probe of Inquiry to try to touch the mind of the mage. I found that it was a woman, and her mind was wide open for any mage to read. However, before I could scan her thoughts for an identity, something inside of her head shattered, something mental. Before I knew what was happening, a burst of power in the form of a mind-scream had struck at my mind, knocking me flat on my back and instantly shattering every one of my shields."

Aidric shuddered involuntarily at the memory.

"The screams were horrible! Even now, I feel a shiver go down my spine at the thought of those screams. Thankfully, they only lasted a few moments or else I have no doubt my mind would have cracked. Once I had gathered my wits again, I went searching through the forest in hopes of locating her. I found her lying sprawled on her face in the center of a small clearing that I never knew existed."

"A clearing in the Forest of Illusions?" Diryan interrupted with a frown. "There are none that I know of except for the ones around the lake, the path we have cleared centuries ago leading from the edge of the palace grounds to the lake, and the site of the Mage-field, of course. How strange that we have never noticed another."

"My thoughts exactly, Your Majesty. The place contained energy particles similar to those of the

Mage-field. I suspect that there *was* no clearing there until the girl appeared, but that is a matter that should be investigated at a later date. Our first concern should be the girl, herself. She was unconscious when I found her, unknowingly reading the minds of everyone within the Lamian borders."

"Unknowingly?" Diryan echoed, his frown deepening.

"She's untrained, Your Majesty. I'm certain of it. That's why I'm so unnerved. I don't believe she even realizes that she has these powers because if she did, she would not have so recklessly left her mind unshielded or damaged herself so severely." He paused dramatically, then forced himself to continue. "What's worse, I don't believe that she is of this world."

"What!" Selwyn exclaimed, startling Aidric because he had forgotten that he was even there. "What in the name of Seni do you mean by that?"

"Exactly what I said," Aidric huffed, a little uncomfortable under the scrutiny of the two. "Of course, I could be wrong, but I don't believe I am. She was wearing strange garments of materials I cannot even begin to identify. They resembled undergarments of some sort, though I'm not certain they are. After all, why would anyone go parading around so indecently clad? Also, her beauty—well, I'll allow you to judge for yourselves."

"Now Aidric," Diryan began, "I don't believe that those reasons are grounds for—"

"There is more," Aidric cut in as Selwyn gaped at him in shock.

Lamian law forbade anyone to interrupt the king when he spoke, the ultimate insult, and it always rattled Selwyn when Aidric did it. He had always been liberal with the king, talking to Diryan as if they were merely friends and not king and underling, and he often forgot how inexcusable others thought his behavior to be. He did try to curb that level of casualness when others, even Selwyn, were present, but he forgot more often than not since Diryan never seemed to notice that type of impropriety, anyway.

"I managed to heal the damage that she inflicted upon herself in her ignorance," Aidric said, "hoping that when she regained consciousness, I could get some answers from her."

The king leaned forward eagerly. "You have spoken with her, then?"

"Not really," Aidric replied with a frustrated sigh. "She spoke a language that was so foreign to me that I couldn't even begin to decipher it. I couldn't read her thoughts either because her mind had been so severely traumatized. There was a very good chance she would have gone mad if I had tried. I had hoped to reveal her existence armed with as many answers to the questions I knew would be raised, but since that's not the case, I came here with different intentions."

Diryan suddenly looked wary. "Which are—"

"Nothing nefarious, I promise. I need you to give Master Zenas your permission to have him magick our language into her memory in order for us to be able to communicate with her."

Some of the tension left Diryan's shoulders. "Of course. I, myself, would have suggested it if you had not. Only the maiden can give us the answers as to her identity, and if she proves to be who you profess her to be, we must do everything in our power to prevent the tragedy the prophecy foretells."

Both Selwyn and Aidric stiffened at the king's words as Diryan stood up abruptly, all visible traces of the fear he had sported earlier gone from his expression, replaced by a look of sheer determination that made Aidric smile inwardly with pride.

We truly are blessed to have such a king—so ready to take on whatever problems Seni wishes to throw at us with hardly a blink. If only I could feel so confident—

"Aidric, thought-speak Zenas. Tell him to drop whatever it is he is doing and to meet us at your suite immediately."

As Aidric nodded and instantly obeyed the king's

orders, Diryan's eyes unfocused as he lost himself in his thoughts. Again, Aidric wished he knew what the king was thinking.

If only he could thought-speak, then he might be more inclined to share them when we're among others if he knew only I would hear them...

"Lads," Diryan finally said with a hint of a smile, "I do believe that we are about to make history."

***

He opened his eyes and smiled, the vision of the pale girl with the golden hair fading into the sight of the dusty stone wall before him that was half-concealed in the shadows of the dim room. Within the darkness of a hood the color of the blackest night, a pair of saffron eyes flashed in a flare of incandescent light as he savored the vision. The very air around him seemed to go still.

"At last, she has come," he said quietly into the gloom. "A mage of legends, one not born of this plane. So it begins."

It was time for him to emerge into the world again, time to push those that were his in the direction that was predetermined. He had waited long enough, observed the lands from afar with scant interference. The Time was near. His plan would succeed.

She would be his. The only question was when.

CHAPTER SIX

"You are certain she is powerless?" Zenas asked uneasily for what seemed the thousandth time during the five depths that they had been waiting outside Aidric's suite while Aidric dismissed the shield he had constructed earlier.

Aidric regarded the aging linguist with impatience, biting back the retort he so desperately wanted to spat at him, and said dryly, "For the last time, Master Zenas, no harm will come to you. I have placed a powerful shield around her mind to block her ability to use her power. She is also quite unconscious and will not wake unless I will it so. There is nothing to fear from her. Now, shall we enter, gentlemen, or stand out here all day cowering like fools?"

Zenas glared at Aidric, clearly insulted, but Diryan only smiled mischievously and nodded. The Linguist often annoyed the king as well with his constant whining. Aidric winced to think of what the old man was like when he was a child if he whined this much now.

However, despite his calm appearance, Diryan hesitated at the door and held his hand out as if to say "after you." Aidric sighed, taking the cue from the king and led the way into his suite, followed by Diryan, Selwyn, and a very unhappy Zenas bringing up the rear.

When Aidric noticed that no one followed him inside his bedroom but lingered in the doorway, his temper flared, and he whirled around and snapped, "For the love of Seni! She's *unconscious!* You are all acting as if you'll be struck dead the moment you step into the room!"

As he glared at the three men, they shrank back in the face of his angry words, looking sheepish. Even Zenas, who, by Aidric's standards, was a stubborn old goat, flinched under the force of his words. People were always quick to comment on how formidable Aidric appeared when in a rage, and not for the first time, he wondered if people really did fear he would snap and cause them harm.

Diryan cleared his throat, breaking the uncomfortable silence that followed. "We have every reason to be hesitant, lad," he admonished. "In that room lies a maiden who could very well level the entire kingdom just by lifting a finger if the words of the prophecy hold any truth. We *do* have much to fear from her."

The venom in Aidric's eyes died down. He was right, of course. They *did* have much to fear from the girl, and he shouldn't be cross with them because of their natural hesitation. So why was he still annoyed?

"I assure you, Your Majesty," Aidric said in a more even tone, "she *cannot* harm you. I have blocked her channels completely. Besides, if to do ill had been her intentions all along, then I would have been struck down the moment I first found her in the forest. When she awoke here, she was only confused and frightened, and yet, she didn't once try to attack me either magically or physically. Now come. We have wasted enough time as it is."

The moment the three men entered the room, they released simultaneous gasps of shock. Undeniably, the first thing that they had noticed was her golden hair. It radiated like pure sunlight in untidy strands on the pillow, a shocking contrast to the stark whiteness of the fabric. She appeared as small and innocent as a child lying tucked into the large bed.

So beautiful, Aidric thought wondrously as he gazed down at her peaceful face. *How can anyone fear such a maiden? How can I?* Despite his reassurances to the others, this maiden stirred a fear within him that he had thought long dead and buried in the past.

"It *is* true," Diryan whispered suddenly, breaking the shocked silence. "By Aidius, the Golden Mage has come at last!"

"Her hair—it really does look like strands of gold," Selwyn said faintly.

Aidric turned his gaze from the girl to Selwyn in alarm. Selwyn's face had become suspiciously pale and he looked as if he was about to swoon. Sure enough, as Aidric called out his name sharply, Selwyn's eyes grew vacant, and he pitched forward. Aidric rushed forward to catch him.

"Typical," Aidric remarked with some amusement as he carefully laid his friend onto the marble floor. "He never could handle shock very well."

He laid his hand onto Selwyn's forehead and with a slight exertion of power, commanded him to awaken. Selwyn's eyes immediately flew open, and for a few beats, he merely stared up at Aidric blankly before sense finally flooded back into his eyes. Selwyn's gaze shifted between Aidric and Diryan in confusion, but then, a moment later, he groaned and quickly shut his eyes again, no doubt seeing the irritation in the king's eyes.

"I did it again, didn't I?" Selwyn moaned, his

cheeks coloring in embarrassment.

"I'm afraid so, my friend," Aidric replied with a smile. "That Empathy of yours does nothing for your nerves."

As he hauled his friend onto his feet again, Aidric glanced over at the faces of the king and Zenas. Everything in Diryan's stiff posture and benign expression told him that he was impatient but trying not to show it. Zenas, however, wore a very open expression of disgust at Selwyn's unexpected behavior.

Sighing inwardly, Aidric turned back to Selwyn and forced himself to say sternly, "Sel, if you feel that you can't handle the current situation, I'm afraid that I'll have to ask you to remain in the sitting room until we finish here. We must have *no* distractions while we are interrogating her. It could result in a disaster in this already delicate situation."

Selwyn swallowed hard, hurt briefly flashing in his eyes, but before Sel could reply, Aidric hastily added, "Sorry for sounding so brusque. I *do* wish for you to stay. Your Empathy is easily ten times more powerful than mine and could be very helpful."

Selwyn nodded. "I'll be all right. I'm sorry. Sometimes I'm so concerned about the emotions of others that I ignore how over-sensitive my own can be. I promise I'll keep it together."

"Fine," Aidric said as he walked over to the bed to position himself for the upcoming interrogation.

The others followed his example and arranged themselves in a line at the foot of the bed.

"Now remember," Aidric warned, "she's extremely confused, and I don't believe she knows where she is. Although I did the best I could to calm her, she will probably wake frightened, so don't make any sudden movements that would alarm her further. I don't want to have to paralyze her again."

"You said she could not harm us," Zenas interrupted accusingly.

"She cannot!" Aidric snapped back, his patience thinning. *Insufferable old goat!* "I say this for her benefit, not yours! Do you not trust me? Is my word no longer good enough for you, Master Linguist?"

"Enough," Diryan commanded sharply.

He turned to Aidric and regarded him with a critical eye.

"You surprise me, Aidric," Diryan said. "You usually do not lose your temper quite so easily..." He trailed off and looked at Aidric with a raised eyebrow.

Aidric stiffened. He knew very well why he was so on edge, and bringing up that particular fear was out of the question in present company. He didn't want to add any more preconceived biases to the situation than they already had. She had yet to even open her eyes, and the fear already in the air was enough to choke even a non-empath.

"Forgive me, Your Majesty," he apologized softly, bowing his head. "This whole situation—I guess I'm more unnerved by everything that has happened than I had thought. Then to have my words so questioned—"

"Have you forgotten *who* she could possibly be, boy?" Zenas interjected. "We would be remiss not to question *everything*, even the assurances from a mage of your knowledge and power."

"No, I haven't forgotten," Aidric replied flatly, bristling at Zenas's continuing refusal to address him with the proper honorific. "I wish that I could, that she was just an ordinary maiden I found passed out in the forest, but she is not. Even if she proves not to be the Golden Mage—which I seriously doubt—you can all plainly see that she is of a race that is alien to our own. She is, by no means, ordinary, but that does not mean she should automatically be treated as an enemy of Lamia. Now, I do believe that we have wasted enough time on this petty nonsense. Shall we proceed?"

Diryan nodded, the barest hint of a smile on his lips as he turned to Zenas and said," You heard the lad, Zenas. Magick our language into her memory."

"As you wish, my liege." Zenas's face went utterly blank and his eyes unfocused until he appeared to be as lifeless as a statue.

Aidric's mage senses could detect the faint whisper of magical energy that Zenas projected from his mind and into the mind of the girl. It always puzzled him how Zenas actually transferred memories from his own mind and could permanently implant them in the minds of others. It was a form of thought-speech, but unlike the thoughts being sent by a thought-speaker, Zenas was able to alter a person's memory banks with the thoughts he projected from his own memory. However, his ability was limited to the transferring of languages, and nobody could discern why.

It was a rare ability. Usually only one with the potential of becoming a Master Linguist was born in a generation, and sometimes there would be none for a couple of hundred years.

"It is done," Zenas announced a few moments later, his sharp voice slicing through the tense silence.

Aidric's heart began to race with both trepidation and rising excitement. He only hoped that she would do nothing that would alarm the others. Having to restrain her with magic again was definitely not the way to earn her trust.

He reached out a hand and gently rested it onto

her forehead, all the while feeling three pairs of eyes boring holes into his back.

He then abruptly turned to Selwyn and said, "Sel, if she shows any signs of distress, I want you to use your powers to soothe her. The last thing we need is for her to refuse to speak out of fear and suspicion. She shouldn't be able to, but if she does start to push back at you, thought-speak me *immediately*."

Selwyn nodded curtly, his entire demeanor stiffening with sudden alertness.

Satisfied, Aidric turned back to the golden-haired girl. *"Awake,"* he sent into the bowels of her unconscious mind.

Her eyes instantly flew open, and he could feel everyone tense behind him. At first, she appeared only confused, blinking alluring green eyes the color of peridot stupidly up at him. Then those eyes widened in shock as they darted from him, to the others, then back to him. She let out a small sound of fear and promptly backed up on the bed until her back slammed into the headboard, trying to unsuccessfully meld into the wood.

"Don't be afraid, milady," Aidric said gently in Lamian. "We mean you no harm."

Instead of the reassurance his words were meant to give her, they only seemed to increase the panicked look in her eyes.

Why is it that nothing can ever be easy? he thought in exasperation as he watched the girl cower in his bed, unsure of how to proceed next.

CHAPTER SEVEN

The first thing Allison saw after waking was the face of the strange, white-haired man. For a few seconds, she stared up at him blankly, her mind still muddled and heavy with sleep. Then movement within the room caught her attention, and she tore her gaze from his face to the penetrating eyes of the three men at the foot of her bed. Her eyes widened as she took in the appearances of her new—visitors.

Like the white-haired man, the others wore similarly strange and lavish costumes, though of different colors and levels of elegance. The one that stood on the outside right wore a sapphire-blue robe completely embedded with gold braiding and jewels. Everything about him screamed "I am in charge," not only in the obvious wealth of his clothing and his noble carriage, but also in his severe, controlled expression as he looked down on her as though studying an interesting new specimen.

The old man standing on the other end of the trio eyed her with open mistrust and something a little like contempt. He wore rather ornate, white robes of the strange silk-like material, and many jeweled rings encircled his bony fingers. His hair was as white as the hair of the younger man standing beside her, except for a few strands of silver.

Standing in the center of them and dressed in garments similar to the younger white-haired man's except for their deep green color, a twenty-something redheaded man stared down at her warily, his face pale and his stance so tense that his entire body quivered. His hand unconsciously fingered the hilt of a sheathed dagger on his belt, and Allison was quite certain that he would not hesitate to use it if provoked.

On the verge of panicking, Allison whimpered and attempted to scramble out of their reach, but the large headboard behind her prevented her from moving back very far.

Who are these people? she thought frantically, cowering against the thick headboard under the intense stares of the others. *Where in the hell am I?*

Then the younger, white-haired man spoke, and Allison nearly choked on a sharp gasp when she clearly understood the strange words. Her mind had interpreted their meaning effortlessly as though he was speaking a second language she had known fluently all her life.

"How—how—" she sputtered aloud in English.

The white-haired man gazed down at her in confusion, his pale-violet eyes burning into her own, but as before, she couldn't seem to tear her gaze away from those eyes—so imploring, so full of—concern? He glanced over at the old man, who merely shrugged, before turning his eyes to her again.

Then his expression changed to one of understanding. His eyes brightened, and a ghost of a smile began to form on his lips. She found that smile unnerving, and she couldn't fathom why it disturbed her as much as it did. She shivered and hugged her body more tightly in a subconscious effort to protect herself as her eyes darted fearfully between the four men.

None of this is real. These people aren't real. This has *to be a dream! None of this craziness can be—*

"I assure you this is *very* real, *we* are very real," the white-haired man suddenly said firmly in that strange tongue.

Allison's mind jolted to a halt. It was as if he had plucked the thoughts right out of her mind. *Coincidence—it has to be a coincidence. My thoughts must have been clear through the expression on my face—nothing more...*

"Your language is unknown to us," he contin-ued, offering her a gentle smile, "as is your appear-ance. Although you may not understand why you can suddenly understand our tongue when you couldn't before, you'll also find that you can speak it with the ease of your native tongue. I ask that you use it, for we cannot understand yours."

This can't be—I do *understand him,* she thought in utter bewilderment. *Is he right? Can I speak his weird language even though I've never heard it until today?* She slowly relaxed her huddled posture and cautiously looked at all the alien faces at the foot of the bed more closely. Although tense and eying her with what appeared to be mistrust, none of the men had made any hostile moves towards her, or, in fact, moved at all.

Yet.

Then there was the strange, yet handsome man who looked to be old, but wasn't. He had assured her that they meant her no harm, but could she trust his words? He seemed sincere enough, his smile genuine, but what had he done earlier to cause her temporary paralysis? Allison was sure he had caused it, but she had absolutely no clue on *how* he had done it.

She looked back at the man beside her. There was no doubt that he frightened her, but at the same

time, her curiosity was peaked. She had too many unanswered questions whirling around in her mind,
questions she desperately needed answers to if she
hoped to make sense of what was happening to her.
She decided to give their language a try.

Clearing her throat nervously, Allison said in a
small voice, "Who are you?"

Immediately after those words left her lips, she
let out a tiny gasp of shock. The words she had just
spoken were not English but in a language that was
both foreign and familiar. She hadn't really believed
that she would be able to speak his language. She had
formed the question in her mind in English, but
when she had opened her mouth to speak, the words
had mysteriously converted to the strangers' language.

Ignoring her gasp, the white-haired man replied
rather amusedly, "I think that the more important
question, milady, is who are *you*?"

The humor in his voice disconcerted her, and
Allison once again shrank away from him in uncertainty. She didn't know what she had expected him to
reply, but it had not been this casual rebuttal of her
own question as if he was mocking her.

Just as fear began to creep in again, a warm sensation enveloped her body, causing her tension to
immediately melt away and her limbs to relax until

she was more or less lying slumped against the head-board. She felt comfortable, at peace, and that nothing would ever hurt her, almost as if someone was whispering those reassurances into her mind.

"My name is Allison McNeal," she said abruptly without realizing that she was going to speak, breaking the heavy silence in the room.

"Allison," the white-haired man repeated as if testing the way the word felt on the tip of his tongue, "such a strange name. Very strange, indeed." He tilted his head to the side curiously. "Not knowing our language, you are obviously far from home. How is it that you came to be in the Forest of Illusions?"

"Where?" Allison asked in surprise, forgetting for the moment that she was speaking their language as casually as her own.

"The Forest of Illusions," he repeated patiently, as if talking to a small child. "Do you not know where you are?"

When she shook her head, he frowned and said, "This is the kingdom of Lamia, but that is not what's important." His eyes narrowed. "*How* you came to be in our kingdom without the level of your powers being detected at our borders is what concerns us."

Lamia? Kingdom...?

"I don't know!" Allison cried, clutching the blanket pooled on her lap. "I've never even *heard* of

Lamia! What do you mean, 'my powers'? Oh, God! Will somebody please tell me what's going on? Why do I suddenly understand your language? What did you *do* to me?"

The fear and confusion had returned with a vengeance, erasing the strange languidness that had overtaken her body. She longed to be able to just melt into the bed, anything other than face this impossible situation.

The white-haired man abruptly reached a hand towards her, and Allison shrieked, causing him to immediately jerk it away as if singed.

"Don't touch me!" she moaned, hugged her knees to her body and shutting her eyes tightly, willing herself far away even as she automatically braced herself for an all-too-familiar blow.

This can't be real! Allison thought miserably, remembered pain and old fears coming to the forefront of her entire being and threatening to strangle her. *We got out! I got out! No one was supposed to be able to hurt me again. This is only a nightmare—just a nightmare. I'm still in bed in my apartment. Soon I'll wake up, and this will all be just a bad memory. Just a—*

Her frantic self-reassurances were interrupted by a loud voice that seemed to emerge from the back of her mind, a voice that exclaimed, *"Selwyn, for Seni's sake, calm her!"* The same security and warmth that she had experienced earlier immediately followed that voice, dragging her out of the dark pit she had fallen into and back into the here and now so suddenly that she knew it couldn't have been natural. With a new-found horrible clarity, she now realized that she was being manipulated.

"Stop it!" Allison shouted, her fear instantly melting away into anger as she lifted up her head to glare at the redhead, whom she inexplicably *knew* had caused her to feel that warmth.

She suddenly felt violated in the worst way. Through all her past beatings and verbal abuse by her once stepfather, at least her emotions, her reactions, had been totally *hers*, something *he* couldn't have, and now this stranger had suddenly changed that.

"Whatever it is you're doing to me, just stop it!"

The redhead visibly paled and took a couple of steps back away from the bed. He swayed a little before he took a deep, audible breath and seemed to control himself with considerable effort.

Satisfied that she had unnerved him, she then turned to the white-haired man, who was staring at her with wide eyes, and demanded, "Who are you? *What* are you? Who the hell is Selwyn?" She pointed to the redheaded man and asked, "Is that Selwyn?"

Before the white-haired man could open his mouth to reply, she continued almost in the same breath, "How did I get here? You *must* know! What was it that he was doing to me?"

Somewhere in the back of her mind, Allison knew that she was only able to face these men and boldly demand answers because the redhead had taken away her fear, and that realization only made her angrier.

The man held up his hands as if he was afraid she was about to go for his throat and said, "Please calm yourself, milady. I'll gladly answer your questions, but only one at a time and *only* when you have settled down. We mean you no harm, as I said before, but we do wish to understand how you entered into the kingdom as well. That's a question that we had hoped *you* could answer."

His eyes narrowed as Allison opened her mouth to speak but immediately bit back on the retort she had been ready to spat at him when she suddenly felt a chill go up her spine.

"If you don't calm yourself," he said slowly, his voice low and warning, "then I'll be forced to spell you into immobility again until you are willing to be civil."

Allison's anger died away, and she shivered when she heard the coldness in his voice. In that instant, she knew that this was an extremely dangerous man. She felt her entire body go rigid as she stared back at him, afraid to even blink.

Nodding with satisfaction at her reaction, the man said, "To answer your first question, my name is Aidric Stanisnik. I am the Mage-general of Lamia and also court mage to King Diryan Lasha."

"—which would be me," the auburn-haired man at the foot of the bed said suddenly, speaking for the first time in her presence and nodding slightly when her eyes acknowledged him.

Her eyes were dangerously close to popping out of their sockets. A King—it was no wonder he had such an aura of authority about him!

As she gawked at the king, a particular word in Aidric's introduction of himself suddenly sank into her shocked mind, and she realized the implications of the title he had introduced himself as.

She turned back to Aidric. "You said you were— a m-mage?" Allison asked, her voice stuttering over the last word that she was certain that she had mis-heard.

Aidric exchanged an unreadable look with the king. "Yes," he answered, watching her face more intently.

"But—you can't be," she whispered, more to herself than to him.

"Is that so?" he asked, raising an eyebrow. "Why?"

"Because mages don't exist," she whispered, more to herself than to him.

"Don't exist?" Aidric echoed in bewilderment. "Of course they exist."

Allison shook her head. "Not where I come from," she insisted.

"Most peculiar," King Diryan interjected. "I have never heard of a land in all of Seni's World that does not possess at least the knowledge of mages in general. Even the most remote village in Sonon knows of mages."

"Seni's World?"

"Yes, Seni's World," the king repeated. He raised an eyebrow at her blank expression and asked, "*Surely* you are not ignorant of Seni as well, milady."

The look of utter disapproval on the king's face made Allison uneasy. It reminded her too much of the looks her stepfather used to give her when she had squirmed too much as a child during the excruciatingly long and often times disturbing "church" services he had dragged all of them to every day. Depending on his mood, the consequence of those looks had led to anywhere from a tongue-lashing to a few whacks across her back with a belt for her "disrespect" to the cult's leader. Was "Seni" the name of their god?

"I'm afraid that I am," Allison said hesitantly,

not daring to meet the king's steely gaze. Something in those piercing smoky-blue eyes unnerved her, but she couldn't quite put her finger on it—something familiar. Yet, she couldn't bear to look him in the eyes for more than a few seconds to determine why.

"Where exactly have you come from, Allison?" King Diryan asked with an edge to his voice sharp enough to draw blood.

She instantly shrank back in renew fear at the sudden cold fury and suspicion that flashed within his eyes.

"Please," Allison pleaded weakly, "I meant no offense—"

Frowning, Aidric opened his mouth to speak, but a sharp look from the king instantly silenced him.

"Answer," King Diryan commanded in a chillingly calm voice, ignoring her words completely as if she had never spoken them.

"I-I'm from California," Allison stammered as she forced herself to form her incoherent thoughts into words.

Now it was King Diryan's turn to look puzzled, his harshness melting away almost as quickly as it had appeared. He turned and glanced at first, Aidric, then Selwyn, and finally at the old man who had not so much as uttered a single word in Allison's presence, asking the others the same, silent question with his eyes. He received the same slight shake of the head in return from each of them.

"Where exactly is this—Cali-fornya?" the king asked, the name of the city rolling off his tongue awkwardly.

Allison's heart sank. She knew there were probably tiny, obscure countries in the world she had no idea about, but for someone not to know about a place as well-known as California...

"In America," she replied, a tinge of desperate hope in her tone.

"I'm afraid that I'm not familiar with the village you call Cali-fornya or the kingdom of America."

"I don't believe we *should* be, Your Majesty," Aidric said slowly. "Don't you see? By her own admission, she is of a place alien to our knowledge just as the prophecy foretold. We cannot deny it any longer. It is she. I'm now completely certain of it."

"Oh?" King Diryan inquired. "And what makes you so certain about her identity now when you had doubts earlier?"

"The name of her homeland," Aidric said without hesitation. "You know as well as everyone else present in this room that I have traveled to the ends of Seni's World and back, and I have never heard of the kingdom she speaks of. Before you ask, let me ease your mind by saying that she is speaking the truth. I took the chance of darting in quickly to read the information directly from her mind. The only questions that really remain are how she ended up in the Forest of Illusions and why did a miniature Mage-field suddenly appear out of nowhere around her?"

Prophecies? Allison thought with confusion. *Mage-fields? What in the world is he talking about?*

"Yes, milady," King Diryan said, turning back to her, "how *did* you end up in our kingdom without being detected by our guards at the Lamian-Sononese border as being one of the mageborn?"

"I really don't know!" Allison insisted, clutching anxiously at the blankets again. "Believe me when I say I don't know! One minute I'm at a local park walking with my sister, and the next minute a bright light suddenly appeared out of nowhere in front of me. A force pulled me inside into a world of complete madness, and then the next thing I know, I'm lying on my face in a place so alien to me that I thought the whole thing had been a dream!"

"You journeyed through a portal, no doubt," Aidric said, "a portal that could have only been constructed by the will of Seni if there truly are no mageborn in your world."

"There's that name again—Seni," Allison said. "You keep mentioning his name. Who is he, or is it a she?"

Aidric and King Diryan exchanged peculiar glances.

"Seni is our divine master," Aidric answered simply, "our creator, and I believe it's by His will that you were brought here as you were. Long ago, a Seer from the Order of the Providence—those priests gifted with powerful Foresight abilities—foretold your coming. Ever since, the people of Lamia have long awaited your coming with much anxiety and fear."

"Fear? They're afraid of *me*?" Allison asked incredulously. "Just *who* am I supposed to be?"

Aidric didn't answer her right away. He exchanged uneasy looks with King Diryan, who merely shrugged and waved a hand in a gesture of assent. Aidric nodded slowly, then fixed his gaze on Allison, his unusual, pale-violet eyes boring so intently into her own that she immediately looked away uncomfortably.

"Can it be so terrible," Allison said quietly, careful not to meet those overpowering eyes, "that you hesitate to tell me?"

"Yes, I hesitate to tell you," came his even reply, "but not because it's necessarily terrible. I hesitate because I'm not certain of your reaction given that you don't believe that I am a mage."

Allison sighed and raised wary eyes to him again. "Given everything I've experienced today, I shouldn't doubt what you've told me so far. You pretty much proved it earlier by paralyzing me and then removing my paralysis later with literally a wave of your hand. I've been running it over and over in my mind, and although it's completely crazy, the only explanation that makes sense is that you *are* what you profess to be."

Aidric moved forward and knelt down at her bedside, and to her alarm, he gently took her right hand in his. She started to pull away, but he squeezed her hand more firmly and she instinctually froze. He then held out his free hand, palm up, and as her eyes darted from their joined hands to his other, a flash of light suddenly appeared in its center. When the flash cleared, a small, golden globe of pulsating light rested within the palm of his hand. Allison could only stare at the ball of light in mute shock.

"Trust me when I say I *am* a mage—as you are as well."

CHAPTER EIGHT

A llison felt her entire body go rigid as she slowly lifted her eyes to Aidric's face.

"W-What?" she stammered in disbelief, her mind still reeling from the shock of the glowing orb he had produced from thin air.

"Whether you realize it or not, you *are* mage-born, Allison, with the potential of becoming a very powerful adept-mage," Aidric said. The orb in his hand abruptly disappeared, and he lowered it to cover the hand he was already clasping. "We all believe you to be the mage named in the prophecy I spoke of earlier, one known as the Golden Mage. *That* is the reason for our fear. You hold much magical potential within you that we cannot even begin to guess how much you *are* capable of doing. I am the most powerful mage in the kingdom, perhaps in all of Seni's

World, and you easily blasted through my strongest shields and laid me flat with the power of a single mind-scream."

Allison jerked her hand out of his grasp, her head shaking vigorously in denial. "I didn't—I can't—" she protested weakly, her stomach lurching as if she was about to become ill. "It isn't possible—"

"But it is, milady," Aidric said firmly. "There is no mistaking the power you have within your hands. Any fool with the slightest inkling of mage potential could plainly see your potential."

"You don't understand," Allison said in agitation. "I *can't* be a mage. Mages are only fantasy where I come from. No one there has the ability to perform *real* magic that isn't only clever illusion, least of all *me*. Sure, we have people who claim to be what we call in my language 'psychics' and 'telekinetics' who are able to predict the future, read minds, or levitate objects with the power of their minds, but those kinds of paranormal abilities have never been proven to actually exist. Now you're telling me that I can suddenly work magic! *Real* magic! It just doesn't make sense."

"Indeed it doesn't," Aidric mused. "I have never known someone to suddenly manifest mage abilities without being born with the ability in the first place. Yet, if you are the Golden Mage as we believe, then anything is possible."

"What made you even think that I'm the one in your prophecy in the first place?"

"The hue of your hair."

"My hair?" Allison said in surprise, raising a hand to finger it in confusion. "What's wrong with the color of my hair?"

"Your hair is golden," Aidric explained. "It's a feature described specifically in the Prophecy of the Golden Mage. In all of the lands I have traveled across throughout Seni's World, I have never seen anyone with hair that is golden."

Allison's brow creased in bewilderment as she took in his words. *He hasn't ever seen anyone with blonde hair? How could he not? Unless—*

She swallowed hard against the lump of new fear that suddenly formed in her throat at the direction her thoughts were leading. It was as if a bolt of lightning had suddenly jarred her awake from her nightmare—into the clutches of another even more terrifying than the first because this one wasn't a dream at all.

"I'm not on Earth any longer, am I?" Allison asked in a flat voice.

A huge gasp instantly brought all eyes onto the king, who was suddenly staring at Allison with an odd expression, something like bewilderment if he hadn't been frowning so severely.

"Your Majesty, what—" Aidric began before King Diryan interrupted, ignoring Aidric completely.

"Did I hear you correctly, milady?" the king demanded. "Did you imply that you came from *Earth*?"

"Yes," Allison answered, her pulse speeding up. "You've heard of it?"

"I believe I have," he replied. The redhead—Selwyn—flashed him a startled look. "My father once told me a tale when I was but a lad about a stranger who suddenly stumbled into a tavern in Lepha about 150 years ago. He was raving like a madman in a strange, fluid language, calling everyone—oh, what was the word Father used—*'monsieur,'* I believe it was."

"*Monsieur!*" Allison exclaimed. "That's—" She broke off helplessly when her excited mind could not find an equivalent word in the Lamian language, but then finished hastily in English, "—French!"

King Diryan leaned eagerly forward. "You know the language?"

"Yes!" Allison answered excitedly. "At least enough of it to know that *'monsieur'* means 'sir.'"

He nodded thoughtfully. "No one in Lepha knew what to make of him. In the beginning, they thought him possessed by demons and sent him to the village temple in order for him to be cleansed. Of course, the Senini found nothing of the sort in him, only a great amount of fear and confusion—much like you. The Senini sent for a Master Linguist, who implanted the Lephan tongue into his memory as Zenas has done to you with ours."

Well, that explains why I'm suddenly fluent in Lamian—sort of, she thought dazedly. *That's one mystery out of a thousand more cleared up, but...what the heck are Senini? Priests? Exorcists?*

"The stranger's name was Alphonse, if I remember correctly, and he said he had come from a land named Paris. He also mentioned Earth as you have, though the word he used was '*Terre.*' He was dressed in clothing similar to our own in that period, but the fabrics were most peculiar, such as have never been seen anywhere. My father told me that Lepha still possesses his garments in their royal archives under spell-lock. They called him *Lans-alamarsk*—the Phantom Stranger—because he claimed that he had been walking in his world when he became disoriented and appeared in the village of Toril just like a phantom."

"What became of him?" Allison asked eagerly. "Was he able to find a way to get back home?"

"I'm afraid not, milady," King Diryan replied apologetically as Allison's sudden hope came crashing down. "He lived out his life in Lepha according to my father."

Somewhere in the back of her mind, Allison had been holding on to the desperate belief that everything would be all right and her current nightmare would be just that—a nightmare, but the king's words suddenly brought reality crashing down on her.

"You mean—I'm stuck here—permanently?" she asked in a small voice, uncertain whether or not she wanted to hear the answer.

Everyone fell silent for a moment, shifting uncomfortably under her watchful, imploring eyes.

It was Aidric that finally broke the heavy silence by answering, "Allison, I'm sorry, but I'm afraid that it is so."

"But—but—can't *you* help me?" she pleaded, grabbing his upper arm. "You're supposed to be a *mage*. Can't you—cast a spell or something to send me back?"

She didn't want to accept his words—she couldn't. Accepting her fate meant that she had to face it, and she was already on the verge of falling apart. She wanted to believe there was still hope, still a way for her to get back home to the new life she had struggled so hard to build for herself, but when she saw the pity in Aidric's eyes, she knew before he spoke that there was no hope at all.

"I'm sorry, milady, but I know of no spell that

can help you. We can only open portals between magical planes within our own world, not alternate worlds. I wouldn't know where to even begin. Until you appeared, I didn't believe it was possible for a portal to be built between worlds. That's why I strongly believe that it was Seni that brought you here, that the ancient Prophecy of the Golden Mage has begun to unfold. It's the only logical explanation. I'm sorry, but you must remain here as Seni wills."

"No," Allison whispered in a barely audible voice. Then louder, "No—NO!" Suddenly she was sobbing brokenly into her hands. "Kat, my mom, my friends...I won't ever..."

As she sobbed, she was vaguely aware of the sound of clothing fluttering softly, of Aidric's presence near her, and then of footsteps echoing across the marble floor. Only when she heard a door click shut did she raise her now pounding head from her hands and regard the room with tears still leaking from her eyes.

Allison froze when she found that Selwyn, King Diryan, and the silent Zenas were no longer in the room, and only Aidric remained, on his feet again and staring at her with the oddest expression. Her sniffles immediately stopped when her gaze met his strange eyes—eyes that were guarded but at the same time, swimming with secrets. They seemed the very eyes she saw every morning when she looked into a mirror.

Then without warning, he reached out a deliberate hand and gently brushed a falling tear from her cheek.

Startled, she shrank away from his touch and whispered, *"Don't."*

He pulled his hand away as if it had been slapped, a puzzled expression forming on his face.

"Why are you so afraid of me?" he asked just as softly. "I mean you no harm; I have *done* you no harm. I only wished to comfort your pain."

"I—I don't know," she replied uneasily, still shrinking away from him while new tears began to shimmer in her eyes.

"I think you do."

"Wouldn't you be frightened if you were in my shoes?" she demanded.

"In your shoes?" he asked, his expression becoming even more perplexed. "What do you mean—"

"Never mind," she interrupted with a shaky sigh. "Where did the others go?"

"I sent them away."

"Why?"

"I could sense your despair. You may not realize it, but you are broad-sending your emotions openly, and with my Empathy, they are as clear as though you were shouting them. I thought that you and I could speak alone for a while without the pressure of having a king watching your every move and an old man's suspicious eyes boring into you. I want you to feel at ease with me, Allison."

Allison looked away. "I don't know you at all," she said softly.

"Too true," Aidric said with a sigh, but he flashed her an encouraging smile. "Then I suppose I should begin by telling you about myself and my kingdom."

Turning to look at him again, Allison slowly nodded.

Aidric cautiously sat on the edge of the bed beside her and began, "Once again, I'm the Mage-general of Lamia as well as the king's personal court mage. My duty to my kingdom and to Seni is to protect my king and people from all threats, as well as to guard the Mage-field from those who would abuse it."

"What's the Mage-field?" she asked curiously before she could stop herself.

"It's the place where adept-mages draw their power," he explained. "It lies mostly along the Lami-an-Sononese border to the south. It's not something that can be seen by normal sight. Only mages that possess Inner-sight can actually see the energy gathered there. To all others, it is merely a clearing within the forest.

"No one knows how a Mage-field comes to be formed, but I suspect that mankind had no hand in their origin. It also serves as the power source to fuel the Shield spell around the borders of Lamia that has thus far been proven impenetrable, even to my power, and I'm yet to find another mage my equal." He grinned suddenly. "Although, I suspect that your mage abilities will one day exceed my own. I can't be certain until you master them completely."

"I still say that I couldn't possibly have any mage powers," Allison said stubbornly.

"That you do is irrefutable," Aidric replied with a chuckle. "What do you think you were doing when you collapsed in the forest?"

She sat up straighter. "You know why I was hearing voices that weren't there?"

This was one of the questions that had been plaguing her since the first time she had awakened in Aidric's bed. She had assumed that her strange journey through the light realm had caused her to go temporarily mad, and the voices had been the product of hallucination. Apparently, that had only been her wishful thinking.

"You were using the magic of a mind-mage," he

said. "You fully opened your mind to every thought within our borders, and they all came rushing into your head at intolerable volumes. Your mind shut down because it could not bear what you were putting it through, thus, your collapse."

"Mindreading?" Allison inquired skeptically.

"Yes, mindreading," Aidric's voice amusedly said inside her head.

Allison gasped in shock and pressed her hands against either side of her head. If not for the fact that his lips never moved when she heard his voice, she *never* would have believed what had just happened.

"How did you do that?" she demanded in a strangled voice.

The corners of his mouth stretched up. *"Simple,"* she heard within her mind again. *"I merely reached for the channels into your mind that are receptive to external thoughts and sent my thoughts through them. Since you share my ability, you can hear me, although it is not mindreading. It's one of the many forms of thought projection. We call it 'thought-speech' and those whose gifts lie in thought-speech, levitation, mind-probing, and mindreading, 'mind-mages.' Go ahead, try it. Just concentrate on placing your whole attention on me, and imagine that an invisible thread links our minds together. Then, just send your thoughts down that imaginary thread."*

"I can't do something like that!" Allison said

aloud.

"Yes you can. Have faith," Aidric sent. *"I know what I'm talking about."*

With a huge dose of trepidation, Allison did as he instructed. She focused her full attention onto his face, did her best to imagine a line linking their minds together, and thought as hard as she could, *"CAN YOU HEAR ME?"* Not particularly clever, but it was all she could think of to say.

To her surprise, Aidric's face suddenly contorted into a grimace of pain, and he grabbed ahold of his head.

"Ah! Not so loud!" he exclaimed, flashing her a pained look. "You don't need to think so hard. Only the barest sliver of a thought is needed in order to be heard. Your thoughts are like your voice—you control the volume in which you desire to be heard. You can send emotions through your thoughts, as well, but that lesson is for another time. For now, is there anything you wish to ask me?"

"Yes…" Allison said hesitantly. "You—you say that I'm this 'Golden Mage' person. What exactly does that mean? What is it that you plan to do with me because of it?"

"I'm not certain how King Diryan will proceed with the situation," Aidric replied thoughtfully after a moment's silence. "Your presence here in our kingdom was unexpected. It's a delicate matter—one that will require much more consideration and discussion. According to our prophecy, the Golden Mage is said to possess great power that can be very dangerous if it's not controlled. More than likely, the king will assign you to me as an apprentice since I am really the only one qualified to teach you to control your mage abilities."

"And after you teach me, what then?" she asked warily.

"You will be sworn as a sacred mage of Seni by our Horae, the priests of politics and warfare. A feast will be held in your honor in the palace as you are presented before the entire order of all classes of mages, but you need not be concerned with any of the ceremonial aspects just yet. Mage lessons usually take two to three years to complete."

Feeling the ground crumbling beneath her, Allison pressed her lips together firmly and turned her gaze away from Aidric to the plain, granite wall, wistfully longing for a window to gaze out of, but the room oddly contained none. She turned so quickly that he did not see the shimmer of tears beginning to form in her eyes.

Allison felt a hand hesitantly rest on her shoulder, but this time, she didn't flinch away. The warmth of his hand through the material of her blouse gave her a little comfort, and she found that he no longer frightened her so much as made her feel unsettled.

"I was going to be a councilor you know," she said softly into the silence, her gaze still turned to the wall.

He said nothing.

"I had such big plans," she continued, her voice wavering dangerously. "I wanted to help other traumatized children the way a councilor once helped me."

"Allison—" Aidric began.

She continued on as if she hadn't heard him. "Then this happens. Suddenly I'm whisked off and abandoned in an alien world by a god whose name I've never even heard before and given some super scary powers that I have no idea how to control. Now, instead of the councilor I've worked so hard to become, I have no choice but to become something I'm not sure I want to be."

As the tears that had been swelling in her eyes began to slowly fall down her cheeks, Allison turned her head back around to face Aidric, her eyes heavy with a heart-wrenching sorrow. His expression somber, Aidric lowered his hand from her shoulder and gently cupped her folded hands into his own. He looked at her as if he wanted to speak, but he seemed at a loss for words.

As the tears continued to fall in eternal streams down the curves of her face, she whispered, "I'm nobody. There's nothing at all remarkable about me, so why...?"

"Seni has many reasons for his actions," Aidric replied quietly, "though He is not overly fond of disclosing them. Take heart, Allison. I don't believe you were brought here only to fulfill the role of our prophecy. Nothing is ever so cut and dry as that. We must simply have faith that all will be well in the end and accept the task given to us."

CHAPTER NINE

A llison regarded Aidric's serene expression when he spoke of Seni with a sense of wonder. There was no doubt that he was every bit as devoted to his god as her stepfather was, if not more so, and yet, he didn't show the same severity that her father did, the fanaticism. There was only a sense of peace around him, and total devotion to the god he called Seni as though it was the most natural thing in the world.

"You're really devoted to your god," Allison said, pulling her hands from his and wiping away all the stray tears on her face. "Is that why the king seemed insulted and furious when I told him that I didn't know who Seni was?"

Aidric nodded. "Though, it isn't just Lamia who is devoted. All kingdoms to the ends of the world devote their lives to Seni, for it is He whom we truly serve. As for the king, the anger he showed is a bit more complicated than a matter of your ignorance. His Majesty has lost much to the will of Seni, more than he cares to admit, and the thought of someone from our world that was spared the burden of devotion, of absolute obedience, by her ignorance infuriated him. That's why he softened when he learned that you came from a different world, but regrettably, the story of his woes is a long one. Maybe someday I'll tell it to you, but for now it is better left unsaid."

"Of course—I didn't mean to—it's none of my business—" Allison stammered, feeling her pulse speed up with renewed anxiety. She hadn't considered that it might be taboo or even against the law to ask personal questions about the king.

"You don't have to look so worried, milady," Aidric said gently. "You may ask me anything."

"It's because I have no idea why you're being so, well, so *nice* to me," she blurted, his assurances making her feel even more agitated. "You, yourself, said that I was dangerous, that everyone was scared of what I might do. Unless that prophecy spells everything out about my life up until now, you don't even know what kind of person I am. Yet here you are patiently answering my probably inappropriate questions instead of demanding answers. Even when I tried to escape, you were nothing but gentle to me when I expected punishment."

"Have you been hurt so deeply in the past that you are surprised to find a little kindness in others?" he cut in with a frown.

Allison suddenly found her hands very interesting. "I'm just confused," she insisted, her voice tight with tension.

She could feel Aidric staring at her almost like a physical touch, making her desperately want to dive under the blankets to hide like a frightened child. She *hated* being scrutinized. It reminded her too much of... Allison sucked in a sharp breath. *No!* She refused to allow her mind to go *there!*

It's not the same. It's not the same!

"I sense a darkness in you," Aidric abruptly said, making her nearly jump out of her skin, "something that has been stirring in your soul for a long while..."

Allison drew in a deep breath in an effort to calm her racing heart. "You're—very observant," she said, attempting to keep her voice light, but the slight tremors in her voice ruined the effect, "but I'd rather not talk about it right now."

She was relieved when he didn't press.

Instead, Aidric suggested cheerfully, "Shall we speak about your homeland, this Earth—or was it California?"

"Both," Allison replied, this time managing to smile a little when he actually pronounced California right unlike the king. "Like you call your world simply 'Seni's World,' we call ours Earth. I'm actually from a place called the 'United States'—I guess it would be the equivalent of a kingdom here but ruled differently. It's broken up into fifty sections and the section, or 'state,' I live in is called California. There's so much to tell. Is there anything in particular that you would like to know about Earth?"

"So much I don't know where to begin," Aidric said eagerly. "Does anyone else in your world have golden hair as you do?"

She chuckled. "Yes, millions probably, but we call it 'blonde.'"

"A rather harsh name for such beautiful locks," he commented, fingering a strand of her hair.

Allison blushed furiously. She never seemed to be able to handle compliments gracefully. They always made her feel ashamed, a result of years of her stepfather punishing her for the "sins" of all her supposed instances of pride and vanity.

"And what about your own hair?" she asked quickly, eager to steer the subject off herself. "I've never seen anyone as young as you look with white hair."

"Truly?" Aidric said with interest. "The hue of

my hair is as common here on both the youth and the ancient as the grass underfoot. It's little wonder why you looked at me so strangely. We must appear as foreign to you as you do to us."

"Not everyone," Allison said. "Just you."

"How so?"

"Besides their clothes, the others look like the people of my world," she explained. "Only you are visibly different with the colors of your hair and eyes. I've never seen anyone with eyes your shade of pale-violet."

"Indeed, not many people possess them here, either," he said with amusement. "I guess I'm just one who is full of oddities."

"I didn't mean to imply—" she stuttered, her cheeks coloring once again in embarrassment.

"Of course you didn't," he said with a brisk laugh. "I was merely teasing you. Forgive me. Sometimes even the Mage-general can forget his manners."

Before she could respond, the amusement suddenly left Aidric's eyes, and they became distant, as if he was deep in thought. Before she could ask him what was wrong, the warmth flooded back into his eyes, and he regarded her with a bemused expression.

"Don't look so alarmed, milady," he said. "I was only listening to King Diryan's Seneschal, Lord Ion. He has summoned me to the Council Room, no doubt to discuss you. Unfortunately, I must leave you now. Feel free to wander about my chambers as you please while I'm away, but I'm afraid that you cannot leave my suite just yet." He looked troubled as he explained all of this to her. "I know that it sounds as if you are a prisoner here, but trust me when I say that it's for your own safety as well as ours."

"I understand," Allison assured him.

She was startled when he took one of her hands and lifted to his lips, planting a light kiss onto the back of it.

"I'll not be long," he promised as he released her hand. "We have many more conversations to engage in that I'll be eagerly awaiting. There is so much about your world that I wish to know, as I'm certain you have many questions about mine. I should have better answers as to your status here as well. Until then, please make yourself comfortable in my absence. If you are hungry, the servants have left food in the sitting room. There are also countless books there that you may want to explore. Many of them contain the histories of Lamia and her surrounding kingdoms. I trust that you will find them of great interest. Now, I must excuse myself. A *long* Council meeting demands my attention."

He smiled wryly and added, "And this was supposed to be my day off!"

Allison shyly returned the smile. Aidric gave her a slight bow before he turned on his heel and briskly left the room. Only when she heard a door bang shut in the distance did she slip from beneath the mass of warm blankets, standing unsteadily in just her socks on the marble floor. Her knees felt as wobbly as cooked spaghetti, not a good prognosis since she also felt a little dizzy.

Now that Aidric was no longer there to capture all her attention, Allison was able to assess her surroundings more thoroughly. A strange device against the far wall immediately caught her eye as she gazed about the room. A large and narrow, rectangular-shaped hole had been carved into the wall starting about a foot from the floor and ending about a foot from the ceiling. Inside, a glass tube as wide as her arm ran horizontally in the very center of the rectangle, marked with numerous equally distanced black notches from top to bottom, two of them thicker and more prominent than all the rest.

On closer inspection, she saw what appeared to be a small amount of dark sand the color of powdered cocoa falling down the tube to settle at the bottom, falling from a hole where the top of the tube met the granite wall. The depth of the sand at the bottom of the tube had already accumulated a little higher than the nineteenth mark.

It could only be a clock. There was just no other logical explanation for it. With a little imagination, it even vaguely resembled an hourglass, though this clock obviously would not need to be flipped over every hour, which brought up a pressing question. There were a lot more marks than twenty-four, so how *did* they manage to tell time on it? For that matter, how did it work? Was magic used? Allison certainly didn't see any electrical outlets anywhere in the room! She would have to remember to ask Aidric about it later.

Thinking about electrical outlets made her suddenly wonder what illuminated the room. Without windows, it obviously was not sunlight. She looked above her and gasped in surprise. A glass lantern hung suspended in the air without the aid of any ceiling fixtures—more magic, no doubt—but that was not what had her gaping up at it like a fool. The flame which the lantern housed was *green*

She had not seen a green flame since her physics class in high school when they had stuck wires dipped in different chemicals into the flames of their Bunsen burners, though the result had looked nothing like *these* flames. The green flames seemed to pulse with energy, creating an uncanny illusion that the flames were some kind of heart.

Allison suddenly had a powerful urge to get out

of the room.

Can this day get any more messed up? she thought dazedly as she hurried out of the bedroom, down a hall, and then into a high-ceilinged chamber almost four times the size of the bedroom. Her eyes widened as she drank in the elegance of what could only be the sitting room Aidric had spoken of earlier. However, "sitting room" hardly seemed fitting words to describe such a place.

As it was in the bedroom, the floor consisted of polished marble, but that's where the resemblance ended and the grandeur began. Four identical, intricately carved marble columns stood at each of the four corners of the room. Delicate swirls were painstakingly carved into the marble in complicated, symmetrical patterns that resembled oceanic waves, beginning from the top of the column to the very bottom. Amid the many swirls, what appeared to be gold was embedded in concert with the patterns. On closer inspection, Allison found that it was indeed gold.

Two smaller columns stood on either side of what was probably the front door to his—apartment? Suite? She vaguely remembered Aidric saying that he was a "court" mage. Did that mean he lived in the king's palace? She filed that question away as one of the thousands she would probably end up wanting to ask Aidric when he returned.

Two creatures that greatly resembled lions, except for the folded wings on their backs and their tall, pointed ears, protruded from either side of each column where it met with the ceiling. They were both terrifying and beautiful to behold. What impressed Allison the most was the fact that they were carved entirely out of solid gold with two jewels that were possibly emeralds as eyes.

In wonder, her eyes drifted from the magnificence of the golden sculptures to the colorful array of jewels embedded into two sets of sapphire-blue curtains that hung over two small, but wide, windows. *At last!* The curtains appeared to consist of the same material as Aidric's cape and breeches.

Jeez, Allison thought amazingly, *do these people have an obsession with gold and precious stones? They seem to be everywhere!*

Furniture-wise, the room was pretty bare. Only a couple of rather plush, but comfortable-looking couches lined the walls on either side of the front door. Two huge, cushioned chairs that matched the couches rested on either side of the two windows.

—and a perfect spot for them. One could sit and gaze out of the windows and dream—NO! she scolded herself firmly. *You're not going to think about your dreams and what might have been. That life's over now, and you should be concentrating on coping with this new one. You did it before*

when Mom and you finally escaped that asshole, and you damn well can do it again!

Before she could work herself up into a panic attack, Allison quickly turned away from the windows and forced herself to once again focus her attention on her inspection of the room. As Aidric had promised, rows upon rows of bookshelves lined two of the walls, their presence adding a "homey" feeling to an otherwise museum-like atmosphere.

She walked over to the set of bookshelves along the eastern wall and began to scan its contents. Not surprisingly, given how she had ended up being able to understand and speak the Lamian language, she found that she could read the strange symbols on the spines of the books. Most of them were labeled as spellbooks of various types, and something in her subconscious mind told her that she should leave those particular books alone until Aidric offered to show them to her.

The others were histories of what she guessed were past Lamian battles, politics, and other related events. A few volumes contained what she assessed by their titles to be local myths and legends. Eagerly, she pulled the thickest of these folklore books off the shelf and began to thumb through it in hopes of finding a section which explained the Prophecy of the Golden Mage. She really knew nothing much about their prophecy, just that she was supposedly a powerful mage that appeared from another world, identified by the color of her hair. Aidric had been frustratingly vague when explaining the details of the prophecy, though purposely, she was not certain. Maybe one of the books in his collection would explain it to her more thoroughly.

To her utter disappointment, within a few seconds of flipping through the pages of the book, she found that the book was not written in the same language Zenas had given her. Pages upon pages of strange rune-like symbols lay before her, reminding her of the first time she had seen Arabic words. Irritably, she shelved the book and pulled out another. It, too, was written in that strange language as the first. She wanted to scream in frustration after a five-minute search through the rest of the folklore books turned up nothing that was readable.

"Why in the hell did they write the titles on the spine in one language when the book was written in another?" she muttered angrily under her breath.

On a hunch, she selected a book on the history of Lamia and opened it to the first page. Sure enough, this book was written in the strange symbols of the Lamian language she knew and could read thanks to Zenas's gift. Allison suspected that the rest of the history books were written in the Lamian language as well.

Strange, she thought suspiciously. *I'll have to remember to ask Aidric about them later. I'm sure there's a special reason why only those particular books are written in a different language.*

Suddenly, the rather insistent growling of her stomach interrupted her thoughts. Only then did she realize just how hungry she was.

God, I'm starving. Kat and I never got around to eating lunch. I have no way of knowing how long I've been here since I was probably unconscious for more than half the time I've been in this crazy world. Aidric said there was food around here somewhere...

She scanned the room again, trying to ignore the stab of pain in her heart that remembering her sister caused her, and spotted the dining table on the other side of one of the couches. As Aidric had promised, a variety of foods covered the table, some recognizable and others not.

Allison selected what she hoped was an apple, an orange, and a small loaf of bread, deciding against trying any of the meats or cheeses no matter how appetizing they seemed because she had no way of knowing from what animal they had come from. She didn't want to find out later that she had eaten the meat of a dog or a cat! She also decided to pass on the fruits and vegetables she didn't recognize. Kat had always said she was a finicky eater.

Her smile was bittersweet as she remembered a time when her sister and she had been in elementary school, and her stepfather had threatened her with a beating if she didn't eat her Brussels sprouts.

"The good lord has given you food when others are starving," he had lectured sternly when she had complained that she did not like them, "so you should appreciate it and clean your plate unless you want a severe penance tonight!"

It had been the first time her mother had prepared them, and she had always loathed trying anything new ever since she'd had a bad experience the first time she had tasted sour cream. Resigning herself for a beating later on, Allison had sat picking at her meal until Katherine slyly scooped up every sprout on her plate when neither of their parents were looking and shoved them into the front of her shirt along with her own helping. Miraculously, that had been one of the few times she had escaped a beating.

No! Allison scolded, giving her head a shake. *I won't think about her.*

With her meal and the book of Lamian history tucked securely under her arm, she moved over to one of the huge chairs beside the window. She resisted the urge to draw the curtains back, not sure if she was ready to see what lay beyond just yet, and settled herself comfortably within the soft cushions to eat and read.

Within a few minutes, Allison was totally oblivious to the world around her as the fascinating history of Lamia quickly unfolded before her eyes.

CHAPTER TEN

A llison was so engrossed in her book when Aidric finally returned a few hours later that she didn't even hear him enter the suite, much less sense his presence, as he approached her chair. When he abruptly spoke her name, she cried out in surprise and dropped the book onto the floor. It fell in an unceremonious heap at Aidric's feet. As Allison blushed furiously in embarrassment and tried to calm her racing heart, Aidric chuckled and bent down to retrieve the book.

I wish I could stop being so jumpy, she thought irritably. *Aidric must think that I'm afraid of my own shadow!* Instantly she reproached herself. *There I go again. Why should I care what he thinks of me, anyway? I've never really cared what people thought of me before, so why should I start caring now?*

Yet, as Allison looked at Aidric, she knew that she *did* care what this strange man thought of her, and that realization left her feeling unsettled.

"I didn't mean to startle you," Aidric said as he handed the book back to her, amusement glittering in his eyes.

"I—I don't usually scare so easily, but after everything that's happened to me today, I'm afraid that my nerves are shot," she explained hastily, annoyingly feeling herself blush again.

"You have the most peculiar way of phrasing your words," Aidric remarked. "Sometimes I have a difficult time understanding exactly what you mean, but at the same time, when I don't take your words so literally, their meaning is clear."

"I could say the same about the way you and your people talk," Allison retorted. "You all speak so formally as if you were giving an important speech in front of a bunch of dried out old scholars."

"I meant no insult," Aidric said apologetically. "In fact, I find it pleasant."

"How so?"

"It brings a little mystery into the conversation," he replied with a boyish grin. "I never know what charming little phrase you'll use next!"

His innocent observation made her shift uncomfortably in her chair. It was a blatant reminder that she was now an outsider again just as she had been when she was a child. When her mother had married her stepfather, she hadn't been allowed to play with any of the neighborhood children, or to really have any friends at all. Her stepfather also had a reputation within the community as being a real asshole. As a result, Katherine and she had often been bullied in school. Their cruel taunts had caused her much grief and pain, so she hated to be reminded of those dark times in her life.

"I see. I take it that your meeting went well since you're in such a good mood," Allison said, quickly changing the subject. She smiled tentatively at him. "Apparently, they decided not to throw me into the dungeon or whatever it is you people do to prisoners around here or else you would be carrying chains and an armed escort instead of those clothes. Are they for me?"

The cheer in his eyes abruptly disappeared, and his expression grew grim.

Alarmed by this sudden mood change, Allison quickly asked, "I—I didn't—say anything *wrong* did I?"

Aidric shook his head. "You wouldn't have said what you said with such casualness had you known just how close your words almost came to be."

Allison could feel the blood leave her cheeks.

"You mean—I—you—they actually were thinking of throwing me into a *dungeon*? You can't be *serious*!"

He nodded unhappily and said, "That and more, I'm afraid. You must understand that the king's councilors were terribly frightened when Diryan spoke of your appearance. They know only too well the threat that you pose to Lamia, to their own lives. I'm ashamed to admit that their first reaction to this news was to demand that His Majesty order you to be put to death immediately."

"But why?" she cried. "I've done nothing wrong!"

"In their eyes you have," Aidric replied grimly. "Your mere appearance in our kingdom poses a lethal threat that *would* justify a death sentence—under normal circumstances. By law, we are required to immediately execute those who would threaten the lives of any in the kingdom, but I explained to them that you are an exception. Since it's obviously Seni's will that has brought you here, it's also His will that you fulfill the destiny He has given you no matter the cost to Lamia. It would be blasphemous to defy Seni's will, and even if it were not, neither I nor Diryan would willfully order the death of an innocent!"

Allison's fear subsided a bit when she heard the steel in his voice.

Maybe he's the only one I can trust now...

However, before she could complete that thought, an inner voice screamed in warning. Could his show of protectiveness possibly be a façade? Aidric had powers after all—persuasive powers that he could at this very moment be using on her to trust him as Selwyn had made her feel calm and protected with his power. She *wanted* to trust him, yet, that nagging suspicion would not go away. How did she know that he was truly sincere?

Can I afford to trust him? Allison thought warily. *Can I afford not to? In a situation like this, he just seems to be too good to be true, or am I just being paranoid? He sounds sincere enough. Oh hell—if I can't trust him, then who can I?*

She suddenly felt eyes boring into her, and she looked up into worried, violet eyes.

"Your emotions," Aidric said with a frown, "they were so open to my Empathy earlier, and now all I sense is numbness, a void. You may not realize it, but you are deliberately blocking me out. Do you not think I speak the truth about what was decided?"

"How can I be deliberately blocking you out and not realize I'm doing it at the same time?" Allison asked, shaken that he could so easily know what she was feeling. She suddenly felt like an opened book, laid exposed for all to see. "You're contradicting yourself."

"Am I?" he said softly. He took a step closer.

"You didn't answer my question."

"No, I'm *not* afraid of you," she said, raising her chin a bit in something like defiance.

"That's not what I asked."

Aidric moved closer. Allison began to tremble despite her best efforts to maintain control. He pried one of her hands from its death-grip on the book in her lap and grasped it firmly. She sat frozen, barely daring to breathe as they stared at one another. It was then that Allison realized she *did* fear—quite a lot. He stirred an uneasiness in her that no one else had ever done before, and what frightened her most was that she really couldn't say why.

"I *do* frighten you," Aidric said quietly.

"N-no—no you don't," she insisted stubbornly, wincing inwardly when her words sounded hollow even to her own ears.

"Yes I do," he said firmly, his thumb gently stoking the back of her hand, "else you would not be trembling."

"All right, yes!" Allison blurted out to her horror, but once the words began to spill out, she found that she couldn't stop the flow. "I don't know why you frighten me—you just *do*. I want to trust you—I really do, but every time you come near me, it makes me uneasy. I don't know why it should because you've been nothing but kind to me." Allison refused to meet his eyes. "My fear must insult you!"

She was rambling, and she knew it.

"It does nothing of the kind," Aidric assured her gently. "I'm a stranger to you, and I expect nothing less. Do we not fear *you*—the powerful Golden Mage delivered to our kingdom by Seni, Himself? It's only natural that two mages as powerful as us should be wary of each other. As you said earlier, trust must be earned." He smiled self-deprecatingly. "I suppose speaking to you about the king's councilors' desire to put you to death is not the best way to go about earning your trust."

Allison shifted uncomfortably in her chair under his scrutinizing gaze and suddenly felt like an idiot. Her uneasiness—was that just her sensing his magic? It had never even occurred to her to think that his overwhelming presence had a physical rather than a psychological cause.

"I'm sorry," she murmured after a moment of tense silence, her shoulders slumping.

"Fear needs no apology," Aidric said, squeezing her hand in reassurance. "Know that I'll do everything in my power to protect you." He grinned suddenly. "After all, you are now my ward."

She tilted her head in puzzlement. "Ward?"

"The king just officially granted my proposal to have you as my apprentice, and everyone knows that

I don't take kindly to my wards being mistreated or threatened in any way. I'll be the first to admit that my temper can be pretty vicious sometimes!"

"I'm your *apprentice*?" Allison asked in alarm. "What does that mean? I won't have to be your servant or anything like that will I?"

Aidric laughed. "Your world must be a strange one, indeed, with all the assumptions you make about ours. Of course you won't be my servant! You are to be my student and *nothing else*. I'll teach you to use and understand your mage powers. You will live here in the palace with me until you reach full adept status. I have a spare room for apprentices that I'm sure you will find quite comfortable. After you are declared a mage by the Horae, then who knows? Perhaps Diryan will give you a palace position, or if by then the tension between our kingdom and the kingdom of Mihr becomes worse—and I pray to Seni that it will *not*—you will be assigned to that area.

"Of course, wherever you are assigned to, you will be given quarters of your own, either here in the Mage Hall or in one of the villages of your choice. In all probability, Diryan will keep you here at the palace because of the threat the prophecy says you pose to us. You, nor I, must ever forget that you are the Golden Mage."

"It sounds as if I don't have a choice in the matter," Allison said bitterly. "It's almost as if I *am* a prisoner."

"You mustn't think of it that way," Aidric insisted. "It is so for *all* mages, not just for you. As I explained before, it's Seni whom we truly serve in the hopes of achieving a place among His Thrones after death. It's His will that all who are mageborn must serve their kingdom however or wherever their king deems best."

"It still sounds like my life isn't mine to live," Allison insisted.

"But it is!" he reasoned. "The king only controls your occupation and even that, only to a point. The rest—family, hobbies, and the like—are for you to choose."

"I suppose…" she said grudgingly.

"You must also keep in mind that our ways are not the ways you have lived by in your world. I, by no means, expect total acceptance of our ways from you right now. That would be absurd and incredibly short-sighted of me. To become an adept-mage takes *years*. You'll have more than enough time to adjust to this new life."

Damn. Why does he always have to make so much sense? she grouched. *I could sit here and argue ethics with him all day, and he would probably have an answer for everything.*

"All right, so I'm your apprentice now," Allison

said. "Are you going to start my lessons today?"

"Not today," Aidric said with a hesitant smile that immediately had her back stiffening. "We've got an engagement to attend, first. Your schooling will begin tomorrow morning."

"An engagement?" she asked suspiciously. "What sort of engagement?"

Aidric cleared his throat uncomfortably and after a moment's hesitation, replied, "It's a presentation to all the members of Lamia's council, consisting of the Circle and King Diryan's councilors." He smiled sheepishly at her. "—your presentation."

Allison could feel all the blood drain from her face even though she half expected him to say something of the sort—but a whole council! She abhorred being scrutinized by just *one* person, and now Aidric was telling her that she had to go before an entire *council* with who-knows-how-many people where she was certain everyone would be gawking at her!

"No way!" she balked. "Aidric, please don't make me go! I can't *stand* to be under that much attention! Just the thought of it is enough to make me feel sick! I'll do anything else you ask of me—just— not this!"

"But you must!" he insisted, his eyes stricken. "All apprentices must be presented and approved before the Circle before they are allowed to be taught. It's one of our laws, so it's something that you cannot avoid."

He leaned down and placed a comforting hand on her shoulder. "It's not as bad as you think. You merely have to stand before the king until he acknowledges you. You will then curtsey as he nods at you, and I'll then present you to him and the Council. Next, he will grant you permission to become my apprentice and also grant you Lamian citizenship."

"That's still—I can't—" she protested, shaking her head and silently cursing herself for making such a big deal about something so trivial.

"Yes you can," he assured her firmly. "It will be over before you realize. Understand, I wouldn't ask you to do this if it were not important. Many members of the Circle don't know that the Golden Mage has appeared. Think of the shock they would have if they encountered you in the palace. Based on your appearance, alone, they would probably react first and ask questions later. Having your presence unknown to the public would be very dangerous for you. You *must* allow Lamia to know who you are. Please Allison, do this, if not for Lamia, then for your own safety."

Allison sighed as she looked into his pale-violet eyes and saw the earnestness, the pleading. Maybe if she zoned out and didn't look at anyone... "All right."

Aidric's pinched expression relaxed as he reached over to pick up the folded garments he had set onto the small table beside her chair earlier.

He handed them to her. "Here. This is the uniform for female apprentice-mages. You must wear it for the presentation and every day from here on out during your official training time until you reach adept status. I'll have the royal tailor make up more uniforms for you later. The only time you don't have to be in uniform is during social engagements such as casual parties, festivals, some holiday celebrations, and of course, in the evenings if I don't choose to give you a lesson.

"It just so happens that today is a holiday—the Eve of the Birth of the World. Tonight the palace will be alive with music and spectacles. A good portion of the kingdom's holdings and villagers will arrive to join in the festivities. It'll be the perfect opportunity for me to introduce you to some of my best friends and acquaintances. It'll also give you a chance to meet many people and perhaps befriend a few."

"I really don't think I'll make any friends here," Allison said sadly. "Judging from the way Selwyn, the king, and that Linguist shrank away from me out of fear earlier, everyone else will probably want to steer clear from me as well because of what I am."

"Only those worthy of your friendship will look past the Golden Mage and see just Allison," Aidric said firmly. "My people may just surprise you. We Lamians are a strong-minded, resilient bunch."

"I hope you're right," she said ruefully, "because right now, you're the only friend I've got."

He stilled. "You trust me enough to call me a friend?"

Allison rose from her chair. "I would be stupid not to. Without you, I would probably still be unconscious in the forest, maybe even dead—Aidric, what is it?"

Color had risen to his cheeks as if he had suddenly remembered something embarrassing, and he had also quickly averted his eyes from looking directly at her, something he had never done before.

"Have I said something wrong?" she asked anxiously.

Still careful to avoid looking directly at her, Aidric replied a bit hesitantly, "No. I—it—you—" He blew out a frustrated breath. "I hesitate to even say this to you because I don't want to offend, but…"

As Allison stepped closer to him, his blush became painfully noticeable through the paleness of his skin. "I swear I won't be insulted," she coaxed, curious as to what could rattle this self-professed Mage-general so much.

"Very well," Aidric said stiffly. "It's your clothing. It's *very* immodest. You reveal too much skin, and it's *very* improper for me to look on you as you are now."

Allison laughed, making him blink at her in surprise, and said, "You think *this* is immodest? I guess your eyes would be popping out of their sockets if you ever went to a beach in my world dress! Shorts are pretty much the norm when it's hot, and California is pretty hot all year round."

Aidric's blush deepened and he hastily explained, "No man who is a gentleman should ever see that much of a woman's skin unless they are intimate." Then sheepishly, "I must confess that I believed that you were wearing undergarments of some sort when I found you."

This only amused her further. *Undergarments, indeed!*

However, Allison's smile faded when she saw how extremely uncomfortable she was making him, and she said a bit contritely, "I didn't mean to embarrass you. If it will make you feel better, I'll go change into the uniform you've given me right now."

"It would. Thank you," he said, relief plainly visible on his reddened face as she turned to go change into what she felt was not only new garments but into a new life as well.

CHAPTER ELEVEN

"I don't know, Aidric," Allison said uncertainly as she fingered the long skirt of the dress he had given her. "I feel like I'm dressed for bed, not to go before an entire council!"

The dress she wore was pale blue and made of the same strange, silky material as Aidric's clothes. It rested against her skin so lightly that it gave the impression that she wore nothing at all. The neckline was moderately high but not so high as to make her feel stifled, the bodice loose and comfortable. The hem of her skirt fell down to brush the tops of her feet, and the dagged sleeves were long and billowy, giving her arms plenty of room for movement. It seemed more robe than dress really.

All I need now is a wand and a pointed hat, she

thought wryly.

Aidric laughed good-naturedly. "Says the girl who thought nothing of showing so much of her legs. However, if I allowed you to go before the Circle and the king dressed as you were, Diryan would definitely have my hide for allowing you to parade around the palace so immodestly dressed!"

"You act as if I was dressed like a prostitute or something," Allison retorted irritably. "If you or I were to go running around the streets in my world dressed in these costumes, people would think we got lost on the way to Comic Con—and please don't ask what Comic Con is because I wouldn't even know where to begin explaining it to you."

"I have offended you," Aidric said ruefully. "I apologize most humbly, milady. I truly meant no offense. I was only trying to put you at ease and as usual, failing miserably." He offered her his arm and said, "Shall we go before the king sends a search party to see what has become of us?"

As she accepted his arm, Allison heard him mutter under his breath, "—and before I make a bigger fool of myself than I already have."

He said it so softly that she wasn't sure if he even meant for her to hear. She started to comment on it but then decided against it. Although talking with Aidric would make for a good distraction from having to think about the horror of her upcoming presentation, she really didn't want to make him any more uncomfortable than she already had.

She glanced up at him as he led her down a dim corridor she assumed was part of the Mage Hall he had spoken of earlier that was illuminated only by a single, green-flamed lantern suspended from the high ceiling. He seemed lost in thought, his brow creased as if troubled.

Feeling a sudden surge of anxiety, Allison was about to ask him what was wrong when he led her through a door at the end of the hall, and instead of the room or extension of the corridor they had just left she had expected to see, a small, indoor garden lay before her in its place. She quickly forgot her questions as she let out a little gasp of surprised delight when she absorbed the extraordinary beauty before her.

A colorful array of flowers, some slightly familiar and others completely alien, grew throughout the room in intricate patterns of such complexity that only a skilled landscape gardener could have arranged the beds. Many of the flowers hugged the grassy path that led across the room to an opened archway and another brightly illuminated room. The bright sunlight shone down into the garden through a glass ceiling.

Many different plants hung from hooks extending out from the walls, giving the illusion that trees aligned the room. It reminded Allison very much of a live butterfly exhibit within a large botanic garden she had once visited as a child on a class field trip. It was all so beautiful.

Aidric smiled down at her and said, "Not something you would expect to find at the end of a gloomy corridor, right? It *is* an odd place to put a garden, but Diryan insisted that this room be converted into a garden when he first took the throne. He said that the palace had always felt so impersonal and cold inside, that it needed something to make it seem wore welcoming. His Majesty always did have a weakness for extravagant gardens.

"He had the ceiling removed and replaced with glass in order for the moonlight and sunlight to shine through. It gives the impression of being outside without all the inconveniences—thunderstorms, insects, and other such nuisances. My mentor, Lord Othos—who was Diryan's court mage at the time—spellcast a shield over it to prevent any intruders from using this room as a means to enter the palace easily and also to prevent the weather from damaging it."

"Now, over there," he pointed to a room on the right beyond the opened archway she had only glimpsed earlier, "is the palace's main courtyard. It's constructed in the same manner as the garden, and it's where we celebrate our holidays and festivals. But mostly, it's a place for leisure and gossip. As you can see, they are preparing it even as we speak for tonight's celebration."

Sure enough, many women and men were hard at work inside the courtyard, busily hanging up decorations, grooming the many plants and shrubs, and setting up dozens of tables that were being covered with every kind of food and drink imaginable.

"You can sneak a better look when we walk through, Allison, so there's no need to strain your eyes now," Aidric said with amusement.

Allison looked at him sharply. "Walk through? You said that the Golden Mage scares people. We'll cause a panic!"

"There's no need to fret, milady," Aidric assured her. "I have already thought of that possibility. I'll simply cast the spell of invisibility over you."

"Will it really make me invisible?" she asked incredulously.

He chuckled. "No. The spell doesn't actually make your body disappear from this plane. It's a glamour, a misdirection of the mind. It causes anyone who looks at you to believe that they see nothing. However, you must be very careful not to bump into anyone, and you must also be silent, or the spell will be broken. Now, stand perfectly still as I cast the spell. It will cause you to feel a little peculiar, so don't be alarmed."

Allison watched in fascination as Aidric made a few wide-swept gestures over her with his hands while muttering a few strange words almost under his breath. Then, true to his word, she began to feel a curious tingling all over her body similar to the pins and needles sensation of the blood rushing back into a limb that has gone to sleep. Yet, she saw nothing of the magical properties he was using. No colorful streams of light emerging from his hands or even a faint glow.

When Aidric lowered his hands in completion, she asked, "Am I invisible now?"

"I should certainly hope so," he said with a smile. "I can still see you, but that's only because I know you are under a glamour. Now, let's go. The Circle and the king are certainly anxiously awaiting your presence."

"Don't remind me," Allison groaned as she unconsciously took Aidric's arm again—now hanging casually at his side as to not arouse attention—and allowed him to lead her down the small path in the indoor garden and into the courtyard. Once inside, the courtyard loomed all around them even larger than what she had believed it to be at first glance. It was easily the length of at least four football fields placed end to end and twice as wide.

She had wondered how they were going to fit so many people into one place, but now she saw that they would indeed have no problem in fitting several towns' worth of people into the courtyard. That a space as large as this was situated within a building made her suddenly question the size of the palace, itself. Maybe later, Aidric would take her outside to see it, to tour the grounds.

As they made their way through the courtyard, Allison noted that everyone immediately stopped what they were doing and either bowed or curtseyed to Aidric as they passed them by. Aidric acknowledged everyone with a slight nod and smile, but he said nothing to them. *Just as if he were a king.* Allison had to bite her tongue to keep herself from voicing the many questions that suddenly arose in her mind.

True to his word, the workers also didn't see her even though she practically walked right under their noses. It made her feel strange to think that she was technically "invisible" to all the people around her.

I'll never get used to all of this magic business, she thought with a sigh.

"*Yes, you will,*" she suddenly heard Aidric say in her mind.

Luckily they were no longer in the courtyard or else she would have surely blown her cover when she let out a little cry of surprise.

"I wish you wouldn't read my mind like that," she told him irritably.

"I didn't," Aidric said with a laugh, not at all taken aback by the irritation in her voice. "You bespoke *me* through thought-speech."

"What! But—I didn't mean to—"

"I gather not," he said, still amused. "It's an easy enough mistake to make, believe me. I, myself, still do it occasionally when my mind is drifting elsewhere during some of the long Council sessions I'm forced to attend. I can assure you that when it happens, Diryan's councilors are *not* amused with my thoughts!"

"But I was only *thinking*," Allison explained anxiously. "Don't tell me you've been hearing every single thought I've had in my mind today!"

To her surprise, Aidric drew her into his arms and hugged her tightly with rough affection before saying, "I can only imagine what has been running through that pretty head of yours to have you so worried about my knowing about it."

"I didn't send my thoughts to you then?" she persisted as she slowly and discreetly moved away from him, blushing profusely at having been so near to him. She dared not think about the heat Aidric's embrace had caused her to feel in case she accidentally sent *those* thoughts to him!

Aidric shook his head and answered, "This was the first time you have bespoken me since the last time we spoke mind to mind. However, if you want to avoid any other thoughts to escape you unknown, then try not to focus on your thoughts so intently when you think of others. Until I teach you how to block thoughts from both entering and leaving your mind, you must be very careful. Your thought-speech is very powerful, and the shield I have placed on your mind to prevent thoughts from both entering and leaving your mind unwittingly cannot prevent a stray thought or two from leaking out occasionally."

"But Aidric," Allison said anxiously, "what if I send a thought unknowingly to everyone when I'm being presented before the court and it's one that they don't like? They'll throw me into the dungeons for sure!"

"I never should have spoken to you about the dungeons," he said with a frown. "It seems that I can't stop putting my foot in my mouth, can I? I didn't mean for it to sound as though you would be broadsending every thought that enters your head to everyone who has the ability to receive them. What you just did happens rarely, usually when someone is highly stressed as you undoubtedly are now. Now that you are aware of what you have done, it's very unlikely that it will happen again. Please don't allow my carelessness to worry you."

"You have nothing to be sorry for," Allison said. "I would rather you tell me the truth than to sugarcoat everything, no matter how bad or scary." She suddenly looked down at her feet as they walked. "I haven't been making it very easy for you to deal with me, have I? My suddenly appearing here must be horribly disrupting to your own life. I'll try hard not to be a bigger burden to you than I already am, I promise."

"A burden?" Aidric asked, sounding truly surprised. "Whatever gave you that impression? I find your company refreshing—someone who can jest, laugh, and cry about things other than that damned silent war with Mihr. Believe me when I say that it pleases me greatly that Diryan has given you to me as an apprentice. I don't want to hear another word about this burden nonsense."

"No matter what you say, I still feel like a burden and not just to you, but to this whole kingdom," Allison insisted bleakly. "I don't know why I was brought here—whether it was by your god or because of some huge cosmic coincidence isn't important. My presence here is far from a welcomed sight judging from the little you've told me about your Golden Mage prophecy. I shouldn't be here, and yet, here I am with no hope of ever returning home."

Upset, Allison quickly turned her head so Aidric wouldn't see the tears welling in her eyes. She wanted nothing more than to just drop where she was standing and release all the anguish she was keeping bottled up inside, but instead, she fought back the tears and struggled to regain her composure. These days, she had no problem with crying in front of people, but the last thing she wanted to do was to make a spectacle of herself in front of this man again.

"Allison?"

"It's nothing," she replied, perhaps a little too sharply to be convincing, as she turned around to face him again. "Sorry," she said almost in the same breath, casting her eyes down. "I'm tired and anxious about the presentation. I know that's not a good excuse for my behavior, but if you'll forgive my bad manners, I think we should go on and get this presentation over with." She raised her eyes and managed a wry smile. "I think I've stalled long enough."

Aidric returned her smile and said, "There's nothing to forgive, milady, but you are right. We should be getting on to the Throne Room. The king allows me a little latitude where his patience is concerned, but even I can overstep his boundaries some-times. This is probably one of those times. No doubt he has already chewed off all of his fingernails and half of his councilors'.'"

Allison laughed as Aidric led her through a door and down another long corridor. Her stomach was tied in knots by the time they stopped again. She suddenly wished that she hadn't eaten anything earli-er because she started to feel a little queasy when she realized that in a few minutes she would be facing the king and an unknown number of his court. It would do little good for her first impression if she threw up her lunch onto the king's feet!

However, she lost some of her anxiety when she set her eyes on the extravagant double doors up ahead that could only lead to the Throne Room. It seemed that the palace would never cease to amaze her, not surprising given the restrictive life she had once led.

The doors were either solid gold or thickly gold-plated, and a mural of an unknown battle was pains-takingly etched into the soft metal to cover every inch of both doors. Light seemed to radiate directly from them so brilliantly that Allison couldn't look at them without squinting. On either side of the doors stood two columns from floor-to-ceiling seemingly cut out of a nearly colorless crystal-like substance.

She couldn't believe that the Lamians had found crystals large enough to create those two monstrous columns.

She pointed over to one and asked, "Aidric, are those columns really made out of crystal, or are they just glass?"

"Neither," came the reply. "Those columns were cut from a couple of diamonds Diryan had hailed in from Sersia. The types of crystals I think you mean have never been found so large. Now, if you would pardon my absence for a moment, I must speak to the guards before we are allowed to enter."

Allison merely nodded dumbly, distracted by the impossibility before her. Ignoring the guards and Aidric completely, she walked over to one of the columns and ran a hand over the smoothness of the jewel. She could see the colors of the spectrum glimmer throughout the flawless, diamond column as she circled around it.

A diamond, she thought wondrously. *Aidric talked about it so casually, and yet, if I tried to cash in on just a piece of this back home, I would definitely be billions of dollars richer! I wonder if they even think of precious stones as valuable here beyond being just another beautiful decoration?*

She took a step back from the column uncomfortably when she noticed that the guard not speaking to Aidric was staring at her intently, his face completely expressionless and unreadable. Hastily, she looked away and wished that Aidric would hurry up and finish talking with the other guard. This guard's total lack of emotion disturbed her more than if he would have gaped at her in horror as she expected.

To her relief, Aidric abruptly motioned for her to come to him, and she hurried over to his side, self-consciously aware that the guard's eyes still followed her every move.

"I don't like the way that guard is staring at me," Allison whispered to Aidric with a nervous glance in the guard's direction. "I feel like he's looking for an excuse to slice me in half with his sword!"

"Pay them no mind, milady," Aidric sent into her mind. *"It's merely their duty to look so fierce. Gaul is a master at looking like a brute. It's his way of safely gawking at you without appearing to be doing so. You must remember that they are as curious about you as you are about them and this world."*

Aloud, he said, "The Circle and the king are ready to receive us. I'll do most of the talking, so you need not say anything unless a question is directed to you. Just remember to curtsey before His Majesty when I announce you. I'll help you through this as much as I can."

CHAPTER TWELVE

Despite Aidric's reassuring words, Allison didn't feel very reassured as both guards each opened a golden door, and Aidric half-pulled her inside after him. She couldn't help jumping a little as the doors banged shut behind them, echoing loudly through the silence of the enormous Throne Room. It sounded so final, as if the closing doors had sealed her fate. She swallowed down her fear with some difficulty and willed herself to appear outwardly calm even though her heart was threatening to tear out of her chest.

Several gasps of shock immediately followed the echoing of the closing doors. Suddenly, Allison felt the weight of dozens of eyes on her as she reluctantly took in the scene before her.

At once, she knew why this group of people called themselves the Circle. Over two dozen elegantly dressed men and women sat side by side on a narrow, elevated platform that circled the entire room along the walls, broken only in the center by the silver- and blue-carpeted aisle leading from the doors up to the dais where the king of Lamia and a silver-haired woman who was probably the queen sat. Inside the circular platform lay several rows of marble benches on either side of the aisle, a setup much resembling that of a church.

Four marble columns similar to those that lined the corners of Aidric's sitting room, rising at least two hundred feet to the high, arched ceiling, lay on either side of the aisle at both the beginning and ending of the aisle where the circular platform was divided. On the wall behind the throne seats hung a magnificent tapestry of a large silver teardrop, a hint of a figure within, against a sapphire-blue background.

The whole effect was just as overwhelming as Allison had feared. It took every ounce of willpower she contained to prevent herself from fleeing from the room and all those penetrating stares that seemed to demand to know the secrets of her very soul. Aidric's grip on her arm abruptly tightened as if he sensed that she might bolt. With his empathic abilities, it was probably closer to the truth than she realized.

It seemed that everyone began to murmur at once when the initial shock of her appearance wore off, until King Diryan shouted for silence. Instantly, the room fell silent. Fighting back tears, Allison hardened her expression and allowed Aidric to lead her up the silver- and blue-carpeted aisle until they both stood only a couple of feet away from where the king and queen sat in regal silence.

Allison's eyes widened as she stared up at the queen. Like Aidric, the woman's appearance seemed otherworldly. She was not young—Allison could plainly see that by the faint lines around her eyes—yet, they seemed to refine the woman's features in a way that probably made her more beautiful now than when she was younger.

She had an agelessness about her that made pinpointing her age impossible, especially when her hair was a lovely shade of silver that seemed to sparkle with its own vitality and not at all like the dullness of the silver caused by aging. Allison suspected that it was the color the queen had been born with as Aidric's true hair color was white.

The eyes that were scrutinizing her so intently were a shade of violet so deep that they appeared almost black. Her expression was curious without even a hint of the fear so many others had shown.

She held herself with such grace and dignity that anyone would be envious. Allison feel ugly and awkward in comparison.

"Your Majesty, My Queen," she distantly heard Aidric say as he bowed gracefully, "my lords and ladies, I present to you Allison McNeal, my new ward and apprentice."

Somehow Allison remembered to curtsey before the royal couple, though clumsily, since she wasn't altogether sure of the correct method, and her only examples had come from movies. *I don't know why I couldn't have just bowed*, she thought irritably. *Even I couldn't mess that up.*

The king and queen both nodded in acknowledgment, and at once the low buzz of voices resumed all around her. She shifted her feet nervously and glanced over at Aidric to see what he would do next.

She really hated to know that all those people were talking about her, and there wasn't a damned thing she could do about it. All she could do was stand there feeling like an idiot and hope that it would all be over soon so she could once again hide out in the relative safety of Aidric's suite.

Surprisingly, it was King Diryan, not Aidric, that next spoke.

"Enough with the formalities, lad," he said in a voice so low that it surely was meant for their ears alone. "You may both go take your seats before the Circle. Now that they have seen her with their own eyes, maybe they will be more inclined to believe all you have told them and listen to reason."

"As thick-headed as some of them are," Aidric murmured mischievously, "I doubt even the sight of her will make them believe."

"You are probably right," Diryan replied just as mischievously. "Now go take your seat, lad, before someone overhears that loose tongue of yours and you suddenly find that you have more to concern yourself with than a legendary ward!"

"My King," he said mockingly as he led a very astonished Allison to one of the two empty seats between the dais and the circular platform. He then seated himself in the other across the aisle.

Allison couldn't believe that the king allowed Aidric to speak so freely and sarcastically to him as if they were merely drinking buddies and not king and underling. For all she knew, they might just *be* drinking buddies. Either that, or her idea of how a king ruled over his subjects and King Diryan's were as different as apples and oranges.

As she took her seat, Allison noticed that all eyes were still on her, some with ill-concealed fear, others skeptical, but most awestruck. She could feel her face burning red in embarrassment under all their scrutiny. This was exactly what she had wanted to avoid when she had first refused to come to the presentation.

Standing before the king and queen had not been as bad as she had thought it would be since her back had been to the dozens of prying eyes, even though she had still felt them boring into her back. Sitting before the Circle where she dared not lower her eyes was infinitely worse. She longed to be able to melt into her seat.

Allison reached for that imaginary line between Aidric and her.

"This was exactly why I didn't want to come here," she sent intently down the line, hoping that she was using her thought-speech correctly. She certainly did not want anyone else to know how uncomfortable she was.

Although his face remained as passive as ever, she saw his lips twitch ever so slightly as if he was trying to hold back a smile.

"How quickly we learn," she suddenly heard him say in her mind, his voice dripping with the amusement he could not outwardly show. *"I had about given up the idea that you would bespeak me with thought-speech without my first initiating the conversation. I see that you have*

also mastered volume control—at least my mind hopes you have! Now you can see firsthand the importance of thought-speech, especially in a situation such as this when conversation is taboo. Now, what is it that's troubling you?"

"All those eyes..." she replied with a mental shudder. *"I wish they would stop staring at me like I was some kind of monster or something. I hate being scrutinized, Aidric. You can't even begin to understand just how much. When will this be over? What happens now?"*

"I'm afraid that it'll be a while, yet. Diryan plans on addressing the Circle about you and how your presence here will affect Lamia. It's extremely important that they see you, Allison. They must accustom themselves to your presence."

"You've been so vague about the prophecy and what's in it that has so many people looking at me with fear and suspicion as if I'm plotting to murder the entire kingdom in their sleep! Even you *look at me warily sometimes. Don't think that I haven't noticed. Do you ever plan on telling me the whole prophecy?"*

Allison marveled that his expression never changed once as they "talked." In fact, he didn't glance in her direction at all.

"I realize that you must be very frustrated about that vagueness," Aidric said, *"but please understand that I had to be so. The Seer in the Order of the Providence who Foresaw your coming also thought that it should be the king of Lamia who would ultimately reveal the contents of the prophecy to the*

Golden Mage when she appeared. Have patience, milady. You'll hear it soon enough, although afterwards, you may wish that you were not so eager to learn the fate Seni has given you."

She struggled to keep her sudden alarm from her face. *"What the hell does that mean?"*

"Patience," was his only reply before King Diryan began to address the Circle.

"You have all now seen with your own eyes the golden-haired maiden in which Aidric spoke of," King Diryan said. "I know that everyone present in this room is very familiar with the Providencen Prophecy of the Golden Mage. For as the prophecy reads:

On the Eve of the Birth of the World,
Through brilliant colors and light,
A mage that hath dwelt in a realm unknown
Will come to the land of Lamia,
A maiden with hair spun like gold
And a beauty meant for no mortal eyes to
    behold.

This mage will possess power that no man has
    possessed,
Bestowed upon her by our divine lord, Seni,
To seal the fate of the kingdom.
The Golden Mage she is named,

And either Lamia's savior or destroyer she will be proclaimed."

Allison's blood turned to ice when she heard the words King Diryan spoke, words she only minutes earlier had demanded to hear.

No wonder these people look at me like I'm the Devil, she thought in horror. *That prophecy all but says I really will murder them all! The savior or destroyer—it doesn't take a genius to know which one everyone believes I'll be. Aidric was right—I shouldn't have been so eager to know the truth. If only I hadn't insisted Kat and I visit that damned park, then maybe none of this would have ever happened...*

She was startled out of her thoughts when she suddenly found King Diryan standing before her. All she could do was blink stupidly up at him in surprise, wondering how his rising had escaped her notice. She could feel herself beginning to blush again. Painfully aware that all eyes were on them, Allison forced herself to meet the king's gaze and not shrink from it.

When he gestured for her to stand, she could do nothing but obey. "Come," he said simply, and she followed him down the aisle until he halted in the very center. Despite her best efforts, she could feel her knees begin to tremble at having to stand so exposed.

"There is nothing to fear," Aidric thought-spoke to

her, but his words didn't make her feel any better.

"As you all know," King Diryan began while Allison suffered silently at his side, "today is the Eve of the Birth of the World, and this maiden," he gestured to Allison, "suddenly appeared in our kingdom within the Forest of Illusions. She also has spoken of traveling through a portal filled with multitudes of colors and light from a world that is not our own, a world named Earth. You also can plainly see that she has hair of gold, a hue no mortal in Seni's world has ever possessed, and no soul here could honestly deny her beauty."

Mortified, Allison could feel her cheeks heat up more fiercely and desperately wished that Aidric's spell of invisibility still concealed her. *I just want to die, right here and now,* she thought miserably.

"The Mage-general has confirmed that she has abilities even beyond his own," the king was saying, oblivious to her distress. "Untrained, she flattened him with the power of a single mind-scream. The evidence is quite compelling. I believe she is indeed the Golden Mage that was Foreseen to come, and we must do everything in our power to see that the disaster foretold in the prophecy never comes to pass. That is why I have entrusted Aidric with the duty of instructing her to control the powers that Seni has bestowed upon her."

He paused dramatically as his gaze slowly swept the entire Circle. "She will be given full citizenship as well. As Aidric has pointed out to me, she is indeed an important asset to our magical defense, so I expect her to be treated accordingly. I forbid any unprovoked acts of violence against her under penalty of death. It is Seni's will that has brought her to us, so it is our duty to see that His will is carried out accordingly. Who are we to defy what He has set forth?"

Questions burned in Allison's mind as she listened, but she didn't dare say a word for fear that the nobles of the Circle would think her disrespectful for interrupting the king. After all, she knew next to nothing about the proper etiquette of a royal court. She didn't want to give them any more reasons to look at her with contempt than they already did.

She stood silently with her back ramrod straight at Diryan's side until he finished speaking.

Allison then cleared her throat and inquired timidly, "King Diryan—Your Majesty?"

His head turned to her in surprise. He had probably not expected her to speak at all. "You have a question for me?" he asked.

"Yes," she continued, relieved that her voice came out steady. "You spoke of an uncertainty in your prophecy, that I will either be the destroyer or savior of Lamia. Is Lamia currently at war?"

She had spoken softly, intending for only the king to hear her question, but then everyone suddenly began to talk all at once while the king frowned in thought, making her instantly regret opening her mouth at all.

"None can be certain of what perils lie before our kingdom," the king hedged. "The prophecy can very well be referring to the silent war we are currently engaged in with the eastern kingdom of Mihr. For years, their mage-king, Roderick, has hungered for the power of our Mage-field. No other kingdom's Mage-field comes near to equaling the power of our own. With the power of Lamia's Mage-field at his whim, he would be capable of conquering not only Mihr's neighboring kingdoms but quite possibly the entire world. However, he would first have to conquer Lamia to even have access to the power of our Mage-field.

"What is preventing him from realizing his tyrannical ambitions is the Shield spell that my ancestor, the great King Ladonis, cast over Lamia at her founding to prevent the Mage-field from falling into the hands of men such as Roderick. Only those with permission may enter our kingdom since the Shield can only be opened from within the borders, and only those with citizenship may remain more than a few days."

Allison must have been making quite the face because the king suddenly laid a comforting hand on her shoulder.

"Perhaps it is to free us forever from Roderick's threat that Seni has sent you here to accomplish," he said kindly before his eyes once again turned introspective. "And yet, there is always the possibility that allowing you to confront Roderick on the battlefield on the kingdom's behalf could also cause our downfall, for the only possible way Roderick could breech our Shield is to have a mage more powerful than King Ladonis, himself, under his power. You have that very potential, milady Allison, as the prophecy has foretold."

Allison felt all the blood drain from her face. "But—but wouldn't it be better, then, if I didn't learn how to use these mage powers?" she stammered. "Couldn't Aidric just keep my powers shielded as he's been doing? That way you can be sure that Roderick can't use me to conquer Lamia."

"Having no control of your powers could very well destroy us all, as well," King Diryan replied gravely. "Aidric's shields can only hold your powers at bay for a short while. At any time, the wild magic of the Mage-field could break through the shields he has placed on your channels and cause many catastrophes. You could even unknowingly destroy the Shield surrounding our kingdom, allowing Roderick's troops to finally cross over into our lands since no mage living today can perform the Shield spell as King Ladonis did. Your powers *must* be controlled, Allison. There is no question of it."

"Then I give you my word that I'll do everything in my power to see that I learn to control these powers," Allison pledged more bravely than she felt.

"And I shall do everything known to man under Seni to see that she receives the proper instruction," Aidric vowed as he rose and joined the pair in the center of the room.

A middle-aged woman, dressed in an emerald-green dress more fitting to a formal ball than a Council presentation, slowly rose and said, "Your Majesty, if I may speak?"

"Of course, Lady Gaelle," Diryan replied. "I shall hear any opinions on the matter."

"Your Majesty," Gaelle began, "you have said that she has spoken of traveling through a portal in order to reach our kingdom from another realm. You know as well as I that any mage with enough power to control the Mage-field can perform the portal spell. Mihr, of course, has its own small Mage-field, but Mage-field it still is. Roderick has more than proven he is capable of performing spells that require the use of great power, even with the limited power of his Mage-field. It's also said that he's a practitioner of the Dark Powers. She could very well be an agent of Roderick, sent here under a glamour more powerful than any of us have seen to destroy the Shield from within."

"Probing her mind for any deception was the first thing I did," Aidric interrupted impatiently. "She speaks the truth on all she has revealed, but suppose she hadn't and was indeed an agent of Roderick's. How then can you explain how Roderick managed to breech the Shield after all these years of failure and open a portal within our forest? Why then not come himself rather than sending a lackey?"

"I have no answer," she replied coolly. "I'm but a *mind-mage*, and you, my dear Lord Aidric, have more knowledge of such things than I. The one thing these years that I have been a mind-mage have taught me is to not dismiss something as impossible. I'm sure you found no trace of deceit in her mind—we wouldn't be standing here in this Throne Room with her a step away from the king if you had. Yet, I would ask Your Majesty's permission to test her myself."

Aidric angrily started to retort, but a warning look from Diryan quickly silenced him.

"We shall hear her out," the king said. "All suspicions will be voiced and addressed right here and now."

Just great. As if these people weren't suspicious enough of me as it is! Allison despaired.

"It's not that I doubt your abilities, Milord Aidric," Gaelle explained evenly. "You would not hold the position you hold if your abilities were not exceptional. I merely wish to subject her to a test with a mind that could not possibly be distracted by her extreme beauty."

"How dare you even imply—" Aidric boomed, taking a step towards Gaelle before Diryan held him back with his arm.

"A word of caution, Lady Gaelle," King Diryan warned, disapproval on his face. "Your request indeed comes very near to being an accusation. However, if it would put all minds at ease once and for all as to her identity as the Golden Mage of prophecy, then I grant you my permission to perform your test before Circle and Council." His attention turned to Aidric. "Aidric, if you would allow her access."

"Understood," he replied, his voice still tight with tension.

Allison eyed Gaelle nervously, wondering exactly what the woman would subject her to. She had no memory of Aidric performing anything like a test on her. Had he performed it while she had been unconscious?

She started when she heard Lady Gaelle's voice suddenly say, "It's done. She speaks the truth."

But how could she have— Allison turned questioning eyes to Aidric, but before she could form the words in her mind for thought-speech, he answered her silent question.

"The test isn't something that is consciously felt by those who don't know what to look for," he sent. *"That's what makes the ability so dangerous. One of the first lessons I'll teach you is how to detect an unwanted mind-probe and how to shield against it. I must apologize for her accusations since I know she will not. They were uncalled for and accomplished nothing but making the Circle unnecessarily wary of you.*

"Lady Gaelle is disliked by many. She trusts no one and thinks herself knowledgeable above all others, even the king. Calling my abilities into question in such a petty manner is just her way of making certain that she is given the attention she believes is due her. It would be wise to avoid her if possible in the future."

"I'll remember that," she sent back, eyeing Gaelle with hidden contempt.

"Are there any others who also wish to speak before me?" Diryan asked.

When no one else rose, he gestured for Aidric to take his seat and commanded Allison to follow him. Puzzled, she obeyed and followed him up to the foot of the throne seats where he told her to stand before the queen and himself.

Once seated, Diryan called out the name, Voytek, and a redheaded youth barely into puberty immediately appeared from the shadows behind the throne seats. He bowed deeply to the king. He then turned to Allison and stared, his blue eyes widening as he looked at her.

Does everyone have to stare at me? Allison thought crossly as she sent to Aidric, *"Who is he?"*

"He's Diryan's page and scribe," Aidric said. She heard his laughter echo through her mind before he added, *"Although I should say he's Diryan's puppy from the way he follows Diryan around ever at his heels."*

"How come he wasn't here before?" she asked.

"He wasn't needed then. My taking you as a ward was already granted and documented in the Council session I just returned from, so my presenting you was only a formality. His Majesty is going to grant you citizenship now, so it needs to be officially documented. Don't worry. All that is required of you is to agree to the terms he speaks before you."

"Do you wish to be granted citizenship, milady Allison?" King Diryan abruptly asked, capturing her attention again. Voytek finally took his eyes off her long enough to begin to scribble furiously on the piece of parchment he carried.

"I do." *I think.*

"Under the laws of Lamia, once citizenship is

granted, you cannot renounce it unless I forfeit it as a penalty for a crime committed against the welfare of the kingdom. You cannot, under any circumstance, seek to obtain citizenship elsewhere while a citizen of Lamia. Do you understand these terms?"

"I understand." *Does this mean I can't ever leave the kingdom?*

"Permission must be petitioned and obtained from this Council if you desire to leave our borders. It is a serious matter since the Shield must be opened in order for anyone to leave the kingdom."

"I understand." *Well, that answers my question. He makes it sound as if I'm a prisoner here, my freedom given up willingly in exchange for the protection of Lamian citizenship. If things were really bad on the outside, I suppose it would be a price worth paying. Apparently these people think it is, or else I don't think they would have given up their freedom to come and go as they please so willingly.*

"Then I grant you citizenship, Allison McNeal. Aidric, come forth and place the seal of our kingdom onto the brow of your ward."

Aidric rose and stepped up to her. Before Allison could even begin to wonder what he was going to do to her, he pressed a hand firmly against her forehead. She felt a curious coolness sink into her skin. A few seconds later, the coolness completely disappeared when he removed his hand.

"What did you do to me?" she whispered anxiously.

"Shh. Don't speak aloud. I did as Diryan said—placed the seal of Lamia, the silver teardrop you see on the tapestry behind the throne, onto your brow so you'll be detected as a citizen by our border guards should you ever need to leave the kingdom. Don't fret. It's not visible to normal sight. Just as it is to see the energy of the Mage-field, Inner-sight must be invoked to see the seal."

Relieved, Allison allowed Aidric to lead her with a hand against the small of her back to her seat. She was surprised when the queen rose to immediately follow.

"Come dear," the queen said gently, holding out her hand to Allison while Aidric smiled encouragingly at them both. "This Council meeting will no doubt continue on for some time now. Your presence or absence will not make much difference."

Allison nodded and took the delicate, ivory hand offered her and allowed the queen to escort her out of the Throne Room. However, as the two women made their way down the aisle, Allison's skin crawled as she felt one distinct pair of eyes out of the many trying to bore a hole into her back following her as though somehow physically connected until they disappeared through the double doors, eyes that held a disconcerting fear.

CHAPTER THIRTEEN

Galen tensely watched the golden-haired woman as she left the Throne Room with the queen. When he had first set eyes on the Golden Mage after the Mage-general and she had walked so dramatically through the golden doors, he had felt an immediate fear. The Prophecy of the Golden Mage had always unnerved him from the first moment he had heard it at the age of five. Then the dreams had come.

For the past two years, he had suffered from nightmares involving the Golden Mage. Not knowing whether they were a result of his Foresight ability or his own twisted imagination, they had truly frightened him, yet he told no one about them, not even his wife.

He had seen Lamia in ruins, bodies of friends and acquaintances littering the kingdom. All had been aflame, green mage-flames eating away at their flesh and clothing. All but he had perished in the flames. He had watched in helpless agony as his wife and children burned to ashes, weeping over the family he could not save.

The dreams, no matter the difference in their beginnings, would always end the same. He would glance up and see the Golden Mage, the murderer of all he had ever loved, staring down at him, her smile mocking and cruel. Her body glowed with that same eerie green of the mage-flames around her. Always, she would raise a hand to strike him dead, but before the blast came, he would always wake up, drenched in sweat and weeping.

Galen had always assured himself that his nightmares were *not* Foresight warnings but mere dreams in an attempt to prevent himself from facing what could be the horrible truth, until he had his first glimpse of Allison McNeal and realized that she and the Golden Mage of his dreams were one and the same. It was at that fateful moment that Galen could no longer deny what his dreams had been screaming out to him in warning—predictions of the possible things to come.

Only years of experience as a mind-mage skilled

in keeping his mind calm no matter how stressful the situation prevented him from screaming hysterically like a fool when Allison appeared. He held his peace with tremendous effort throughout her presentation and King Diryan's subsequent monologue. He almost lost control of himself when the king asked if there were any who wished to voice their opinions concerning the girl. Even now, he wasn't entirely certain how he had managed to remain silent.

His dreams were a matter that could only be discussed with His Majesty and His Majesty, alone. After Lady Gaelle's suspicions were proven to be nothing more than her usual show of arrogant superiority, he didn't think the Circle would give his claim of Foresight dreams a second thought, especially since his Foreseeings had been wrong a couple of times in the recent past.

Furthermore, judging from the venomous way Lord Aidric had glared at Lady Gaelle when she had challenged the honor of his ward, only a fool would have said an ill word against the girl in the Mage-general's presence. That was one mage Galen preferred not to cross directly.

After the queen led The Golden Mage out of sight, Galen wasted no time in drawing the king aside and asked if they might have a word in private. King Diryan nodded and left his counselors in charge of the discussion he had begun regarding the latest strategy in forcing Roderick's troops from the Kemosian border.

In the farthest corner of the Throne Room where they were well out of earshot, the king demanded, "This had better be important, Galen. Border conditions in Kemos are continuing to worsen, and I don't have the time to spend on minor concerns."

"It's *very* important, Your Majesty," Galen assured him. "It concerns the girl, Allison."

"I thought we had finished with that business, Galen," Diryan said impatiently. "You had the opportunity to speak earlier when I called for voices. Why didn't you speak up then?"

"This is something I couldn't discuss before the Circle," Galen insisted, "especially in the presence of the Mage-general. What I wish to say is for your ears alone, Your Majesty."

"Very well," Diryan invited. "Speak your mind, but I warn you that I can only spare you a few moments. We have given enough time worrying over the girl and her destiny when it's in Seni's hands, alone."

"I have been sent a warning," Galen said. "For two years, I have had dreams of the Golden Mage, dreams filled with visions of horror and suffering that would drive any sane man mad. In these dreams, the whole kingdom has perished, consumed by the girl's mage-flames. I am convinced that these were not mere nightmares, but a Foretelling of the tragedy that will certainly befall us if we allow that demonspawn to breathe another day!"

His expression hardening, King Diryan asked in a fierce whisper, "Have you gone mad? I never thought you to be so heartless. Nothing, even the potential danger that poor child poses, would justify the murder of an *innocent!* You know as well as I that it was by Seni's will that she was brought here to our kingdom as the Golden Mage, and fate, alone, will decide which path she is destined to follow. We can only pray to Seni that it isn't the dark path that fate will choose."

"But I have *Foreseen* the destruction of Lamia!" Galen cried. Did he not understand? "Surely you won't idly stand by and allow this! Is the life of one girl worth the life of millions more?"

"Since you are clearly frightened and allowing your emotions to speak for you," the king said slowly, a note of warning in his tone, "I shall forget that last part. Foresight dreams warn of only one possible future *as you know very well.* Yours may never come to pass if we do everything in our power—which *morally* we can do—to take the correct cautionary steps to protect the Golden Mage from falling into the wrong hands."

"Then you will do *nothing*?" Galen asked incredulously.

"Nor will you," Diryan said darkly, his eyes narrowing coldly at the stranger the normally genial man before him had become, "because mark my words, if I find that you have taken it upon yourself to be judge and executioner to her, then *you* will not live to breathe another day."

Galen shuddered at the anger in Diryan's voice as the king silently stalked away without another glance. Never in all the years he had known the king personally had he ever seen such ire and coldness in him. He had been so certain that His Majesty would see things as he saw them, and now that he stood rebuked, he didn't know what to think or do. King Diryan had said that his dreams might not come to pass, but those words meant to assure did nothing to relieve the terror festering in his heart.

If I can't destroy her without having to face a penalty of death, then I sure as the six hells can watch her every move, and when she turns to evil as I know she will, I'll be there to do what should have already been done!

As he glanced over at the king and his fellow members of the Circle, he had one last fleeting thought before he walked over to join them again. *Even though you may not wish it now, My Lord King, when this is all finished, the demonspawn will lie dead at your feet by my hand and you'll be begging most humbly for me to accept* your *apology!*

***

"Aidric tells me that he plans to take you to tonight's celebration of the Birth of the World," the queen chatted gaily as they made their way up a flight of steps and to Allison's astonishment, straight through the wall behind a large, golden statue of a man in a crown that rested at the top of the stairs. The queen laughed cheerfully at Allison's gasp of surprise, and explained that the wall was merely an illusion spell cast over the doorway.

"I believe that it's a splendid idea to attend the festivities as your first social engagement as a citizen of Lamia. I'm sure you will meet and befriend dozens of people. However, I do believe Aidric has not even given thought to what you will wear. You can't very well go dressed in your apprentice uniform! It's not proper. Until you can be fitted for your own garments, I'll lend you some of mine since we are near to height. Accond, our palace tailor—Seni, bless his heart—is indeed very skillful in his trade, but I must confess that his one flaw is that he isn't very punctual with his orders."

When Allison merely blinked at her, the queen smiled and said, "Oh, but listen to me, jabbering on when I haven't even properly introduced myself. How ill-mannered of me to have not done so earlier. My name is Ileanna, and don't you dare address me as 'My Queen,' 'My Lady Queen,' or other such nonsense unless we are at court where the law demands such foolish courtesies. I dislike all these formalities having a crown demands."

Allison could hardly believe what she was hearing. This beautiful woman, a *queen* no less, was chatting away as if they were old friends, even though they had only first met moments before. More importantly, she showed no signs of the fear and suspicion that everyone else seemed to have when they looked at her.

"Why is it that you aren't afraid of me when so many others obviously are?" Allison couldn't help asking in bafflement.

The older woman looked at her kindly and said, "My dear child, any fool who bothers to look at you with a clear mind could plainly see that you are as frightened as they are. Why should I fear someone who is so obviously as much a pawn of Seni's will as we, ourselves, are?"

Allison lowered her eyes uncomfortably. "You're being so nice, and you don't even know me..."

"My dear, when I've seen how kindly Aidric looks upon you, how can I do anything but treat you the same? Aidric is a dear friend to both Diryan and me, and we value his opinion of others. However, that isn't the only reason. I could see you needed a friend other than the friendship Aidric can offer." She smiled wryly at Allison. "He is a *man* after all, and not knowledgeable in womanly things."

"I'd like that," Allison replied a bit diffidently.

"Now come. I'll introduce you to my ladies-in-waiting, as well. They should be gathered in my chambers awaiting my return. We needn't hurry selecting a proper dress for you to wear since it is still many sand-marks until nightfall. While my husband and the Circle tend to matters of war, we'll spend the afternoon happily answering as many questions as you like about palace life and our kingdom."

"Thank you," Allison said, her head spinning from Ileanna's chatter. "I do have dozens of questions to ask about Lamia, especially since it seems I'll be living here in this world for the rest of my life."

"You sound so sad, child," Ileanna remarked, tilting her head with concern. "You are missing loved ones, no doubt, and all this talk about the Golden Mage and doomsday prophecies cannot be easy for you to accept. I promise you that I'll do everything in my power to make you feel more at home here."

"You already are," Allison replied gratefully as she followed the queen to her chambers.

CHAPTER FOURTEEN

H idden within the shadows behind the throne, a figure watched the king and the mind-mage, Galen, as they moved to a secluded corner to speak. Perfect. Knowing Galen, they would be occupied for a few moments on whatever grievance that sniveling fool had this time. Luckily, a few moments was all that was needed.

After one final glance in Diryan and Galen's direction to make sure they were still occupied, the silent observer settled comfortably onto the cool, marble floor and prepared to thought-speak the Master. Since three of the most powerful thought-speakers in Lamia aside from the hidden observer currently occupied the Throne Room—Aidric, Galen, and Gaelle—the Observer needed to be extremely careful this time sending his message. If his mind-shield was anything less than perfect, then one of the three would likely sense that someone was using thought-speech and investigate because of the distances involved in the sending. The distance, alone, would instantly condemn him. The Observer couldn't allow carelessness to ultimately sign a personal death warrant.

"*Master...?*" the Observer carefully sent after a few moments of concentration.

"*Speak,*" came the faint, immediate reply.

"*I've learned something today that I think you'll find of interest. There's a great uproar in the palace concerning the mysterious arrival of a maiden into Lamia.*"

"*A maiden?*" The Master asked skeptically. "*How could the arrival of one maiden, no matter how unusual she may be, cause such an uproar? I find the idea absurd. Why are you bothering me with that courtly gossip? I sent you to Lamia to learn Diryan's military strategies, not to wag your tongue with those arrogant fools.*"

"*Oh, but Master,*" the Observer said hastily, "*she's not just any maiden. The Lamians think she's the Golden Mage of their ancient prophecy.*"

"*What!*" Roderick exclaimed loudly, his voice echoing painfully throughout his spy's mind like thunder. "*Can this be true?*"

"*I've seen her with my own eyes, Master. She has hair of gold, and from what was said in court, she lived within a realm different from our own before appearing here this morn-*"

ing. She was also given to the Mage-general as an apprentice, so her mage powers must be great to warrant such a teacher."

Interesting, the Observer heard his Master think to himself, a trick the Observer's master had no idea he could do. *Most interesting, indeed. If that claim holds true, I may yet still have a chance of claiming Lamia as my own. If I were to have the Golden Mage under my power, and if the prophecy holds true, then nothing would ever stand in my way again. Lamia's Mage-field would be mine to control at last!*

Hearing the Master's thoughts while they thought-spoke over great distances, and *only* over great distances, was a surprising side effect that the Observer did not feel inclined to disclose. Any edge held over his master, no matter how small, was an edge that no sane person would relinquish willingly. The Observer refused to even contemplate what would happen if his master ever learned this secret.

"What will you do, Master?" The Observer asked innocently.

"For the moment, nothing," the Master replied, his mind-voice distant. *"She must be untrained if she was given to Aidric as an apprentice. Untrained, she is of no use to me, and I don't have the patience to train her myself. No—let the Lamians deal with her for now, but in the meantime, I do believe that I have an addition duty to add to your plate. Since you obviously have an ear for gossip and the access to court, you will keep an ear out for word that this so-called Golden Mage*

is near to adept status. If the legend holds true, it shouldn't take long at all. You must contact me immediately the moment you hear word. The Horae must not proclaim her a mage, else I cannot hope to control her mind, thereafter."

"It'll be done. I swear it."

"Good. Now go before you are discovered."

The Observer slumped over in exhaustion as the link to Roderick's mind was released and shuddered weakly as he tried to push away the darkness that was starting to seep into the edges of his vision. It took a considerable amount of concentration and power to thought-speak with his master. The Master was not a powerful thought-speaker, so the Observer had to search for his thoughts and extend their range in order for the Master to be heard. It was a highly complicated and energy-draining process, so it often left the spy feeling like a piece of chewed meat that had been dragged through the six hells of Ter-ob.

He softly groaned and forced his trembling legs to carefully rise to equally unsteady feet. He swayed a little as a fresh wave of fatigue washed over an already greatly-fatigued body that was dangerously close to collapsing in exhaustion. Nevertheless, somehow, the spy managed to keep all bearings by grabbing the back of the king's throne seat and leaning a little weight towards it for support.

The Observer closed aching eyes and breathed

deeply for a couple of depths before cautiously peering out from behind the throne seat to see if any eyes were looking anywhere near his direction. The Circle was deeply engrossed in a discussion, so it was unlikely that any of them had noticed the shadow lurking behind the throne seat. Most of the pompous bastards never looked past their own nose long enough to notice the knife about to cut their lordly throat.

At the moment, all eyes were on Lord Caith, the Arms-general of King Diryan's army, who was outlining to the Lord Commander the newest attack strategy that he planned to use along the Kemosian-Mihran border. That strategy was old news as far as the Observer was concerned.

His attention turned once again to the king and Galen. They were still talking animatedly. The two men appeared to be in an argument. King Diryan's body was tense, and from the king's tightly balled fists held at his sides, the spy knew that the king was fighting to control his temper. They spoke in whispers, so the Observer couldn't hear any of their discussion. Galen gestured in frustration with his arms. Apparently, Diryan was less than impressed with whatever the mind-mage was saying.

After Diryan whispered one final retort, hidden eyes watched with amusement as the king turned on his heel and silently stalked away, leaving Galen to stare with a stupid look on his face at the retreating figure and muttering angrily to himself.

It was all too easy, really.

***

Sitting in the comforts of his study, Roderick stared at a painting of a particularly gruesome battle scene mounted on the opposite wall, lost in thought. The knowledge of the Golden Mage's unexpected arrival had come as a fierce shock to him, affecting him more deeply than he cared to admit to himself, and that fact really infuriated him. Seldom ever had any news from the many spies he had planted in various kingdoms outright shocked him, and because he had been caught so completely off-guard, he had allowed himself to show emotion to that fool in Lamia. But that was the least of his worries now.

What disturbed him the most about the news of the Golden Mage was the uncanny similarities of that particular Lamian prophecy to a series of dreams he had been having for some time now. In each dream, the landscape was the same, open plains similar to the terrain of southwestern Mihr, skies filled with dark, angry clouds ready to release their fury onto the world, and an army—his army—stretched seemingly from horizon to horizon.

In several of his dreams, Roderick had been leading his great army against the Kemosian army or sometimes, against the Na'aran army, kingdoms that bordered Mihr in the north and west. In all of them, Mihr always triumphed in the end, the enemy armies either annihilated or captured.

However, in another dream, the dream that re-occurred the most, it was the infamous Lamian army that he had faced. In the Thrones above, the storm had raged as usual. Only a span separated the two armies as they had readied their initial charge.

That's when the maiden in the sapphire cloak had stepped into view, her face hidden within the folds of a cowl, and beneath, wearing the sapphire robes of a Lamian adept-mage. The soldiers on both sides had seemed frozen into place, transfixed by the mysterious maiden as she had slowly glided into the center of the grasslands between the two armies with complete disregard for her safety. Then she had raised her hands and shouted into the very voice of the storm in the ancient language of magic an incantation whose meaning was irritatingly just beyond Roderick's understanding.

Her upraised hands had then come alive with a brilliant, golden light that somehow wasn't blinding, parting the storm clouds until the rays of the suns had shone down upon her and engulfed her, had *be-come* her, transforming her into a being of pure light that was beautiful beyond comparison. Her body had become the sun and the long, wavy hair spilling from within her cowl its sunbeams. Like the rising of the first sun, the golden light had begun to radiate from her body, illuminating the lands around them until not a trace of the once raging storm had been evident.

It was at that point that Roderick had heard the voice, a male voice that seemed distinctly familiar, seemingly coming from the very air around him. It was a voice that only he could hear, urging him to approach the powerful creature before him, this light incarnate.

Each time he had the dream, he would hesitate suspiciously, and the voice would whisper that claiming her was necessary, that it was the only way he would win against the force of the Lamian army. The voice always insisted that the mysterious maiden was the key to his ultimate triumph. Urged by the voice, Roderick would always venture forward, hungry for the power he sensed within her. Yet, she would always turn to face him just before he reached her.

He could never distinguish her features, just that her face and body were proportionate to a woman's, but he had definitely been able to feel the heat of her eyes boring down into the very depths of his soul, searing the terrible coldness of the Dark Powers within with the heat of her rays.

Roderick would wonder who in the six hells she was before being overwhelmed by the pain and beginning to scream—only to wake up in a cold sweat, occasionally with his lip bloody where he had bitten it or an offensive spell ready to cast in his hands. He had never understood the meaning of those dreams, though he was certain that a hidden meaning did lay somewhere beneath the theatrics. Now, he knew only too well.

The Golden Mage...

For years Roderick had hungered after the power of the Lamian Mage-field, and for most of those years, he had devoted his life entirely to the conquest of Lamia. Yet, no matter how organized his military strategy was—how large and powerful his army of fighters and mages—they couldn't penetrate that damned shield around the kingdom. His army might as well have consisted of a child's toy soldiers for all the good they did against the Shield.

Nor had he been successful in forcing Diryan to surrender by invading many of Lamia's allied kingdoms and threatening to destroy them. Lamia's army always drove his forces back, mostly on the account of that accursed mage, Aidric, who seemed to wield ungodly powers.

Damn him!

Roderick sometimes suspected that Aidric wasn't even human. His appearance was certainly uncanny, especially those pale eyes that seemed to find and pluck the deepest, darkest secrets directly from your soul. Rumors floating around Mihr said that he was a demon wearing the guise of a human, Summoned by Lord Othos, Diryan's former Mage-general, on his deathbed.

That particular account served only to amuse him. Roderick had done his fair share of Summoning creatures from Ter-ob over the years, and he doubted that the late Mage-general would have had the courage to do such a blasphemous thing. Well, demon or not, Roderick was determined to dispose of Aidric.

I have labored too long and too hard to let that bastard upset my plans any further.

Ever since he was a boy old enough to understand the ways of the world, Roderick had lusted after power. From that first taste of power he had experienced at the tender age of seven when his father had allowed him, as his first duty performed as the prince-heir to the throne of Mihr, to pass judgment on a prisoner who had been caught stealing from the palace, Roderick wanted to savor even more. There was nothing compared to the feeling of holding the power of life or death over another human being. The only way he could accomplish that, his young mind had reasoned, was to become king, himself, far sooner than his father had anticipated.

To draw attention away from himself, Roderick never disclosed to his father that he had any ambitions of his own. He made a big show of being the lazy prince who cared nothing for the kingdom and only for his own pleasures. It had been disgustingly easy to convince the king that he cared nothing for the crown and was content on being the pampered prince. It was insulting, really, that a man of his blood could have been such a fool. The thought still made Roderick gnash his teeth in disgust.

When, at age ten, Roderick's channeling abilities awakened, his father had eagerly sent for a Domnae, a mage-priest from the Temple of Seni, to instruct him, thinking that perhaps the discipline of the Domni would shape up his son to accept his responsibilities as heir to the throne. Roderick sulked and whined at every given opportunity, refusing to give his maximum effort during his lessons, but secretly he hung onto every word that emerged from his teacher's lips and practiced hard on his mage lessons, determined to learn everything the Domnae had to teach him before he made his move for the throne. He stole spellbooks from the Domnae's library and studied them at night when no one dared to disturb him.

Domnae Nelek had been surprised at Roderick's magical potential, and was frustrated to no end when his pupil seemed to not want to develop his powers to their full extent. Quite by accident, Roderick learned that Domnae Nelek had secretly desired to steal him away to the Temple to become a Domnae when he had completed his training, but as long as Roderick refused to cooperate, he was upsetting those plans.

After that, Roderick had made sure to keep a more careful eye on his teacher, lest he had suddenly awakened one day to find himself confined in the novice wing of the Temple under a submission spell.

For nearly a decade, he had managed to keep up his pretense of being the brat prince in the public eye to the fury of his father and his mentor. Behind closed doors, he plotted and schemed against his father, deliberately creating factions within the noble houses and the ranking occupants of the palace until the entire kingdom was at the brink of a civil war. No one, even Domnae Nelek, had dreamed that their lazy, self-centered brat prince could possibly be the mastermind behind all the turmoil that had suddenly sprung up out of the blue to torment Mihr.

Thus, when the king was found murdered one

night when Roderick was nineteen, the guilty finger never once was pointed in his direction. His father had been found burnt to just a few bones and ash in his bedroom. His night clothes didn't have even a single burnt thread. Even the sheets beneath him had not burned. Only magic could have accomplished such a remarkable feat.

Since Roderick was reputed to be so bad at magecraft that he couldn't even light a lantern with his power, the guilt had been thrown on the only mage in the kingdom who had unlimited access to the king's chambers—Domnae Nelek. Roderick signed Nelek's death warrant himself the very day of his coronation as Mihr's new king. It had pleased him to no end to see the Domnae being led to the gallows wearing only his skin and shackles. In the end, Domnae Nelek couldn't even use his magic to save himself since Roderick had instantly ordered his hands cut off and his tongue cut out.

Executing a Domnae had caused him trouble to no end with the Brothers in Divinity. By divine law, it was forbidden to execute a Domnae without first a trial in the Temple and a death warrant signed by the High Priest, himself. Roderick had scoffed at them and promptly announced the Domnae's plan to kidnap him from Mihr and force him to become a Domnae against his will.

The Temple abhorred scandal. That had shut them up for a little while, at least. It was with that accusation that Roderick had broken from the Temple forever.

The people of Mihr had been shocked by this sudden transformation in their brat prince and also by the power he wielded. Within days, Roderick had united the noble houses and held their loyalties. He had set up sterner laws and new peasant taxes. For a while, it had even seemed as though the peasants would revolt.

He put a stop to such annoyances by demonstrating the extent of his powers. Sometimes he burned houses, but more often than not, it was bodies that lay strewn on the streets of villages, consumed slowly by green mage-flames that could not be extinguished.

Roderick had also immediately enlarged his army, snatching any able young man as young as ten to begin military training. He hired many mercenary mages from the far eastern kingdoms of Bar'taiver and Rathtyen. He also forbade any citizen to leave Mihr, stationing troops all along the borders to prevent any attempts of escape. He thought of the people as his property, and all *would* bend their heads to his will or pay a cruel price for their insolence.

Then the stranger in black robes, his face concealed within the folds of a hood the color of the blackest night, had appeared. Roderick considered that the best day of his life. The stranger introduced Roderick to the dark god, Arioch, and to the seductive world of Ter-ob, Arioch's dark kingdom known commonly as the six hells.

For two summers, the stranger taught him the ways of Arioch and the Dark Powers. Never had he felt so consumed by power, so invincible, as when he wielded the powers of Arioch. It was understandable why he had hated so see his mysterious visitor leave him.

Never once had Roderick seen the stranger's face. Sometimes he liked to fancy that it had been the great god, Arioch, himself, who had been his mentor.

With the help of his newfound powers, Roderick drove the Temple completely out of his kingdom, casting a spell over the lands that saturated the very air and earth with the dark energy of Ter-ob, which would drive any of the Brothers in Divinity mad should they set foot on Mihran soil. The spell had also taken its hold on his people, making them completely his by binding their souls to the land—and to Arioch.

When the hunger for power grew beyond the power he already held, Roderick had aimed his sights on Lamia and their legendary Mage-field, which could give him the power to rule the world. The only thing that stood between him and that Mage-field was that cursed Shield around the kingdom.

All attempts to shatter the Shield had failed miserably. One such attempt had left him bedridden for a quarter-moon after in a fit of rage, he had tried to channel more of the dark energy of Arioch than his body was capable of handling. In that attempt, Roderick had nearly drained the Mihran Mage-field completely.

Then to make matters worse, Aidric and the mage troops he commanded were making it increasingly difficult to attempt more attacks on the Shield, and that left him ready to spit nails.

Now, not only did Roderick have Aidric to worry about, but he also had this mysterious maiden whom the Lamians believed to be the Golden Mage to deal with, as well. He would be a fool to think that he could easily twist her will to do his bidding, but…

Even now he could hear the mysterious voice in his dreams whispering that the maiden he had seen enveloped within the light of the two suns was crucial to the success of his plans. Could the dream have been Foresight of a different flavor, bestowed not from Seni, but from Arioch, himself? Just because Arioch had not rewarded him with a Foresight sending before did not mean those particular dream had *not* come directly from him.

With the Golden Mage in his power, his options were limitless. Roderick could very well conquer all of Seni's world, especially if he had the near limitless power of the Lamian Mage-field to draw from—the Mage-field in which the Golden Mage *would* help him to obtain.

With a smug smile, Roderick sat back into his chair and began to relax the tension in his shoulders as endless images of grandeur flashed through his mind. The more he contemplated it, the more he believed it could be done. No matter what the prophecy foretold, Roderick believed that every mage had at least one weakness. One just needed the fortitude to uncover it. After all, he had found Aidric's strongest weakness. A pity that his attempt to exploit it had unexpectedly blown up in his face, and that method was now closed to him forever.

That was one of the many reasons he had been willing to lose so many of his best spies in his efforts to successfully plant one within Lamia. He had wanted to try to uncover Aidric's weaknesses no matter the cost. However, it had taken the sole spy that had finally managed to cross into Lamia much longer than Roderick had expected to uncover anything useful and even longer to use that information to his advantage.

He simply did not have the patience to wait quite as long this time. If what his current spy had conveyed was true, then perhaps it would be simpler to uncover the weakness of the Golden Mage since she was untrained and ignorant to the ways of magic. Perhaps that, in itself, was her weakness.

Life has just suddenly become more interesting, he thought with glee, gazing at the painting again and imagining that the soldier whose head was being torn off by an enemy's bare hands bore Aidric's face.

CHAPTER FIFTEEN

"Aidric?" a hesitant voice called out from the sitting room, causing him to look up from the map of Kemos, Mihr, and Na'ar he had been studying.

Allison... Aidric smiled as he rose from his chair to go out to greet her, his spirits immediately lifting. She sounded so uncertain, not at all like the majority of Lamian women who were more headstrong than gentle. He found her occasional uncertainty to be a charming quality.

In fact, Allison had not been far from his thoughts during the last few sand-marks he had been working in his study. His mind should have been on the ambush they were planning on Roderick's troops in Kemos, but he had found it very hard to concentrate.

There was no doubt that he was attracted to her. That Lady Gaelle's dig at him had gotten under his skin so badly that she had actually gotten the rise out of him she had desired had made this rather obvious. That realization had piled on an entirely new set of problems to his already overflowing plate.

He didn't know what to think or even if he should explore these newfound feelings at all. They were still practically strangers. Her trust in him was, at best, tentative. The last thing he wanted to do was possibly make things awkward between them, especially since they would be working together closely on a daily basis on her magecraft. Even the smallest distraction during lessons could be dangerous.

Then there was the little matter of *him* trusting *her*. After what had happened with Alina, he didn't know if he could ever fully trust a woman again. Pursuing that type of relationship at this point would be incredibly stupid. It was probably best to just put his attraction out of his mind and continue on acting the mentor only.

Aidric left his study and headed for the sitting room where he found Allison standing near the front door as if she was afraid to enter the room any farther. She wore a dazed expression, her attention focused inward. At the sound of his approach, her eyes immediately darted over to him. She smiled, relief washing over her face, and she took a couple of steps away from the door.

"I was afraid you weren't here," she said shyly.

For a long moment, he said nothing as his eyes took in the stunning vision before him. Allison was no longer wearing the apprentice uniform he had given her. Instead, she was dressed in one of Ileanna's most elegant gowns, obviously intended for the coming night's celebration.

The gown was a deep shade of green that matched her eyes perfectly. It was of the new style, its neckline cut lower and the bodice laced even more tightly in order to accentuate every curve. The hemline in the back, though still long, full, and modest as ever, hung slightly longer than the front until it nearly brushed the floor as she walked. The dress fit as though it had been made especially for her, yet she kept unconsciously smoothing out the material at her waist as if wearing the dress made her uncomfortable. Considering the type of clothing she had arrived in, he couldn't imagine why.

Aidric couldn't take his eyes off her. Her beauty was so astounding that for a moment, he forgot that she had spoken. He couldn't think. It was as if she had cast a submissive spell over him, and he no longer had a will of his own.

"Aidric?"

Her voice shook him out of his fool's paradise, and with some difficulty, he managed to gather his wits again. Aidric offered her an apologetic smile at the questioning in her eyes as he cleared the distance between them and took her hand, lifting it up to his lips to greet her with a light kiss. He delighted at the blush that suddenly colored her checks, lighting up her entire face with a radiance that enhanced her beauty more than he thought was possible.

"I see Ileanna has kept you very busy for the past few sand-marks," Aidric said conversationally. "I trust you enjoyed her company?"

"Oh, very much," Allison replied. "She and her ladies filled me in on a lot of the customs of this world, but mostly on palace life and the life of the surrounding villages." She sighed. "It's—a lot to take in."

She suddenly looked worried, uncertain. As Aidric watched her, he had an impetuous desire to draw her into his arms.

Aidric gave himself a mental kick in the back-side. *What are you thinking? She is to be your apprentice. Unless she shows any interest, then that is all she will be.*

"Don't worry," he said. "As I've told you before, no one will expect you to adjust to our ways so soon. Now, let us sit and talk for a moment. There's so much I wish to know about your world, and I'm certain you still have many questions about Lamia and your duties as a mage that the queen could not answer. We still have several sand-marks before nightfall and the start of the festivities."

"Yes, I *do* have questions," Allison said slowly. "I think maybe I'll never stop having questions, but I'm sure you must have other, more important, things to attend to. I don't want to keep you from them. I'm determined not to be any more of a burden to you than I already am. I can just sit in here and read some of your books. Don't feel as if you have to spend every waking moment with me."

"I thought that 'burden' nonsense was settled," Aidric said in mock consternation. When she merely adverted her eyes, he sighed and shook his head in frustration. "It really does please me that you are staying with me. Rattling around in this monstrous suite alone is not my idea of a good time, mind you. I have never had the pleasure of having a fulltime apprentice. You are my first simply because no other potential mage came even remotely close to the level of my abilities and could be taught by any other mage. The king thought my abilities would serve the kingdom better in military and diplomatic pursuits rather than instructing all the youngsters."

He shrugged. "However, over the past few years, I *have* occasionally taken up a ward. Both were young men who were about to be proclaimed a mage by the Horae that had shone extraordinary skill. I served as a kind of final mentor to them, polishing their techniques and learning their limits, yet they weren't anything like a true apprentice. You will be the first I'll instruct completely from start to finish."

"But your other duties—" Allison protested.

"You are *far* more important than any other duty I might have, Allison," he replied firmly. "Without the proper training, you could very well destroy the kingdom, and only I have the knowledge and ability to give someone has potentially powerful as you that training. But that's not the only reason. Over the last few years, I have grown extremely weary of politics and have longed to go along another path. Your arrival here has finally given me the perfect excuse to do just that."

Aidric smiled down at her, but her eyes still reflected a great amount of uncertainty.

"Okay," Allison said hesitantly, "if you're sure I won't be taking up too much of your time, then I'm glad for the company. To be honest, I—don't want to be alone right now."

She then abruptly pulled her hand out of his and sharply turned her back to him as though she was about to cry and didn't want him to see her tears. Yet, when she spoke again, her voice was surprisingly steady.

"I still don't know what to make of all of this. It's just so overwhelming, especially after everything Queen Ileanna has told me about this place. I'm still having a hard time coming to terms with the fact this place *exists* much less everything else. It's just so different, and—I guess I'm just afraid that I'll *never* fit in…"

Allison walked over to one of the windows and sighed as she gazed out into one of the indoor gardens.

Aidric waited a couple of beats before following. He stopped directly behind her, uncertain of whether he should touch or even speak to her. Finally, against his better judgment, he placed a hesitant hand lightly onto her shoulder and then was surprised when instead of flinching away as he half-expected her to do, she reached up and covered his hand with her own. Her unexpected touch sent a pleasant shock through his body.

He started to speak, but before he could utter a word, Allison's shoulders tensed, and she said in a wavering voice, "A-Aidric—I don't—it's too much—I can't—"

"It's all right," Aidric crooned softly, wanting to take her into his arms to comfort her but making no move to do so. "You can tell me."

With a shaky sigh, she slowly turned to face him, her lovely face now stained with tears. Her eyes carried a very familiar haunted look. It made his heart ache. Seeing the despair in her eyes was like looking into a mirror. He stared down at her mutely, wanting to say something to ease her torment, but unable to find the right words.

"I'm scared, Aidric!" Allison said bleakly, desperation creeping into her voice. "I feel it—all this power within me I don't understand pushing hard against your shields, wanting to break out and cause all sorts of terrible things! I was terrified it would happen when I was with the queen! I just want it to *stop*, to wake up from this nightmare!"

Allison then crumbled before him so quickly that Aidric nearly missed preventing her from falling to the ground. The moment he grabbed her, she immediately threw her arms around him, holding onto him tightly as though he was her anchor in the sea in which she was now drowning.

This time he didn't hesitate as he drew her closer to his body, enfolding her protectively in his arms as she trembled and began to sob quietly into his chest. He carded his fingers through her golden hair gently in an attempt to soothe her tears, bending his head to whisper words of reassurance into her ear.

Aidric silently held her until her body stopped

shivering and her sobbing ceased, bearing her weight as her body slumped against his in exhaustion, her breathing reduced to ragged gasps.

Holding her so close to him, sharing a moment so intimate, left Aidric feeling conflicted. His emotions were in utter turmoil, partly because his Empathy was picking up Allison's emotions and they were bleeding into his own.

So much for his earlier determination to keep her at an arm's length. Sharing such an intense, emotional moment made that virtually impossible now. He had never longed to make love to a woman more than he did at that moment.

Seni help me, it has been so long, so damned long—

He gazed down at her as he lovingly stroked her hair. Her eyes were closed tightly against the world, her lips still trembling with unreleased anguish. He could feel her arms still holding him tightly in their death grip, the feel of her warm breath on his chest. It was maddening!

Aidric glanced longingly in the direction of his bedroom. He knew he merely had to lead her over to it, and she probably would not hesitate to follow.

He didn't move.

Lamia's Mage-general at his finest, he thought sarcastically. She would follow him yes, but not because it was what she truly desired. She was merely feeling incredibly vulnerable and as a result, longed for his companionship. Nothing more.

Aidius, I've been far too lonely for far too long! he thought, disgusted with himself. *Seni condemn me to the lowest hell of Ter-ob if I ever think anything so depraved again! I'll not have her unless she comes to me out of love!*

A few beats later, Allison pulled away from him, still visibly shaken, but now her expression was more embarrassed than frightened. He didn't know whether to be relieved or disappointed.

"I-I'm s-sorry," she stammered, her tear-stained eyes refusing to meet his gaze. "I'm not making a very good first impression, am I?"

"Nonsense," Aidric replied firmly. "You shouldn't be ashamed of doing what any other would do in your situation. Allison—look at me."

Slowly, she raised her eyes to meet his. They stared at one another for a long, tense moment, almost as if they were trying to read down to each other's soul. Whatever Aidric had meant to say was lost in the heat of that gaze.

Finally, Allison blinked and smiled wryly as she wiped away all the stray tears from her eyes and said almost casually, "I've ruined your shirt."

Taken aback by her sudden shift in mood, Aidric looked down at his clothing dumbly and saw that his shirt was indeed ruined. The front of his shirt was

soaked with Allison's tears and heavily wrinkled beyond salvation where she had gripped him so tightly.
Had anyone seen him in such a disheveled state off
the battlefields, they would have been shocked.

"So you have," he agreed with amusement.
"Strange your dress received no such damage. If I did
not know better, I would think the queen had all of
her wardrobe spell-protected. You don't have even a
single wrinkle."

"It's a gift all women have, I suppose," she said
with a smile.

Aidric laughed but then immediately sobered
when he saw her face turn serious again.

"Thank you," she said softly.

"Whatever for?"

"For just being here," Allison said, "for giving
me a shoulder to cry on when I needed it. I would
have lost it a lot worse if I would have been alone,
and who knows how many bad things I could've inadvertently caused with my mind so unstable."

"I'm not going anywhere," Aidric said gruffly.
"Do you wish to speak a bit more, or would you rather rest until tonight?"

She paused, her eyes flickering towards the en-
tryway to the hall before she shook her head. "Let's
talk."

He nodded and gently took her hand, leading her

over to one of the couches. Allison sank into it in exhaustion, and Aidric seated himself beside her, consciously keeping about an arm-span's distance between them as much for his sake as for hers. He was still unnerved by the emotions she had roused in him earlier, and her closeness was only tormenting him.

"You said you could feel the power pushing against you mind?" Aidric prompted after a moment of silence when it was clear that she would not initiate the conversation.

"Yes," she replied with a shudder. "Even now I can feel it, a sort of tingling and pressure against my awareness—against my soul—or something. It's hard to explain."

Aidric shook his head. "No, I understand. That feeling is the energy of the Mage-field fighting against the shielding I have placed between it and the channels within your mind. It is an energy that is naturally attracted to all mages that have ventured near. You don't yet know how to control this great power, so instead, it roams freely. You must first Bond with the Mage-field before it will succumb to your will. Until then, it will attempt to control you. Unfortunately, my shields cannot prevent you from feeling the turmoil this wild magic is causing within you."

"But what if the magic breaks your shields?" Allison asked fearfully. "You said so yourself that this power broke the shields around you once before."

"Then I'll be there to reset them," he replied simply. "Until I teach you to control your abilities, I'll not let you roam far from my sight, so you would do good to learn quickly unless you wish me to become your new shadow!"

Instead of smiling, as he had hoped, she only appeared more worried. "What if I *can't* learn how to control these abilities?" Allison asked anxiously. "I'm still having trouble accepting the fact that I have them, much less actually using them to do God-only-knows-what." Her hands fisted tightly in her lap. "I don't know if I can do this. I'm just an ordinary college student, not a soldier. Never in a million years did I imagine that I would suddenly be capable of performing *real* magic, much less *battle* magic. It's just too much, too soon for me to deal with right now."

"I *could* postpone your lessons until you feel that you are ready to embrace them..." Aidric offered.

"No," Allison said with a wry smile. "If you allowed me to do that, then my lessons would *never* start!" She sighed heavily. "There's no use crying over what can't be changed, is there? I've had my one allowed freak-out for the year, so I guess it's time for me to pull myself together. I swear I don't usually lose it like I just did. I guess—I guess I just needed it."

"Please, milady, don't apologize," Aidric said in exasperation. "You don't need to justify anything to me or anyone."

"I just feel so, well—embarrassed," she insisted, her cheeks coloring. "I used to scold my younger sister 'til I was blue in the face when she would act just as I did. I don't like to think that I'm suddenly turning into the world's biggest hypocrite!"

Pain entered her eyes when she spoke of her sister. It was obvious that they had been close.

"You miss her," he said gently.

"More than I thought I could ever miss anyone," Allison said, closing her eyes as her face scrunched up as though she was about to start crying again, but then she took a deep, steadying breath. "When I first left for California, I could practically feel the separation like it was a physical thing, but it's nothing compared to how I feel right now. Knowing that I won't ever see her again is just as bad as if someone had just told me she was dead. Knowing that she's alive out there and I can never see her for the rest of my life seems crueler, somehow."

"What is her name?"

"Katherine," she answered simply, offering no further details.

"And your parents?" Aidric prompted, deciding

on a different approach. "What of them?"

Allison shifted uncomfortably and lowered her gaze as she said, "I'd rather not talk about them if you don't mind."

"Of course," he said quickly even though he burned with curiosity, but now was definitely not the time to press. "Perhaps I shouldn't ask this, either, but I would like to know what caused you to lose your composure so thoroughly just now? I worry—though obviously afraid in the beginning, you seemed to be handling things just fine until that moment. Was it the presentation I forced you to attend? If so, then I wonder if having you attend tonight's celebration is such a good idea..."

"It wasn't just the presentation," she assured him, to his relief. He still felt guilty about forcing her into a situation that had obviously distressed her greatly, especially after everything she had already been through. "It was a lot of things—King Diryan's explanation of the prophecy, that Circle member, Gaelle, suddenly wanting to poke around in my head, my terrifying experience in the portal that brought me here, but it was mostly everything that the queen and her ladies explained to me."

When Aidric frowned, Allison abruptly leaned towards him and placed a hand on his forearm. "No—don't misunderstand me. I'm *not* putting any of the blame on Queen Ileanna. It was just that her words suddenly made me realize that all of this wasn't a dream but my new, frightening reality because there was *no way* my own imagination could have come up with something so detailed and convoluted. My mind just couldn't accept it." She pulled her hand back and started to wring them anxiously in her lap. "I'm scared, confused, and there's not much I can do to change that right now."

"I can't imagine being transported to another realm as you have," Aidric said gravely. "I don't know how I would react if I did. This can't be easy for you, Allison, but I'll help you to adjust any way I know how."

She smiled slightly and said, "I appreciate that more than you'll ever know. Speaking of, there's this question I've been meaning to ask you. I feel as if it's been daytime forever, or is it just my imagination? Even considering the circumstances, this day seems to have dragged on forever." She nodded towards one of the windows. "It's only now starting to grow dimmer, or since that one looks out into an indoor garden, is it only an illusion?"

Aidric tilted his head in confusion, not really sure what she was asking. The day seemed as long as any other day to him, but—maybe since she came from another realm, time was different for her.

231

"Perhaps in your world the days are shorter," he suggested. "The first sand-mark of the day begins when the first sun is visible over the horizon. A few sand-marks later, the midday begins when the second sun has risen to its peak. Early evening begins when the first sun has set, and when the second has set, nightfall has come. This whole process between the rising of the first sun to the next rising of the first sun that signals another day is during a forty-nine sand-mark time span. Is it not so in your world?"

"Do you mean to tell me that one of your days is equal to forty-nine *hours*?" she asked incredulously.

"'*Hours*'?"

"I mean sand-marks," she corrected, then added with uncertainty, "I think."

"We were in the throne room for about half a sand-mark to give you some idea of that measurement of time," he said.

She pursed her lips in an utterly adorable way. "Since I was so nervous and uncomfortable, my sense of time might have been warped, but I think your sand-marks and my hours are pretty close to the same length."

"Is a forty-nine sand-mark day so strange?" Aidric asked

"Really strange," Allison said. "One Earth day is roughly equal to twenty-four sand-marks! No wonder this day seems to have gone on forever. To me, you have a full day of daylight! That would mean the night is just about as long as the day."

"Yes," he said, shaking his head in bewilderment. *This Earth really is a most peculiar place.* "How do your people ever accomplish anything with so little daylight sand-marks a day?"

"God knows," she replied dryly. "No wonder I'm so tired. I should be sleeping right now!"

"Maybe you *should* nap before we attend tonight's celebration. We can always continue this conversation at a later time."

"A nap *does* sound great," Allison said carefully, "but I don't really think I want to go to your celebration tonight. In fact, the prospect scares me. I don't know if I can handle being scrutinized by all those strangers so soon after what I endured at my presentation."

"I was worried before, but seeing as how something as basic as the length of a day is unknown to you, I now believe it would do you much good to attend," Aidric said. "Observation is always a better teacher than merely explanation. Plus, you cannot hide from your new people forever. Going to this evening's festivities will be the first step you must take in your adjustment."

"But all those strangers—" she protested weakly.

"—are my friends and acquaintances," he finished for her. "What better way to make friends than my introducing you to them? I'll not force you to go, but I strongly believe you should. Please, milady..."

For a moment, the rebellion in Allison's eyes made Aidric believe she would flatly refuse to attend again despite his insistence, but her anxious expression suddenly changed to one of mischief as she said, "All right. I'll go, but first you must promise to do something for me."

"I'll do anything that you wish of me," he said, relieved that she had agreed. Then remembering the mischief in her eyes, he quickly amended, "Provided, milady, that it's legal, of course."

Allison made a face. "Please stop calling me 'milady'!"

CHAPTER SIXTEEN

"All right, Aidric, spill it out. I want to know every single detail!" Selwyn demanded impatiently as he and Aidric lounged in Selwyn's quarters. Selwyn's wife was currently out on an assignment in Biros and wouldn't return until later that evening, so they had the suite all to themselves.

"About what?" Aidric replied innocently with a tired smile.

"Oh, for the love of Seni!" Selwyn boomed in frustration. "You know 'what.' The Golden Mage— what's she like? You have spent sand-marks with her alone, so you must have some sense of her true personality."

"Her name is Allison, *not* 'the Golden Mage,'" Aidric corrected him, rubbing his temples a little in an unsuccessful attempt to ward off the headache he felt rising. "Aidius, she's just a maiden, Selwyn—a very frightened maiden to be truthful—and none of this Golden Mage business has been easy for her to accept. It makes me want to laugh when I think about how you and everyone else were so afraid of her when I know she's more frightened of you!"

"Are you serious?" Selwyn asked in disbelief. "With all the power she has at her call, she fears *us*?"

"Quite," he said, "and shouldn't she be frightened? It's *she* who is the stranger in our kingdom. Her life is ours to decide because of that fact, and she damned well knows it."

"I hadn't even considered that," Selwyn said thoughtfully. "I suppose you are right, but that image of her sure doesn't correspond with the larger-than-life image the prophecy makes of her. However, her beauty could surely make any man forget that she could very well kill him—or that he were married!"

Aidric felt heat rise to his cheeks at Selwyn's words and then shifted uncomfortably when Selwyn narrowed his eyes suspiciously at him, inadvertently causing him to blush more deeply. Aidric silently cursed himself.

Then Selwyn suddenly laughed gleefully and said, "Bright thrones above! I do believe that Seni has declared you ruler of the Thrones! You've fallen in love with her, haven't you?"

"Not so loud!" Aidric hissed, annoyed. "You'll have the whole damned court gossiping with your loquacious tongue!"

"Ha! So I assumed correctly," Sel said triumphantly. "Of course it had to be the Golden Mage. No simple, lowly maiden would ever do for His Pickiness, am I correct?"

"Hush, or I'll spread throughout the court that you fainted out of *fear* at the sight of a beautiful maiden!" Aidric warned.

"I stand rebuked," Selwyn said in mock horror, "yet, you haven't denied that what I've said is true!"

Selwyn's look of triumph suddenly turned to one of dumb surprise as he suddenly found himself landing firmly on his backside on the hard, marble floor as his chair flew out from beneath him.

Aidric laughed at the bafflement on Selwyn's face and said mischievously, "Poke fun at me, do you?"

"Completely unfair!" Selwyn shot back irritably, rubbing his sore bottom. "I don't have the ability to do the same to you!"

"Ah, the privileges of fate," Aidric replied with a chuckle as he stood and offered a hand to his friend, who took it grudgingly and hoisted himself to his feet.

"One of these days—" Selwyn threatened.

"Not so fast, my friend," Aidric said with a grin. "I do believe we are now even. Compensation, you see, for knocking *me* on my ass this morning."

Selwyn smacked his forehead and said, "Ho! I stand rebuked again! Shall we call a truce then, oh Mightiest of Mages?"

Aidric grimaced at the playful title. "A truce," he agreed as they took their seats again, Selwyn carefully sitting down in his chair as if he suspected Aidric of pulling it out from under him again, truce or no truce. Aidric decided to be merciful. He didn't think his friend's backside would take another fall without consequence.

Aidric sobered a little, the amusement dying down from his eyes as he stared at his best friend, uncertain if he should confide his feelings to him when he, himself, wasn't altogether sure about them. He didn't think what he felt for Allison was as deep as love—something a little beyond affection, maybe—but love? If he was being honest with himself, he knew it would be very easy to fall in love with a gentle and playful soul like Allison.

The question was, *could* she ever come to love him as more than her mentor? Was it even possible for her to see him as more than a figure of authority, as just a man, or was he only raising his hopes to only have them come crashing back down on him? He didn't think he could handle that kind of crushing disappointment after what he had gone through with his last relationship. Point in fact, he wondered if he could even handle another relationship period!

"Aidric, what is it?" Selwyn asked, alarm creeping into his tone.

Aidric sighed. He *needed* to share his fears with someone before they became a burden too heavy to carry alone, and who better to help him rid himself of some of that burden than his best friend? He carried the weight of too many painful secrets as it was.

"Sel, I'm at a loss of what to do," he confessed, letting his agitation show. "I admit that this mysterious maiden has stirred my emotions to the point of distraction, but love?" He laughed tightly. "It's just too soon to be bandying that word about. I have only known her for less than a day!"

"But you know that doesn't matter," Selwyn said pointedly, all the teasing gone from his voice. "You know that some people have fallen in love from the first moment they laid eyes upon one another. Aren't Raya and I proof of that? Is it so difficult for you to believe that the same has happened to you? I suspected that you were at least attracted to her from the vicious way you were ready to defend her honor at the slightest provocation, as though she was a lifelong friend rather than a dangerous stranger. The king probably has his own suspicions as well, from the strange looks he was giving you from time to time. Despite what you believe, I wasn't cowering in fear the whole time we were in your bedroom!"

Aidric smiled despite himself. "My own feelings are not the only thing that has me troubled," he confessed. "It's *hers* that are what really matter here. What if all she ever sees me as is a friend and mentor? Aidius, she is to be my *apprentice* after all! I should respect that relationship between us more than my thoughts are allowing me to!"

"Horseturds," Selwyn snapped impatiently. "You and your bloody ethics! You know as well as I that no one would think the less of you for bedding your student. Aidius, you know Patrym practically has a harem in his bed every night, most of them his bardic students, and no one thinks the less of him for it." He smiled wryly at Aidric. "No one, that is, except for *you*. Aidius, Aidric, as virtuous as you've become lately, sometimes I think you should just give up magecraft and take vows. I heard the Order of the Providence is looking to recruit more virtuous souls. With your Foresight, you most certainly could—"

"Sel, can you be serious for at least a couple of depths?" Aidric growled in annoyance. "I'm in a very serious bind here!"

"Sorry." Sel actually sounding a little guilty. "I'll

behave, I promise."

Ha! I'll believe it the day Roderick takes vows!

"And of all the people you could have chosen as an example, it had to be Patrym," Aidric added in disgust. "That self-centered spawn-of-a-demon has the morals of a pig—no, I'm being unfair to the pigs—and you are comparing *him* to *me*! Now I feel worse!"

There was no love lost between Aidric and Patrym; it was no secret. Aidric had never liked the arrogant young bard, and he tolerated him only because for what the distasteful man lacked in personality, he more than made up for it in music. Patrym had a voice that seemed to have originated in the Thrones, and few could match his skill with various instruments. Only two men could claim to be his better. As far as Aidric was concerned, the only time Patrym was actually tolerable was when he was performing.

Then, there was also the matter of The Song—

"All right, so Patrym was a bad choice," Selwyn agreed, "but my point is still there."

"No one must forget that she is *not* a normal maiden," Aidric said darkly, "least of all me, although it's damned easy for me to do just that. Her training is very important to the welfare of Lamia, and I *cannot* allow my personal feelings to interfere with her schooling. I mean, say I do pursue her and she turns down my advances? You know I would never be comfortable in her presence again, nor she in mine. That could be disastrous for us all. Do I dare take the risk? Especially after what occurred with my last liaison..."

"Of course you do," Selwyn replied firmly without hesitation. "Aidric, no man alive can compare to your chivalry, nor, Seni help me, do I dare say to your looks. I don't believe any of that would escape her notice. From what I observed in court today, she already trusts you, which is already a big plus in your favor. Her whole demeanor made it perfectly clear when she was near you."

Aidric frowned. "But—"

"No 'buts,'" Selwyn cut in. "You've never had a problem catching a woman's eye before, and before you say it, the 'time' thing will not be an obstacle for either of you. You most certainly will be spending a fair amount of time together for the next year or so. That fact, alone, should make your chances better than usual. I also hardly think that she will be another Alina."

Aidric winced inwardly at the mention of Alina, but he held his peace. He was in no mood to get into yet another "discussion" about *her* with Sel.

"Come now, Aidric, live a little. It's high time you emerge from the protection of the shield you have cast about you and take a chance. After all, is life not anything but chance?"

"I wish I shared your confidence," Aidric said wistfully.

"And why shouldn't you?" Selwyn demanded. "Damn it, Aidric, you wouldn't have the position you hold now if you weren't *majorly* confident. You face armies numbering in the thousands almost every day, spitting in Death's face, and yet you can't face one woman!"

"Don't you *dare* laugh at me!" Aidric barked angrily, glaring over at Selwyn with such fierceness that Selwyn shrank back into his chair, looking cowed.

"Aidric, I didn't mean—" Selwyn stammered, his face growing pale.

"Oh, Aidius, Selwyn, I didn't mean to—" Aidric babbled, stricken, as he laid his head into his hands. "I'm sorry—I—oh, damn it! Do you see what this is doing to me? I feel as if my insides have been torn out!"

"Aidric," Selwyn said carefully, making him lift his head, "don't torture yourself over this. It accomplishes nothing but causing you pain. If you feel this strongly about her, then just rid your mind of all your 'what ifs' and court her, or talk this over with the king if you are still unsure of what to do. He's a lot better at easing your mind than anyone. Just forget about all that other teacher/student nonsense, and for once think of yourself!" He smiled weakly at Aidric. "After all, I don't believe the courting of one maiden will be the downfall of the kingdom. If that were the case, then we would've been in trouble long ago!"

Aidric chuckled at the absurdity of that thought, his spirits beginning to rise a bit. *Sel's right*, he thought reluctantly. *I have been neglecting my own needs for far too long. It's time I did something for myself for a change. I only hope that I'm not about to repeat the worst mistake of my life.*

He offered Sel a smile. "You are right as always, my friend. It's no wonder Raya married you. You probably pestered her until she grew weary of it and said yes!"

He ducked as Selwyn threw an apple at him and retorted, "That shows what you know you pompous, arrogant, poor excuse of a mage!"

Aidric grinned as he ducked to avoid the second apple Selwyn shot his way.

***

"So, what's your opinion of her?" Diryan asked his wife with a tired sigh as he sank into an overstuffed chair in the sitting room of their suite.

"She's a sweet child. There's no doubt of that,

but she's also a bit strange," the queen replied with a half-smile as she placed a hand lovingly onto his shoulder. "I suppose the strangeness is to be expected. She is, after all, not of our world. However, others may not be so quick to see it as I do. I'm afraid that one's preconceptions are far too often exercised over one's reason—especially in this court."

"Too true," Diryan replied gravely. "I had a rather unpleasant conversation earlier—to be truthful, an argument—with Galen regarding the girl. That's why I asked your opinion of her—to see if any of Galen's arguments had any sense to them, however farfetched they may have seemed at the time. Frankly, although I defended her, I'm not entirely certain how I feel towards her or what to even think about this whole mess. There are so many unanswered questions about her mysterious arrival. It's gotten to the point where I'm at the brink of pulling out all my hair over the matter!"

"Then why don't you ask the child, herself, these questions?" Ileanna asked gently.

"I have," he said with a snort of frustration, "and she is as puzzled over them as I." Diryan began to rub his temples, feeling another headache coming on. *I don't need this*—

"Perhaps you should consider a Seer of the Providence to ease your mind," Ileanna suggested.

"After all, it was one from their order that Foresaw the coming of this so-called Golden Mage."

Diryan laughed dryly and said, "What good would come of it? They would only speak their endless riddles and say that Seni's will must not be questioned, just accepted. Be damned with all that nonsense! I need answers, not riddles! What I really want to know is why *now*? Why did the Golden Mage appear today and not at some future time? What is the significance? I'm sure there is one since there always is. With a silent war going on, why did Seni—if indeed it was Seni who sent her and not some demon from Ter-ob—burden me with yet another grievance? If what the prophecy speaks of is true, then she could very well cause our downfall, and Lamia would be in the hands of a man who cares nothing for anyone but himself.

"When the people get wind of her presence, Roderick no doubt will hear of her existence. That, I could not possibly prevent, and that's what has me so worried. Armed with this new information, wouldn't he double his efforts to breach the Shield? If Roderick was to have her under his control, he would no doubt be unstoppable, but that's not the only thing that makes me uneasy."

Diryan paused, unsure if he should mention anything to her. Ileanna raised an eyebrow at his obvious hesitation but said nothing. That's what he loved most about her. She knew with almost a Seer's awareness when she should and should not press him. He was glad that she was willing to tell him where to stuff it even when in a rage if she felt it was necessary.

"I'm afraid that Aidric has become infatuated with her," Diryan continued finally with a sigh, deciding that it was something his wife needed to know.

"I know," she replied softly to his surprise. "Yet, is it really so surprising? She's very beautiful, alone, and vulnerable. The only person she seems to trust is him. Isn't it natural for him to develop *some* feelings for the child?"

"Some feelings, yes," Diryan replied, "but what I have seen goes much deeper than a desire to protect, or even just plain interest in a lovely maiden. I have never known Aidric to give his heart so freely in so little time to anything, especially after that little incident with the last woman he took up with."

"I would hardly call that bitch nearly destroying his life a 'little' incident," Ileanna cut in heatedly.

Diryan chose to ignore that comment. The last thing he wanted to do was get into another discussion with his wife about the infamous Alina affair.

Instead of the retort he wanted to snap back at her, he said, "Aidric practically struck Zenas down every time he said a negative thing about the girl, and it's that behavior that has me so worried."

"Why?" Ileanna asked, clearly surprised.

"Because his involvement with a mage with the potential power the girl has could be disastrous for all of us. No—hear me out, my dear. If indeed they become romantically involved and any of our enemies learned of the pairing, they could very well use that information to their advantage. I don't need to remind you how Roderick has used such information in the past.

"*Everyone,* including our enemies, knows how vulnerable Aidric is with matters of the heart thanks to that damned bard, Patrym, and his accursed song. If something was to happen to the girl—after all, we cannot keep her confined within the palace forever— Aidric would probably never recover. He's had too much heartache in the past to survive another large blow. Without Aidric, our magical defenses would suffer greatly, and Roderick would stand a better chance of laying siege over Kemos and Na'ar, thus forcing me to make a decision I much rather not contemplate making."

"My beloved, I'm sure it wouldn't ever come to that," Ileanna said. "Do we dare deny Aidric any happiness—or Allison? Look at all the happiness we have found together when many thought *our* marriage would only bring disaster."

Diryan remembered only too well how much his father had tormented him because he was in love with and wanted to wed a woman of low birth. Among monarchs, that simply was not done—at least Diryan's father insisted that it was not. In the end, Diryan eventually won over his father and his father's councilors when he pointed out that several monarchs in the past had indeed taken a woman of low birth as their queen and as a result, completely won the favor of all the peasants. During his grandfather's reign, there had been many peasant revolts, one of which almost succeeded in removing his grandfather from the throne.

And of his life, he thought gravely.

Diryan's father had been thirteen when that particular revolt occurred, so he knew only too well that if he would not allow his son to marry Ileanna, the people would be outraged and probably revolt again. However, he was insistent on the fact that Diryan was making a terrible mistake, and she would only bring him grief. Sure, there had been grief, so much that Diryan had toyed with the notion that his father had cursed him, but there was also much happiness. In the end, the happiness of their partnership greatly outweighed all the heartache.

"That's all well and good, but what if she doesn't

wish to have the lad's attentions?" Diryan asked with a worried frown.

Ileanna regarded him with a peculiar smile, causing him to look at her suspiciously. When it became apparent that she was not going to enlighten him without some prodding, he demanded, "All right woman, out with it."

"With what?" she asked innocently, her face in a mask of complete puzzlement.

"By Aidius, if you were not my wife and love, I would seriously consider thrashing you!" he grumbled irritably.

She laughed good-naturedly and wrapped her arms snugly around his neck. "My dear," she said warmly, "you are taking the situation much too seriously. Aidric is an adult and perfectly capable of making intelligent decisions on his own. Bright Thrones above, you act as if he is still in swaddling clothes!"

"However, in matters of the heart, he is as foolish as a lovesick minstrel!" Diryan insisted.

"Come now, Diryan, give the lad more credit than that! After his last disastrous tryst, he has taken to guarding his heart more closely. Besides, I happen to know the girl, Allison, feels the same towards Aidric as he does her."

"She has confided this to you?" Diryan asked in disbelief. "By the Thrones above, you clever woman, if I had known you could extract information such as that so efficiently and quickly, then I would have had you assigned to interrogate prisoners the moment you became my queen!"

"No thank you," she replied dryly. "I would much rather keep my distance from that nasty lot. Besides, Allison didn't actually confide this to me. It was my own observation of her behavior and words when Aidric was mentioned that led me to conclude this."

"Perhaps you could have been mistaken?" Diryan said skeptically.

Ileanna laughed dryly and said, "Hardly, my dear husband. Even though I believe she doesn't realize it yet, there's no doubt in my mind that she is falling in love with her gallant protector."

Diryan looked amusedly at Ileanna's determined expression, smiled indulgently, and drew her to him for a tender kiss. "Women," he breathed into her ear, "always thinking they know all when it comes to love."

"Oh, but don't we?" she replied slyly as she began to caress his cheek seductively in invitation.

Diryan laughed and said, "Keep this up, my beloved, and I'll not accomplish anything else today!"

"Duty, duty," she sighed in mock disappointment. "Were we but simple peasants—"

"At times such as these, I sometimes wish I *had* been born a regular man," Diryan replied wistfully, "but then, perhaps you would not have been interested in me—seeing as how I would be just a peasant and not a king!"

"You beast!" Ileanna exclaimed, feigning insult.

Diryan smiled wickedly at her and said, "Tonight is a night for celebration. Shall I make it up to you by having our own little 'celebration' here tonight?"

Ileanna blushed as deeply as any young court girl and replied, "In that case, milord, I'll forgive you your remark. Go now and attend to your business, and I'll attend to mine. I must admit that I have much to do before tonight's celebration, but before you go, I want you to promise me one thing, Diryan."

"I'm yours to command, milady."

"Diryan, I'm serious!" she exclaimed in exasperation. "You must give me your solemn oath that you will do nothing to come between Aidric and Allison should a romance suddenly blossom between them."

"You know I cannot possibly promise you that," Diryan replied unhappily. "You know as well as I that my kingdom must *always* come before anything else. If I deem it best to forbid them from pairing, then it will be because the wellbeing of the entire kingdom depends on it, but I'll promise you this, Ileanna. For the time being, I'll let the matter be. Whether I intervene or not depends upon how Roderick will react to our newest citizen."

Ileanna still looked unhappy, but she nodded reluctantly and said, "Good enough, I suppose, but it doesn't mean I have to like it."

"I know, my dear," Diryan crooned softly as he rose and took her into his arms in an affectionate embrace. With Ileanna in his arms, his burdens never seemed quite so heavy. "I don't like it either. The Thrones know we have all had more than our fair share of heartaches around here, but Aidric knew he would have to make some sacrifices when he made his vows to the Horae. We can only wait and see what comes of all of this and hope that my interference will not be necessary."

As he held Ileanna tightly in his arms, he thought, troubled, *...and hope that Aidric will not hate me to his last dying breath if the time* does *come for me to interfere.*

CHAPTER SEVENTEEN

A slight fluttering sensation in her mind roused Allison from her fitful sleep. She groaned sleepily, her senses momentarily confused. *What an odd and horrible dream*, she thought as she struggled to awaken her foggy mind. *For a minute there, it seemed so real.*

As her mind began to clear, she suddenly felt something soft, but with an uneven surface, beneath her body. Her eyes flew open, and she groaned despairingly when she saw that she was not in her room in her California apartment but in the room the Mage-general of Lamia had given her. She felt her eyes tighten with threatening tears.

So it wasn't a dream, Allison thought miserably as she squeezed her eyes tightly shut, willing the world away with everything in her.

As if to confirm her thoughts, she suddenly heard Aidric's cheerful voice say in her mind, *"Wake up, sleepy."*

"I am awake," she sent back with her mind crossly. *Unfortunately.*

"You sleep as soundly as a cat," he teased. *"I touched your mind several times before you even stirred."*

"So Lamia has cats," she thought bemusedly, before realizing she had probably sent that thought to him.

"Pardon?"

"Never mind," she said. *"It was a thought I didn't mean to send. I suppose you woke me up because it's almost time for the celebration?"*

"Yes, but I had hoped you would be in better spirits about attending after you had rested a bit." She could almost see his disappointment in the thought.

"I'm sorry Aidric, but it's hard for me to be enthused about going. I've never liked going to that sort of thing. Large crowds just make me nervous for a variety of reasons, but don't worry. I'm not backing out. I promised you I would go, and I will."

"Then if you are to be ready in time, I should let you be," he sent cheerfully. *"I'll be eagerly awaiting your presence in the sitting room."*

I wish I could just lie here in this bed for the rest of my life, Allison thought wistfully as she forced her reluctant body to rise from the warmth and comfort of the mass of blankets and feathers. She grabbed a robe-like garment from a nearby chair and wrapped it securely around her body.

God, I don't know if I'm ready to face this celebration thing right now! She blanched as she thought of the enormous amount of people she would have to face in an hour or so. Every one of them would no doubt be scrutinizing her the whole time, all those strange eyes boring into her, searching, weighing—

I can't do it! Allison thought frantically, feeling the panic start to possess her body before she could stop it. Suddenly she couldn't breathe, feeling as if an invisible hand was slowly squeezing the air from her lungs while fear gripped fiercely at her heart.

Panic attack, she thought through the fear. *Not again—I can't let it happen again! Dammit! Just one slow breath at a time—*

However, the more calmly she tried to draw a breath, the more it seemed her throat constricted on her windpipe. With a strangled gasp, she collapsed onto her knees, her hands frantically clawing at her throat as she tried to coax a breath into her aching lungs.

The room began to darken and spin despite her futile efforts to breathe, and in a last attempt to save herself from unconsciousness, she mind-called

Aidric, all her fear and panic laced into his name as she fell over onto her face, too weak to even attempt to draw another strangled breath.

Before the darkness could fully claim her mind, she distantly heard the door fling open, and a second later, a hand gently touched her forehead. A wave of peaceful warmth washed through her body, and before she knew what was happening, she was on her back and noisily drawing in huge breaths. As Allison began to cough fitfully, she felt herself carefully lifted from the cold floor and enveloped into a pair of strong, protecting arms.

"It's all right," she heard a male voice say soothingly into the chaos of her mind. *"I'm here, and everything is going to be all right."*

It took a few moments of confusion before she realized that it was Aidric's voice that had spoken in her mind and the arms that now held her belonged to him. Then with horror, Allison realized what had happened and that Aidric had seen her once again at her lowest. She tried to pull away, humiliated to the point of tears, but it only caused him to hold her more tightly.

"I think not," Aidric said softly. "You are *not* going anywhere until I get to the bottom of what just happened here."

"I—" Allison started to say before she lost what

little ounce of dignity she had left and burst into tears, burying her face into the now familiar silkiness of his shirt. He said nothing, not even little words of reassurance as he had before. He just merely held her, sensing perhaps that she needed his closeness more than his words.

"Why does this always happen to me?" she whispered miserably through her tears. "Why can't I just get over it?"

"'Get over it'?" he repeated questioningly, causing her to raise her head that suddenly felt two sizes too large and stare up into his pale-violet eyes, her tears momentarily forgotten.

Allison was a bit taken aback. She had only been babbling.

"I—never mind," she said shakily.

"Allison—" Aidric said firmly, staring down into her eyes so intently that she had to look away.

Although the fingers that grasped her chin were gentle, the pressure was firm as he turned her chin towards him until she was forced to look into those penetrating eyes again. When Allison tried to avert her eyes a second time, Aidric shook his head and demanded, "Allison, look at me."

Feeling overwhelmed and at the verge of tears again, she reluctantly obeyed. As he gazed into her eyes, Allison suddenly realized what he was doing.

She could vaguely feel his presence in her mind, like a faint whisper in the back of an enormous cathedral.

In a panic, she shoved at the alien presence in her head in an attempt to expel him. To her immense relief, all traces of the presence left her mind. Aidric blinked at her questioningly, clearly surprised that she had flung him from her mind.

Allison expected him to be angry, but he just sighed and asked in a neutral tone, "Why did you do that?"

She tried to pull away, but his arms were like steel bands. "I can't let you know…"

"Know what?"

"Please," she pleaded weakly, feeling the tears suddenly start to leak from her eyes again, "don't ask this of me. Just—promise me you won't ever try to read my mind again unless I say it's okay."

Something akin to hurt flashed briefly in his eyes, but it had come and gone so quickly that she wasn't entirely sure she had seen it in the first place. "The anxiety attack you just suffered was severe enough that it nearly caused you to lose consciousness. I was only trying to find an answer." Aidric said quietly, his eyes now unreadable. "I'm sorry. You will have my promise, of course."

Allison's heart clenched. Yes, she had definitely offended him. A fine way to repay his kindness.

"No—*I'm* sorry," she said, lowering her eyes in shame. "I didn't mean—you just—surprised me. No, that's no excuse. Here you are trying to help me, and I just shove it right back in your face. You must think I'm such an ungrateful bitch."

"No, the fault is mine, alone," Aidric said ruefully. "You're right. I shouldn't have probed your mind without your permission. I forgot that you aren't accustomed to our ways. I'm somewhat of a *calendae*—a soul-healer—and one of the first things we are trained to do is probe the mind for the source of mental turmoil. I didn't think. I should have told you what I meant to do."

Wishing she could just sink into the floor, Allison mumbled, "Don't I feel stupid, now. I should've known you wouldn't have done something like that without a good reason. It seems like lately all I've been doing is apologizing, crying on your shoulder, and ruining your shirts!"

Aidric smiled at her and said, "That you have, mil—Allison. I think a compromise is in order here. I'll accept your apology if you will accept mine."

"Deal," Allison agreed as she tried to release herself from his embrace, but once again he held fast to her.

"Not so fast, little cat," he said with a grin as she looked up at him with startled eyes. "You still haven't told me why your anxiety affects you so severely. I'll release you when you answer."

"I told you that I didn't want to talk about it. Not now," she said, shifting uncomfortably.

Now that she was clearly thinking again, Allison felt the nearness and warmth of his body all too well. She gazed up into his face, and blushed when she suddenly felt a strong urge to kiss that sensuous mouth that was only mere inches away from her own.

My God, what the hell am I even thinking? she thought with horror. *He's only trying to comfort me. That's* all.

Abruptly, Allison began to wonder about the nervousness from the very beginning that he seemed to cause her to feel just from simply looking at her. Had it *really* been out of fear? *Am I*—falling *for him? But*—*but*—*I can't! He's not*—human—*is he?* She felt the blood filling her cheeks suddenly drain from her face as panic began setting in again. *I can't let him know! I can't*—

Instantly, she built a purely mental wall between her feelings and his. She knew only too well that he was capable of knowing her every emotion as well as her every thought.

It was no wonder she hadn't recognized her feelings, a deeper attraction, for what they were earlier.

She had been too busy freaking out about everything to figure out the turmoil of emotions that had swirled within her.

Aidric seemed to sense her withdrawal from him because his eyes suddenly narrowed and he held her more tightly. "You don't have to be afraid to tell me," he said quietly. "I want to help you, Allison, but I can't do that unless you let me in, if even just a little. I suspect that it has something to do with the reason why the thought of me probing your mind terrified you."

Allison stilled. "I—only used to have attacks like this, bad ones I mean, when I was a little girl," she began softly, ignoring his last comment. "It usually happened when I had to do oral reports in front of my class at school. Just the thought of all those eyes on me was enough to reduce me to tears, but it hasn't happened to me in years."

"Ah," he said with sudden understanding. "That's what happened to you today. The presentation must have reawakened your fears, and your earlier breakdown was just a belated response. You were no doubt thinking of all the scrutiny you would be under tonight at the celebration when you had this attack, weren't you?"

"Yes," she admitted in a small voice. "I just started thinking about all those eyes boring into me and panicked." She shuddered. "What am I going to do? I know I can't avoid everyone forever. Yet, I can't bear the humiliation of having an attack in public, either!"

"I can help you forget your phobia for a while," Aidric said thoughtfully, "but in order to block it, I must know the source of all your fear. Surely you must have some idea of what it is that causes your fear of scrutiny, and don't tell me that you don't know. Every phobia has an initial cause. We are not born with them."

"I d-don't know what you m-mean," Allison stammered.

"I think you do," he replied patiently, "and if you want me to help you, you must tell me."

I can't tell him about my stepdad, she thought stubbornly. *I'd rather suffer through these panic attacks than tell him about all the horrible things he did to us!*

"Your stepfather?" Aidric asked, his tone puzzled.

"You're reading my mind again!" she accused him angrily, this time succeeding in breaking free from his arms, pushing away and glaring at him with blazing eyes. "You *promised* you wouldn't!"

"I wasn't!" he shot back at her just as angrily. "I don't know what you think I am, but a liar, I'm not! When I give my word, I keep it!"

Allison immediately clamped her mouth shut on her retort at the vehemence in his words. *Crap! I accidentally sent my thoughts to him again*, she realized with a sinking heart. *Now he's really pissed at me!*

As she saw the anger and hurt in his eyes, she clamped down on the sob that wanted to burst forth and stumbled onto her feet, intent on the door, of just getting away before she made things worse.

What he must think of me... she thought despairingly as she clenched her jaws more tightly together against the nearly overwhelming urge to cry noisily. *Dammit, why do I always,* always *have to botch things up?*

Just when she reached for the door handle and the floodgates in her eyes shattered, Allison felt a hand grab her arm.

"Hey, enough of that," Aidric said gruffly from behind. "Come here."

Before she could protest, he pulled her back into his arms again, his other hand reaching up to stroke her hair soothingly as he pressed her head against his chest. His gesture of unmistakable forgiveness suddenly made her begin to cry even harder with guilt.

"I'm sorry," Allison blurted out between sobs for what seemed like the thousandth time that day. "God, I'm sorry! I was being such a *bitch*. I had no right—you have every right to be pissed at me. I'm just an ungrateful, self-centered, short-tempered, stupid—it's just that I didn't want you to know about my stepdad, about me, how much he despised me, how he—"

"Whoa," Aidric interrupted with a chuckle. "Slow down a bit! You are babbling in your native tongue, and I can't understand a word of it! Please don't cry. I can't bear to see such a lovely maiden cry."

"I'm *not* lovely," she protested, sniffling. "I'm just an ungrateful, self-centered—"

"Come now, we'll have none of that kind of talk," Aidric said firmly. "You are *not* any of those things."

"Yes I am," Allison insisted bitterly. "I blamed you for something I did myself. There's no excuse for what I said!"

"What do you say we just forget the whole incident and just start over?" he suggested. "Pointing fingers never gets anyone anywhere, in my experience. We still have the little matter of solving the problem of your phobia. I can't leave things as they are, but I also can't help you unless you are willing to confide whatever secret you have convinced yourself should not be told. On my honor, it will never leave this room if that's what you desire, and I'll not judge you by it."

"I want to tell you," Allison replied wearily.

"God, it would be such a relief to tell someone, to unburden myself, but it's just so hard! There are only two other people besides my mom who know about it—my sister and my best friend. You must understand that it's hard for me to confide something so personal, that scarred me so badly, to someone I've only met today."

For a long moment, Aidric regarded her with a peculiar expression that she couldn't quite decipher before he said slowly, "I pray to Seni that it's not what I'm beginning to suspect."

At first, Allison stared at him blankly, but then her eyes widened in horror when she realized what it was he was implying. "No!" she said quickly, "it's not *that*. It was bad, but thank God it wasn't *that* horrible…"

She gritted her teeth. Crap, she was rambling again, and neither one of them needed that right now. He was right. She just couldn't go on pretending the problem didn't exist. That was no way to live, especially now that she had so many more important, scary things to deal with.

Taking a deep, shaky breath, Allison proceeded to tell Aidric about all the years of hell she had endured under her stepfather's hand. She told him about his fanatical devotion to his religion and what she had come to realize was a cult that he belonged to, how he had forced Katherine and her to read their Bibles and pray for hours before and after school, and if they disobeyed, how he had beaten them into submission.

When she told him how her stepfather had always looked down at her with his hard, suspicious eyes, trying to decide if she had sinned enough that day to warrant punishment (which he always did), Aidric abruptly stopped her. "That's what I need. It's your stepfather's eyes that you see in all eyes that regard you with scrutiny. You see them and subconsciously expect punishment, but you don't need to fear him tonight. I can block those certain memories from surfacing, and all you will feel is the natural anxiety one with your diffident nature always feels when meeting a large number of strange people."

Allison closed her eyes briefly as a surge of relief flooded through her. Did she dare hope?

"However, I'll not block those memories forever," he warned. "You must come to terms with your stepfather's abuse before these attacks you've been experiencing will be but unpleasant memories. I'm not a true *calendae*, but I can send you to one if you wish whom I'm confident can help you sort through your feelings."

"Someday," she agreed. "For now, if you're sure you can keep me from freaking out so badly, then it's more than enough."

"Positive," he assured her as he hugged her affectionately, causing her to blush furiously.

To hide her reaction, Allison looked down at her bare feet and mumbled, "Some legendary mage I'm turning out to be. I can't even face a bunch of regular people at a party. I bet the prophecy never said that the Golden Mage was also going to be such a pain in the ass."

"—or so emotional," Aidric teased. "Now, if I have your permission, little cat, I must tap into your mind to place the blocks on your memories."

Her face coloring, Allison muttered, refusing to meet his eyes, "You don't have to ask my permission. I only said that because I was afraid you would find out about my past abuse. Just as long as you don't make a habit of doing it all the time, you can read my mind whenever you feel you should."

"You should take care with what you offer me," he said with mock seriousness, his eyes shining with mirth. "You may find me in your mind when it's least convenient for you. Sometimes I have trouble sleeping, and I could keep you up all night with requests for stories of your world!"

"You wouldn't," she said in alarm.

"You think so?" he countered with a raised eyebrow.

"I don't believe you're that cruel."

He sighed and said, "Too true, but I bet you didn't know I was just in your head."

Allison raised a hand automatically to her temple and said, "You mean—"

"—it's done," Aidric finished with an amused grin.

He blocked some of my memories, she thought wondrously, still unable to grow accustomed to all the seemingly miraculous things he was able to perform—things that she would soon learn to perform as well. *But, I can't remember which ones—oh, how stupid can you get, Allison? Of* course *you can't recall which ones. That was the whole point!*

"You look a little unruffled," Aidric commented with a slight frown.

"It's just that I can't get used to all the things you can do with just the power of your mind," Allison explained. "It's all a little unnerving, that's all. I just need time to adjust."

Aidric released her and took her right hand into his, squeezing it gently. "Allison, I know it may seem like an impossibility at the moment, but believe me when I say you *will* adjust, and maybe then things will be a little easier for you."

She couldn't help but notice that he still held her hand firmly in his own with no signs of releasing. She chanced a glance up at his face and saw that he was staring down at her intently, his eyes narrowed and unreadable. Her heart fluttered a little at the intensity of that gaze.

Could he—no. You're only trying to see something that isn't there. Why in heaven's name would someone so amazing want a crybaby like you?

The sound of someone clearing their throat shook Allison out of her thoughts, and both Aidric and she instantly turned their heads in the direction of the sound. Allison's eyes fell on their unexpected visitor, and she drew in a sharp breath, her heart sinking to the bottom of her feet.

CHAPTER EIGHTEEN

A beautiful, raven-haired girl stood in the doorway, regarding both Allison and Aidric with what appeared to be a sly grin. She looked around Kat's age, although the eyes that stared back at her held a wisdom that seemed to suggest her initial assessment was laughably wrong. Her manner was relaxed, casual, but she still managed to convey an air of elegance about her. Allison was startled once again when she realized that the girl's eyes were a rich, golden color.

She must be Aidric's girlfriend or wife, even, she thought, feeling her chest tighten painfully. *Of course she is. She's exotically beautiful and far more sophisticated than I could ever be.*

"I hope I'm not interrupting anything," the young woman said in a slightly accented, musical voice.

"Not at all, my friend," Aidric replied as he quickly dropped Allison's hand as if it had suddenly burned him.

"Well, beast, aren't you going to introduce us?" she asked as she regarded Allison curiously.

Aidric smiled sheepishly at her and said, "Of course I was. Raya, I would like you to meet Allison McNeal. Allison, this is Raya Phelanike, one of my closest friends and also the wife of another one of my closest friends, Selwyn, the redhead you nearly frightened out of his wits earlier."

The wife of…huh? Allison thought in confusion as she stared at the woman whom she was so certain had been Aidric's girlfriend. She was *married*. Allison couldn't help feeling relieved that this beautiful girl would never be competition to her.

Raya, thankfully oblivious to her thoughts, smiled warmly at her and said, "So we meet at last, Allison. Funny, I pictured you to be much taller— considering all the tales I heard while I traveled through Biros earlier."

"Bright Thrones above! Some of the villagers already know of her existence?" Aidric exclaimed with a worried frown.

"So far, I believe only those of Biros know," Raya replied with a chuckle, "but knowing how much *those* villagers love to wag their tongues, I suspect the whole kingdom should be well informed by now!"

"Aidius, I can well imagine what tales must be circulating around with the townsfolk. I had hoped we could have kept her presence here a secret until tonight to avoid such rumors from beginning."

"Ha!" Raya snorted in disgust. "No such luck, beast. Not with all the gossips here in the palace, and you know very well how most of them are prone to exaggeration. As I was riding into Biros, a small mob immediately surrounded me to 'warn' me that the Golden Mage had been found and captured just out-side the palace. According to them, she was—oh, let me see if I remember correctly—'eleven handspans tall, had golden hair that reached the ground, crimson eyes as bright as any demon's, and had cast a spell over the Mage-general, bewitching him to become her slave!'"

She laughed heartily as Allison cringed. "Well, at least the hue of your hair was true enough. It was all I could do to prevent myself from laughing in the poor fools' faces! Hellsfire, sometimes I'm convinced the villagers have read one too many Ter-ob chroni-cles in the dead of night. If you ask me, any such chronicles should all be destroyed! They practically pleaded with me to send an army to protect them from her!"

"That most certainly won't prevent them from showing up at the celebration tonight to gawk at her," Aidric said dryly.

"That's only too true," she replied with a sigh of the long-suffering.

"Great," Allison muttered angrily, more to herself than to them, "just what I need. Everyone here seems to think that I'm some kind of monster!"

Raya flashed her a sympathetic smile and said, "Don't pay them any mind, milady. They are simple folk who fear anything and everything they don't understand. I'm sure when they see with their own eyes and not their ears and imaginations that you are just a normal woman, their fear will subside." She tilted her head to the side with a wistful smile. "That is, a normal woman with not-so-ordinary golden hair. Aidius, what I would trade—who I would *kill*—to have been born with your tresses!"

"My hair's not as extraordinary as you all seem to think it is," Allison insisted uncomfortably.

"The six hells it's not," Raya said excitedly. "Why, you'll be the envy of every maiden in the kingdom!"

"All the more reason for people not to accept me," Allison said with a painful smile. "I don't think I'll ever truly belong here."

"Nonsense," Raya said gently. "I, too, came here

from a far-off, strange land." She smiled wryly. "Well, not as strange as *yours*, but strange enough for these stiff-necked old goats. Everyone took one look at me and decided that I was a barbarian that needed to be shooed away."

"Why?" Allison demanded. Somehow, she couldn't picture anyone *ever* calling someone as beautiful and poised as Raya a barbarian. "A barbarian is the last word I would use to describe you."

Raya laughed airily and replied, "Oh, I didn't always look and speak the way I do now. I come from a land far beyond Sarim called Hrefna."

She spoke the name of her homeland with enough emphasize to suggest that the name alone was explanation enough, and Allison stared at her blankly, the name of the two kingdoms meaning nothing more to her than a couple of random names she had run across while reading earlier.

Raya suddenly slapped her forehead in understanding and said, "Oh, how forgetful of me. You, of course, know little of our lands, and you probably haven't heard the stories of my people—at least not *yet.*" She grinned wickedly. "We don't believe in wearing clothing or finery of any kind. Both men and women go about either stark naked or with a mere loincloth if they are not wed. Only in winter do we wear animal skins to keep warm.

"When I appeared at Lamia's borders, I wore only a loincloth and my hair to cover my nudity. Had it not been by the will of Seni that I knew a bit of the Lamian tongue, I most definitely would've spent my first night here in the dungeons. As modest and proper as these Lamians like to *think* they are, you can well imagine the shock. Yet, despite our differences, I was allowed to become an apprentice-mage.

"At first, I fit in here at the palace as well as a Seninae does in a brothel. That is, until I met a certain young man named Aidric who happened to introduce me to his best friend. Well, what can I say? Selwyn managed to 'civilize' me and win my heart all in the same instant."

"Although he wasn't too thrilled that his wife's assets had been displayed for all to see," Aidric said with amusement.

"Hush beast, or I'll tell Milady Allison all about the time a certain Mage-general had one too many 'sips' of wine and stripped—"

"Ah! You wouldn't dare!" Aidric interrupted with a horrified expression.

"Oh, wouldn't I?" she purred sweetly.

Aidric suffered for a few more beats before Allison laughed at his expression and rescued him by saying, "Although I'd *very* much like to hear that particular story, I think I'll wait and let Aidric tell me all about it himself."

Raya pouted in mock disappointment and said, "Damn, and I was looking so forward to finally humiliating His Highness for all those times he's done so to me. Oh well, mark my words, beast, I'll have my say another time when you least expect it, and when I do, no one will be there to rescue you!"

"Yes, yes," Aidric said with a dismissive wave of his hand.

"*Anyway*, as I was saying before His Highness so rudely interrupted me," Raya continued, "a few people have even forgotten that I arrived here practically nude and that they once called me a barbarian, and they'll soon forget that they ever called *you* the Golden Mage."

"I really don't think people are bound to forget how *I* came to be here and who I am," Allison said unhappily.

"Sure they will," she insisted. "After the initial excitement of your arrival dies down a bit, a little time passes, and they see for themselves that you aren't going to grow another head or other such nonsense, you'll be nothing more than another Lamian mage to them."

"She's right," Aidric cut in with a nod. "It's as

I've told you. You just need to allow yourself and us enough time to adjust."

"And speaking of time," Raya put in, "if any of us intends on being on time for the celebration, then we had better cease gabbing and get ready. That's why I came here in the first place, to see if Allison needed any help to prepare herself for her first social engagement here. And Aidric," her lips stretched up into that same wicked smile she had used earlier, "I hope for the love of Seni that you aren't going to show yourself in public dressed as you are. I suggest you at least go change your shirt. What would the court say if they saw you now?"

For the first time, Allison noticed that Aidric's shirt was still damp where she had cried on his chest and heavily wrinkled in several places where she had clung so tightly to him. That's when she realized how she must have appeared to Raya, though the younger woman was probably too polite to comment on it. Her face was still no doubt stained with tears, her hair likely disheveled beyond belief, and she was dressed in nothing but a robe over her underwear. *So much for first impressions*, Allison thought with a grimace.

"Why do I suddenly feel as though I'm being pushed out the door on my backside?" Aidric said with a laugh.

"How remarkably perceptive of you," Raya replied dryly as Aidric took both her hand and Allison's for a departing kiss and disappeared from the room before Allison could even blink.

"He's such a charmer," Raya commented with a warm smile as Allison regarded the other woman curiously.

She felt a bit embarrassed when Raya turned her gaze to her again and caught her staring. "I—I'm sorry," Allison apologized quickly. "I didn't mean to stare. It's just you're probably as different to me as I am to you, and I guess I couldn't help it. I hope I haven't offended you."

"Oh, *pash*," Raya said cheerfully. "I've been doing my own fair share of staring as well. After all, it's not every day one gets to meet a legend."

"I'm no legend," Allison insisted, suddenly feeling very awkward. "Just look at me! You know damned well that I've been crying. The evidence is still probably visible all over my face as well as on Aidric's shirt."

"Care to talk about it?" she asked.

Before she realized she was going to do it, Allison blurted out, "I don't know how or why this has happened to me. Aidric told me who was likely the one who brought me here, but I'm not sure I'm ready to believe that it was your deity that did it. I'm not sure of anything anymore except that I'm probably never going home. I—"

Allison abruptly cut off what she had been about to say. *Why the hell am I telling her all of this? A moment ago, I thought of her as a prospective rival, and now I'm confiding in her as if she's my best friend!*

It had just seemed so natural for her to confide her fears to the young girl. In a way, Raya was a lot like Aidric, confident, strong, so maybe that was why Allison had warmed to the girl as quickly as she did. She wouldn't at all be surprised if she and Raya really did become good friends over the next few hours.

"Oh, listen to me, babbling on and on about my troubles like an idiot. I'm sure you don't want to listen to all of that."

"I don't mind," Raya assured her. "I understand how lonely you must feel—here amidst a sea of strangers without any family or friends. Sometimes it helps to talk to someone else who has experienced being in a similar situation. Sel's told me a little of how you came to be here and what little Aidric has told him about your world. Most of it is almost too incredible to believe."

"I know how you feel," Allison said. "When everyone here insisted that magic was real and that I, myself, had the potential to become a powerful mage,

I couldn't believe it was true. I *still* don't believe it, really. I feel like I've stepped back in time, or more accurately, into the pages of a fantasy novel. I keep thinking that any moment now, I'll wake up and find that this has just been a horrible nightmare."

"I can't even began to imagine everything you must be going through," Raya said sympathetically. "I wish I could offer a solution that would help you to return to your homeland, but I can't. What I *can* offer you is my friendship if you'll accept it."

Allison stared at Raya in mute surprise. She hadn't really expected the other girl to say anything like that so soon, and she didn't know quite how to respond. She had known Raya for less than an hour, and Raya was already offering her friendship. It made her feel a little ashamed. She really didn't deserve all the kindness given to her so far.

"I—I don't know what to say," Allison admitted softly. "I mean, you hardly know me."

"I know you well enough," Raya said firmly. "Trust me, Aidric will be the first to tell you that I don't offer my friendship lightly. We Hrefnans, by nature, are a solitary lot."

"I'd very much like for us to be friends," Allison said with a smile.

"Good," Raya said, returning the smile. "Now that we've broken the ice a bit, let's see about getting you ready for tonight's festivities. A robe, although glamorous in the bedroom, wouldn't be so popular at a courtyard gathering!"

"I agree," Allison said, feeling relaxed for the first time that day. "Queen Ileanna gave me a dress to wear tonight since I obviously wasn't given the opportunity to pack when I was so graciously dragged here. Could you possibly help me with my hair, though? I just usually brush it and let it hang wherever it happens to fall. I don't know the least bit about Lamian hairstyles, and I don't want to embarrass Aidric or you by looking disheveled."

Raya's eyes lit up. "Of course!" she replied eagerly. "By the time I'm finished with you, no handsome young suitor will be able to keep his eyes off you!"

The thought was appalling. "Um, I was kinda hoping to attract as little attention as possible," Allison explained hastily. "You see, I'm not very good at socializing, and large crowds make me nervous."

"You'll do fine," Raya assured her. "With Aidric as an escort, you don't need to speak much at all. He'll speak enough for the both of you! Believe me, once he introduces you to a few people, you'll start to feel more comfortable, and before you know it, you'll be having the time of your life. Of all the things the people of Lamia are not, they most certainly make up for it with their celebrations and festivals! Now, enough of my gabbing. You need to be off to the bathing room if you want to be presentable at a decent sand-mark. Everything'll be ready for you here when you return."

"Thank you, Raya—for everything," Allison said sincerely as she headed towards the bathing room in good spirits.

CHAPTER NINETEEN

As she walked down the garden path towards the palace courtyard, her arm snugly intertwined with Aidric's, Allison fidgeted nervously, suddenly feeling very shy and awkward despite the assurance his presence gave her. In just a few moments, she would face the majority of the kingdom of Lamia for the first time, and no matter how many times she told herself that it wouldn't be so bad, she could already feel her stomach muscles knotting up with tension as Aidric and she, followed immediately by Raya and Selwyn, crossed the threshold of the arched doorway that separated the indoor garden from the courtyard and into the midst of celebration.

Allison's senses were immediately overwhelmed as she was suddenly bathed in light and color, greeted by the sounds of lively music and a chorus of a thousand voices. Her eyes widened in wonder as they soaked in the near havoc of activity going on before her, her anxiety instantly forgotten.

What seemed like thousands of people swarmed aimlessly around the courtyard, each dressed in an elaborate assortment of costumes of various colors and design that seemed, to Allison, to come straight out of medieval Europe. The women were all dressed similar to her, either in elegant, ruffled gowns made of lace and wool or the silk-like material that the queen had identified for her as *sholkie*, a thread derived from the fibers of the giant leaves of a tree located in the Forest of Peri along the northern borders of Lamia.

Ileanna had explained to her that the only way anyone could depict a noblewoman from a peasant at a celebration or festival was by the material used to make their gowns and the type of stones used in their jewelry.

"Every maiden, no matter how poor or young, owns at least one elegant gown suitable for social events," Ileanna had said with a laugh, "and unless one looks closely, it's virtually impossible to tell the peasant from the highborn maiden. Bright Thrones, one could almost believe it's required by law to own an extravagant celebration gown when listening to a few women speaking of them!"

Allison had regarded her skeptically then, but now that the very mixture of both highborn and peasants confronted her, she surprisingly found that you indeed could not discern between the two classes by a glance alone.

The men, however, were far easier to determine their social status by their clothing. The nobles were dressed far more elaborately than the peasants—in *sholkie* shirts, breeches, and tights of bright colors and heavily adorned with precious and semi-precious jewels that sparkled brilliantly with their every movement. Long, flowing capes completed the look, some even trailing a few feet behind them.

Allison absently wondered how they managed to keep people from stepping on them. Aidric, thankfully, donned a cape that only reached to his ankles, so she didn't have to worry about accidentally stepping on it and embarrassing herself.

The peasant men wore similar outfits but without the capes. Nor did their tunics or shirts sport any gems or the elaborate designs of their lords, but despite those small differences, they were just as elegantly dressed as the highborn.

However, the costume-like clothing was not what truly amazed Allison. It was the fact that everyone seemed to be mingling with each other despite the class in which they belonged. She saw several groups of women, containing both peasants and highborn, gossiping and giggling together with none of the superiority or airs that many of the noble class throughout history tended to express while in the presence of peasants.

When she asked Aidric about it, he just looked at her peculiarly, and answered simply, "It has been that way for some time now."

She waited for him to elaborate, and when it became apparent that he wasn't going to oblige her, she shrugged and turned her attention from the Lamians to the courtyard itself. She could always ask Raya about it later.

Allison was surprised at how different the courtyard now seemed to her in comparison to the state it had been in only hours before. It seemed as if the servants had converted it into a huge garden of paradise. Strange fern-like plants and flowers in various shades of blue, violet, and rose, resembling honeysuckle blossoms but at the size of basketballs, lined the walls and walkways throughout the yard.

Huge lanterns, burning with the same eerie, green flames that illuminated Aidric's suite and the palace corridors, hung from lines that were stretched high above from the enclosed walkway leading to King Diryan's suite to the east and west walls, bathing the courtyard in a faint green glow that somehow gave the scene a dreamlike quality.

"Why are the flames in those lamps green?" she asked Aidric as the four of them headed towards a group of people.

"It's not true fire," Aidric explained. "They are mage-flames, fueled by the power of the Mage-field and not by such things as lamp oil. Firestarting will be one of the many things I'll teach you, and I'll explain mage-flames to you more thoroughly then. As for now, there are some friends I would like you to meet."

As Aidric led her deeper into the courtyard and into better light, Allison heard many gasps of shock as the people they passed realized who she was. All conversation around them seemed to cease all at once, and she suddenly felt a thousand eyes burning into her back. She began to feel nervous and awkward again under their scrutiny, and something in the back of her mind, some bit of information, was struggling to emerge—something very important—

"Ignore them, Allison," Aidric whispered into her mind, distracting her from what she was trying to remember. *"Just smile at them, and show them that they have nothing to fear from you."*

Allison nodded, and did her best to smile, if feebly, at all the people they passed. She immediately noticed that some inched away from her when she passed them and tried not to attract her attention to them. Whenever she happened to glance at someone, an intense look of fear flashed across their face, and they hastily tried to lose themselves in the surrounding crowd.

By the time they reached the targeted group of Aidric's friends, Allison was struggling not to cry. The group of seven immediately stopped talking when they caught sight of her, and most of them gazed at her with widened eyes of shock and fear.

"Oh, for the love of Seni, stop looking at her as if she's going to strike you dead," Aidric snapped impatiently. "I know the villagers don't know any better, but as mages, *you* should. I brought her over here for introductions, *not* for you to insult her with your foolish fear."

Looking sheepish, the man closest to her, a brunet that looked to be about Aidric's age, took a tentative step towards her and said, "My apologies, Milady Golden Mage. We meant no insult." He inclined his head slightly. "I am Maldon, of the House Felan."

"I-I'm Allison," she stammered shyly.

Her obvious shyness and Maldon's boldness seemed to cause the other mages to lose most of their initial fear of her, and one by one, they introduced themselves to her. Aidric wore a peculiar half-smile as the mages were introducing themselves to her, and she suspected that he was thought-speaking with them, likely answering all of the questions she *knew* they must be flinging at him about her.

God, it's like they're talking about me behind my back, she thought, annoyed, *except it's worse since they're standing right in front of me! If they're so damned curious about me, I wish they would just ask me their questions and not Aidric.*

As if reading her mind, the mages suddenly turned to her all at once and bombarded her with questions. What world did she come from? How did she get across the Lamian border undetected? Was her hair really golden? Was it Seni, Himself, who had sent her?

"You asked for it," Aidric's amused voice said in her head, *"and before you ask, you accidentally thought-spoke me again. We must do something about these little mishaps and soon, but for now, I do believe you have your hands full at the moment with this curious bunch. I would have answered their questions, but since you were so annoyed that they were not asking you—"*

"All right, all right, I did ask for it," Allison sent, struggling not to laugh. *"You don't have to rub my nose in it, though!"*

"Then how else shall I amuse myself?"

"I'm sure you'll think of something."

She heard ripples of laughter over the surface of

her mind as she once again turned her attention to the group of mages to answer their questions as best she could. They continued to play their little question and answer game for perhaps thirty minutes or so before Aidric decided that she had suffered their questions enough and rescued her from them with the excuse of wanting her to meet a few other people.

"There's a couple of bards I would like you to meet," Aidric said loudly over the music and voices as they headed towards the center of the courtyard. "They have been singing ballads of your coming since they were old enough to wail in pitch, and they insisted that they *had* to meet you."

"Insisted my rump," Raya said dryly. "It's more like 'demanded' with those two. They probably just want to either grill her for stories of her world to put into their wretched songs or try to court her."

Was it her imagination, or did Allison suddenly see a flash of what looked like jealousy in Aidric's eyes? It had come and gone so quickly that she wasn't entirely sure that she hadn't just seen what she had wanted to see.

However, if Aidric had been jealous, his voice betrayed nothing. "Too true, barbarian. I'll have to keep a watchful eye on them."

"Hey! That's my wife you're calling a barbarian,"

Selwyn retorted in mock anger. "Say it again, Mage-general, and you might find yourself on your ass again!"

"Aidius, help us all," Aidric lamented with a grin as Selwyn playfully punched him in the arm while Allison and Raya giggled.

As they reached the center of the courtyard, Allison saw a group of bards, flamboyantly dressed in gold and silver robes of a more flowing, wider design than Aidric's mage-robes, sitting in the grass and busily playing fiddles, lutes, harps, wooden flutes, and a strange u-shaped reed instrument that emitted a hypnotic, low-pitched sound that was similar to a male bass voice but nothing she had ever heard an instrument produce. She had a sudden image of a group of Gregorian monks chanting in a majestic cathedral.

Before them stood four mages that were busily entertaining the crowd with what appeared to be a laser and light show to Allison but accomplished with magic instead of laser beams. She stared at the glorious spectacle in awe, watching the mages skillfully weave the colorful lines, flashes, and showers of light into various shapes and patterns to the accompaniment of the bards' music.

Aidric pointed to the young, silver-haired man playing the strange instrument and to the man sitting next to him playing a lute. Allison started when she realized that they were identical twins.

"Those are the two that I want you to meet," Aidric told her. "The one playing the lyra is Keldan, and the lute player is Aren. Despite the fact that those two were born—or should I say we were curs- ed—with the largest wagging tongues in all of Lamia, they are quite a remarkable pair. They aren't simply bards, but bardic-mages. Until they were born, Lamia had not seen a bardic-mage for four centuries.

"From the moment of their birth, they were treated basically the same as you are now being treat- ed—with much fear and uneasiness because bardic magic is a powerful force when cast in concert, and Seni only sends those with the ability to wield power- ful magicks when great chaos is about to befall us and there will be great need for such magicks. Fur- thermore, a certain prophecy also mentions the birth of bardic-mages. They won't look on you with fear since they have walked the same path you have be- gun."

Allison didn't in the least like the way Aidric's voice had tensed when he had spoken of this "bardic magic." She suddenly had the strangest feeling that he had not told her the whole reason why he wanted her to meet the twins.

She eyed him suspiciously and said, "Something tells me that there's more to it than you just wanting me to meet them because everyone was as scared of them as they're now scared of me." The surprise in his eyes was all the confirmation she needed.

"I thought so," she thought-spoke to him. *"All right, Aidric, what's going on?"*

"No longer timid, are we?" Aidric replied lightly. The casual expression on his face never changed.

"Not when I'm in the dark about something that concerns me," she sent, *"and don't try to change the subject, Aidric. I want to know what you're hiding from me."*

"I'm not 'hiding' anything from you, Allison," he said with a mental sigh that echoed throughout her mind and said volumes more than a normal sigh would have. *"I only wished to confirm my suspicions before I spoke to you about them."*

"What suspicions?" she demanded. *"And what do those bards have to do with—oh—"*

Her eyes suddenly widened, and she felt all the blood drain from her face when she realized exactly what he had implied.

Aidric nodded at her expression as Raya and Selwyn eyed them both curiously, and sent, *"Exactly. Now do you understand why I didn't mention this to you before? While you slept and your mind was free from torment, I took the liberty of probing your mind to view the extent of your abilities. I wanted to have a good idea of what exactly I needed to teach you before your first lesson tomorrow. That's when I discovered that the section of your brain that houses the ability to control the greater bardic magicks was not dormant. I've asked Keldan and Aren to confirm this, and they have agreed to instruct you in learning to control this magic if indeed you possess the ability, for I have very little knowledge of bardic magicks."*

Allison sighed audibly, feeling that she should be angry with him for probing her mind without her knowledge, but not able to feel even a hint of annoyance. *I have enough to worry about without getting mad at every little thing,* she thought, suddenly feeling weary to the bone.

She sent, *"To tell you the truth, Aidric, at this point, nothing you say will really surprise me. I swear, if it's not one thing, it's the other. Why me?"*

"Why you, indeed," Aidric agreed sympathetically. *"The burden that rests on your shoulders is more than any mortal should ever have to carry. If I could, little cat, I would bear this burden for you willingly."*

Before Allison could reply, Raya suddenly stepped between them and demanded, "What have you two been talking about? I've been trying to get your attention for at least five depths now. What's so secret that you have to use thought-speech?"

"No one but I and the twins know of your possible bardic-mage ability, and it must remain that way," Aidric warned. *"If the people should get wind of this, it would cause*

a chaos that could only end in disaster. Reveal this to no one."

Even as he was thought-speaking her, he said cheerfully to Raya, "Nothing, nosy. Allison was only asking me about the bards and a few other things, and it was just more practical to use thought-speech than trying to make ourselves heard over the noise. And if you must know, I was also warning her about Keldan and Aren's—*hem*—none-too-subtle attentions whether they are wanted or not."

Allison blushed as Raya turned to her, her eyes dancing with amusement, and said, "That's advice I wouldn't take too lightly. Believe me, with your beauty, they most likely will be circling you like two dogs in heat over a bitch!"

Allison blushed even brighter at Raya's bluntness as Aidric scowled at her and gave her a hard nudge with his foot.

"Sel, how many times have I told you to keep a leash on that barbarian tongue of your wife's? Hellsfire, her bluntness is enough to make *me* blush!"

"If I'm not mistaken, wasn't it you who brought up the subject in the first place?" Sel asked with a raised eyebrow.

"Damn, so I did," Aidric admitted sheepishly, "but that doesn't change the fact that you still need to keep that blunt tongue of hers on a leash."

"Beast," Raya growled.

"Barbarian," Aidric countered.

"I warned you—" Sel threatened menacingly.

"Try anything, and I'll be forced to allow Allison to have a stab at you!"

"Hey! Leave me out of this!" Allison retorted as she glared at Aidric in mock anger, her lips twitching as she tried to keep herself from laughing.

"I thought you were on my side," Aidric pouted, doing his best to look hurt, but failing miserably.

"Well, I suppose I have no choice but to be on your side," Allison said, her eyes bright with mischief. "If I don't, then you'll kick me out of your suite, and where would I live then?"

"I hear Patrym still has room for one more in his harem," Selwyn offered.

Both Allison and Aidric glared at Selwyn who looked at them innocently for a split-second before he ruined the façade by bursting into laughter.

As Aidric made to strangle Selwyn, a new voice suddenly said from behind Allison, "Always fighting—typical. What am I to do with you two?"

Allison started at the unexpected voice, stifling a shriek, as she whirled around to face the new arrival. It was one of the twins, though she was not certain which. She stared at him with wide eyes, willing her racing heart to slow its hectic pace. He tilted his head to the side as he looked her up and down with his piercing blue eyes, smiling at her expression with amusement.

As he stared at her, that little nagging thought in the back of her mind stirred, trying once again to surface. She shivered at the feeling and hastily shoved the thought away. She had the distinct feeling that she was better off not knowing what it was.

"My pardons, milady. I didn't mean to startle you," the bard said with the most melodic voice Allison had ever heard, at least a hundred times more melodic than Raya's. "I am Keldan, a friend of Aidric's. You, of course, can be none other than the Golden Mage, Allison. It's a real pleasure to meet you at last, and you are most definitely as beautiful as the prophecy says the Golden Mage would be."

Allison mumbled a greeting and fidgeted uncomfortably under his intense, certain that she was blushing scarlet by now. She suddenly wished that she was somewhere far away. This man intimidated her. *And he's supposed to be one of my prospective teachers!*

To her immense relief, Aidric came to her rescue by stepping between them and slapping the bard on the back in greetings. Allison used the distraction to slowly and inconspicuously inch herself as far away from him as she dared without being rude.

"Where is Aren?" Aidric asked.

"Getting us food and drink," Keldan replied as

he nodded his greetings to Selwyn and Raya. "At least he is *supposed* to be getting us food and drink. I wouldn't be too surprised if he's off in some dark corner right now entertaining some poor, unsuspecting maiden."

As if you should talk, Allison thought darkly.

"I heard that," a voice pretty much identical to Keldan's called out above the noise, and a few seconds later, Aren appeared beside his brother as if he had conjured himself there magically, his hands loaded with plates of food and a wide bottle of what appeared to be wine balanced precariously underneath his arm.

For all I know, he probably did conjure himself up, she thought with an unpleasant jolt.

"Now, now, you know I was merely teasing," Keldan insisted innocently.

"Bah! I doubt that, big brother," Aren said dryly as he handed his brother one of the plates. "I shouldn't even give this to you after such an insult."

Then he seemed to notice Allison for the first time, and Aren immediately ignored his brother and sauntered over to her, his eyes looking her over hungrily as if he planned to devour her instead of the food he had brought. It took every ounce of willpower she had within her to prevent herself from turning on her heal and running away from him.

Allison groaned miserably to herself and thought, *Just great. I thought Keldan was bad enough. Aidric was right—they* are *a curse. Why doesn't he go bother someone else?*

"The prophecy doesn't do your beauty justice, Milady Allison," Aren purred sweetly. "Not too surprising, really. After all, what would a pious, dried out old Seer know about women anyway? It's a real pleasure to make your acquaintance. I am Aren."

I'm sorry I can't say the same about you. "It's nice to meet you, too," Allison replied evenly, careful to keep the annoyance she felt out of her voice.

"Aidric, Aidric, you are one damned lucky bastard to have such a beautiful woman living under your roof! You must be careful lest you wear yourself out!" Aren said, grinning slyly at Keldan as Aidric flushed up to the roots of his hair, though in irritation, if the murderous gleam in his eyes was anything to go by, rather than embarrassment. Allison had frozen and could only stare mutely at Aren in shock.

"And you accuse *me* of having a barbarian tongue!" Raya chided Aidric.

"Come now, little brother, you're embarrassing her," Keldan said. "I apologize, milady. Aren loves to tease. We promise to behave from henceforth."

Ha, I'll believe it when I see it, she thought darkly as she sent to Aidric, *"Where in the world did you dig up these two—uh—gentlemen?"*

Although Aidric's face remained passive, his reply was layered with laughter. *"What, you don't find them charming?"*

"As charming as a snake, perhaps."

Aidric choked when he heard her reply, and the twins suddenly eyed him suspiciously as he struggled to control himself.

"What's so funny?" Aren demanded.

"Nothing," Aidric replied casually. "Aidius, can a man not choke anymore without one getting suspicious?"

"Not when the man in question is you," Keldan said dryly.

"You're no fun," he said with mock disappointment, and then to Allison, *"Hissssss."*

Allison lost her entire composure then, doubling over with laughter as everyone eyed her strangely. Then all eyes turned to Aidric who gazed back at them innocently with eyes that seemed to say "who me?"

"I was right," Aren said accusingly to Aidric. "You *were* talking about us!"

"Prove it," Aidric challenged.

Aren muttered a few words under his breath in a language Allison didn't understand, but they sounded suspiciously like curses. She couldn't recall a time when she had ever laughed so hard. *And to think you didn't even want to come to this celebration at all,* she chided herself as she watched the twins advance towards Aidric, their eyes threatening all kinds of violence.

Then, without warning, Allison was suddenly knocked to her knees by a mental blow that left her mind reeling in pain and utter confusion. She opened her mouth to scream, but no sound emerged.

One gasp, two, and then just as suddenly as the blow had come, her mind abruptly filled with terrible images of what appeared to be countless soldiers being slaughtered by dozens of creatures straight out of her worst nightmare. They looked like enormous clouds of smoke, except for the fact that two very solid, very large fangs, at least a foot in length, were clearly protruding from within each of those hellish, swirling masses.

Impossible—they are impossible—

CHAPTER TWENTY

M en and women were being disemboweled and decapitated everywhere, and to Allison's horror, she could actually feel both the fear and the pain that was thick in the air. The creatures, it seemed, were trying to slash their way through the group of soldiers to get at what Allison *knew* was a village that had been the creatures' main target all along.

Vaguely, through the haze of the madness, she could feel herself retching, sickened by the bloodbath she had just witnessed, and trying to scream. She distantly heard somebody shouting her name as if they were a mile away, but she couldn't answer while her mind was still lost within the tight grip of madness.

It was only when Allison felt the sting of a sudden, violent slap across her face did she break free from those horrifying visions and come back to herself to find Aidric's frightened, pale-violet eyes staring down into her own.

"Aidric! My God, the people!" she cried frantically. "Those *things*—they're dead—dear God in heaven—they ripped them to shreds—so much blood—blood—"

"Damn it, she's in shock!" she heard what sounded like Raya's voice cry.

"The people! You've got to help the people!" Allison shrieked over and over desperately, until someone slapped her face again.

She immediately stopped her hysterical ravings and fell silent when she felt the shock of the blow. The sharp pain was something she could focus her mind on, and Allison soon found herself thinking more coherently and realized that she was freezing. At the same moment, a bone-deep exhaustion swept over her body, and her vision darkened alarmingly along the edges.

"I'm cold," she whispered, no longer having the strength to manage more than that.

Immediately, Allison felt blessed warmth flow throughout her body, and a little corner of her mind that was still thinking rationally knew that someone was healing her. She could feel the familiar warmth destroying the unnatural coldness that had invaded her body, and as the healing wiped out the last bits of coldness, sense returned to her.

She blinked up at Aidric in confusion and rising fear and whispered, "My God, what happened?"

"Bless the Thrones, she's making some sense," Aidric said with a heavy sigh of relief. "I don't have the time to explain now, Allison, but I need you to relax because I'm going to probe your mind for the images you saw. We may yet prevent whatever horror you've Foreseen from coming to pass."

Allison didn't understand everything he was saying, but she obeyed him and tried to relax as best she could. She immediately felt Aidric's now familiar presence probing around in her mind, a light feathery touch on the surface of her thoughts. A moment later, Aidric withdrew his probe, and when she saw the haunted look in his eyes, she knew he had seen what she had seen. His face had paled considerably, and he looked sickened.

"It's Roderick!" Aidric exclaimed in both horror and anger. "He plans to Summon a *dyani* swarm and release them on Idona!"

Allison heard several gasps, and then it seemed as if everyone began to talk at once. She looked around and noticed that a large crowd now surrounded her and that she was lying flat on her back on the soft grass. A few familiar people—Aidric, Raya, the king and queen—and many not-so-familiar ones knelt or stood in a tight circle all around her.

At Aidric's revelation, King Diryan's expression hardened, and then he stood up abruptly and ordered, "Someone find me the Lord Commander and General Caith, and send them here immediately!"

"Majesty, I am here!" a gruff voice called out a split-second before a tall, brown-haired man shouldered through the crowd and presented himself before the king at strict attention. Allison noted absently that his face was covered with scars. This man practically screamed military.

"Rally your troops as swiftly as possible to ride to Idona," Diryan commanded. "The mages and healers will follow shortly after. I'll have Aidric thought-speak the stables and have them saddle the horses."

"There's no time to ride there completely by land," Aidric protested. "We must go by portal, for Roderick plans to attack within the sand-mark!"

Diryan cursed loudly. "Very well. General Caith, have your men report back here when all is ready. Lord Pyrs will issue you further instruction then—if he ever gets here! Now go, and make haste!"

General Caith bowed his head and disappeared into the crowd within the blink of an eye. Allison could soon hear him barking orders somewhere in the distance.

"Everyone clear the way so that I may cast the portal spell!" Aidric shouted. He then turned to Keldan and Aren and said, "My friends, I need your assistance with the portal spell. I don't dare risk draining myself too much before this battle. The Idonans, Seni help them, will need every drop of strength we mages can give them."

They both nodded solemnly. Allison was amazed at the twins' transformation from the loud, obnoxious men who had teased her so crudely to these serious men. Aidric turned once again to King Diryan and began to silently confer with him. After a while, a man who was probably the Lord Commander the king had called for and a few more people joined them in the conference.

Raya stayed beside Allison, helping her to sit up, and explained a little of what was happening. What she understood was that she had somehow been given a glimpse of the future, but Raya wasn't sure how it had happened since Aidric had blocked all of her abilities ever since he had found her unconscious in the forest.

Whatever it was that had happened to her, Allison felt as if she had been dragged facedown through the pits of hell. Her head throbbed painfully in sync with the rhythm of her heartbeat, and it took every last ounce of her strength just to sit up.

"Raya, what were those—*things?*" Allison asked tremulously, shuddering at the memory.

"*Dyani,*" Raya replied grimly. "They are demonspawn from the first hell of Ter-ob."

Allison had no idea what Ter-ob was, but she knew by the look in Raya's eyes that she didn't want to know.

Instead, she asked, "They looked like a swirling cloud of smoke with teeth. How is that possible?"

"When conditions are right between the magical planes," Raya explained, "a dark-mage has the ability to Summon creatures from any of the six hells of Ter-ob. However, the light of Seni prevents them from entering completely into our world. Only a hint of the darkness from their realm—the swirling smoke as you call it—and their fangs are able to become completely substantial and only when night falls across the lands."

She nodded, wishing she had not asked. Allison knew that she wouldn't sleep a wink that night, especially if she was going to be alone in Aidric's suite. Maybe Raya wouldn't mind having her over for the night—that is, if she could make herself actually ask. She hated to intrude, friend or no friend.

As Allison watched the Lamian army, now equipped in armor, helms, and swords, gather into the courtyard, Aidric suddenly turned away from Diryan and hurried over to where Raya and she sat.

"Are you all right?" he asked her, his brow furrowed with worry.

"I think so," Allison replied uncertainly, "except I feel like I was just trampled by a mob of crazed people. My head's throbbing something fierce!"

Aidric nodded and said, "You should since you've just suffered through both a mental and magical shock. Even though we should have expected Roderick to try something like this in the midst of our celebration, none of us actually Foresaw this coming. According to Seer Penrith, even the Providencen priests had no Forewarning." He then turned to Raya and said, "Can you please stay with Allison and make certain she's properly taken care of? I don't know how long this battle will wage on, and I don't want to leave her alone so soon. Seni knows when and if I'll return."

"Of course, if you're sure I won't be needed," Raya said.

"At the moment, I believe we have mages enough, but I'll bespeak you if the need suddenly arises. Now, I must be off. I believe we are ready to depart."

"May Seni guide and protect you," Raya said softly.

Allison could say nothing as Aidric gazed down

at her solemnly, nodded his good-byes, and rejoined the army.

"Will he be all right?" Allison asked fearfully as she watched his retreating back.

Raya tilted her head to the side and regarded her with a little shrewd smile. "You care for him don't you? I mean, more deeply than just friendship?"

Allison looked away, feeling the blood rising to heat her cheeks. Did she dare?

She refused to look at Raya when she answered, "I think—I think—yes, I like him, more than I probably should."

"I thought so," came her answer.

Allison started and turned astonished eyes on Raya, who was smiling. "Don't look so surprised," Raya said gently. "It's clear how you feel about him every time you look at him. Even a blind fool could see it. My only question is, why haven't you acted upon it?"

"I don't think I could ever be that bold!" Allison replied anxiously. "Besides, I don't know how he feels about me, and until I do, nothing will happen *at all*. I don't want to make things awkward between us, so promise me that you won't say anything to him about this!"

"But why?" Raya asked, puzzled. "You love him, and yet, you don't want him to know?"

I didn't say anything about love*!* Instead of arguing the point, Allison merely pleaded, "Please, just promise me."

Raya sighed and said, "All right. Although I don't understand why under the Thrones above you would wish it so, I promise I'll say nothing to him, but I wish you wouldn't keep your feelings to yourself. I admit that I don't know Aidric's feelings towards you, except that he obviously sees you as a friend, but he's been long without a lover. He's overworked and lonely. I think you would be good for him. He's been brooding much too often these days."

"As handsome and kind as he is, I'm surprised he has no one."

"Oh, he could have any number of lovers if he chose, but he's been hurt too many times in the past and is wary to give his heart to anyone. I'll let him tell you about it if he chooses. It really isn't my place to speak of his past, personal troubles."

Allison nodded and turned her attention to Aidric once again, who, along with Keldan and Aren, was beginning to cast the portal spell. She watched in spellbound silence as Aidric suddenly began to glow with a brilliant, golden incandescence. He raised his hands high above his head and began to gesture with them in a series of complicated patterns. She could see his lips moving, but his words were lost in the strong hum that had suddenly filled the air. A few seconds later, both Keldan and Aren began to glow with that same brilliant light when they each placed a hand on either side of Aidric's shoulders.

Allison felt a slight tingling along her arms as the glow of power illuminating the trio brightened to the point where she had to shield her eyes with her hand. Then, to her amazement, a beam of sparkling, golden light emerged from the palms of Aidric's outstretched hands, and with a sudden sweep of both hands in a circular motion, the power left his hands and formed what appeared to be an outline of an oval of golden light.

As Aidric began to move his hands in various weaving motions, Allison suddenly understood what it was he was doing. He was literally "sculpting" the power into the shape he desired, although she couldn't even begin to imagine how he was accomplishing it.

Criss Angel, eat your heart out, she thought, awestruck.

When the last empty space of the oval was flooded with power, there was a loud boom that sounded as if a cannon had gone off, and the very air within the oval seemed to tear in half amidst a brilliant flash of colors. Aidric dropped his hands to his sides, looking not at all tired from his efforts.

Before him stood a more refined version of the "rip" that had transported her from her world to this one. Allison shivered at the thought of traveling through one of their portals again. *Never again! Not if I can help it!* she promised herself fervently.

Allison watched with a sense of dread as one by one, whole groups of people walked into and disappeared within that brilliant, shimmering light until only Aidric and the twins remained. As Aidric stepped towards the portal, he turned to gaze in her direction, winked, and was gone. Then, before she could so much as blink, the portal dissipated in a great flash of colorful light.

Raya must have been watching her expression when Aidric had walked through the portal because she suddenly said in a reassuring tone, "Don't worry. Aidric is a powerful mage, and if there's anyone who can survive a battle without so much as a scratch, it's him."

Allison stared at the spot on the lawn where the portal had been only seconds earlier and said grimly, "I just pray that you're right."

Yep, she would definitely not sleep that night.

CHAPTER TWENTY-ONE

"*S*he *what!*" Roderick exclaimed in disbelief after his spy had reported all the recent events occurring in Lamia, nearly causing the spy to lose contact with him.

His mind-voice laced with fear, the Observer repeated, "*The Golden Mage has warned them of your intentions to eliminate Idona. She just suddenly had a—fit of some sort and started raving like a woman possessed. The Mage-general managed to extract what she'd Foreseen from her mind, and now, as we speak, Diryan is preparing to send troops to Idona by portal.*"

"*Damn it! I thought you said she was untrained!*" Roderick boomed furiously.

"*S-She is,*" the Observer sent, mind-voice sounding small and cowed.

"*Then pray tell me how she managed to Foresee some-*

thing that I have kept blocked from even the most powerful of the Providencen Seers," Roderick demanded.

Fools—they are all fools!

"The Lamians are as baffled as we," his spy said defensively. *"Apparently, not even Aidric knows quite how she did it, and if I understand correctly, Aidric had shielded her from having the power to use her abilities. She was* not *supposed to've been able to use her Foresight under those restraints."*

Roderick's temper quickly simmered at this newest revelation. *Well, well, not even His Mightiness can keep a leash on her power,* he thought smugly, not being able to resist feeling a great deal of satisfaction that someone—even if that someone had not been him—had finally proved more powerful than the bloody bastard.

Roderick ran his fingers through his hair and frowned as a very troubling thought suddenly occurred to him. If Aidric, who—he admitted grudgingly—was more powerful than he, could not hold her powers at bay, then what chance had he? *He* was no fool. He knew his magical powers had their limitations.

Yet—no one is infallible, Roderick reminded himself. *Certainly even a legendary mage has her weaknesses. I must find out what they are.*

"I have a new task for you," he sent. *"You must trail*

*the Golden Mage and learn all you possibly can about her—
her loves, her darkest fears, and more importantly, her closest
friends."*

"But the palace guards keep the strictest eye on her," the
Observer protested weakly, *"not to mention the Mage-
general, himself. Under that much attention, I couldn't possibly—"*

"I don't wish to hear your pathetic excuses!" Roderick
"snapped" impatiently. *"You'll do as I bid! If you cannot
get near her, then invade her mind and steal the information I
require."*

"But, Aidric—"

*"You damned fool! You have been bespeaking me without
detection for moons! Surely the task of probing one girl's mind
while escaping detection is within your power, and if it isn't,
then you damned well better make it within your power! You
know the penalty for failure…"*

Roderick smiled sadistically as he "felt" all the
blood leave his spy's face. The last spy that had failed
to deliver was now encased behind a walled-up dungeon cell suffering the agonies of starvation and suf-
focation but unable to die since Roderick had used
the Dark Powers to keep him alive for as long as it
amused him. It was a trick only a dark-mage of Arioch knew. At night, his screams could be heard quite
distinctly throughout the servant quarters.

"Yes, milord," the Observer sent, the spy's mind-
voice betraying fear, though the spy tried hard to

cover it.

"You may go," Roderick said absently, his mind already forming an alternative plan for Idona as he quickly turned his attention to thought-speaking the mage he had sent to Idona. *"Kion, hear me."*

"I'm here, 'Highness," Kion's raspy mind-voice replied in the same thought, startling Roderick, to his annoyance. He didn't like to be reminded of how many of his subjects had stronger thought-speaking abilities than he possessed. Damn fate and its vices!

"There's to be a change in the initial plan," Roderick sent. *"Lamia has inconveniently become aware of my plan to attack Idona, and they are preparing to transport an army to aid the Na'arans. You will release the* dyani *onto the village now, and when Diryan's army appears, turn the slaughter onto them as well. The mages, however, are to be captured and brought to me alive as planned."*

"And what of Aidric, milord, should he be amongst them?" Kion asked passively.

Aidric, Aidric, Aidric. Roderick was growing increasingly weary of that name, more so in just the past sand-mark.

"I want Aidric captured especially," Roderick replied firmly. *"Abandon your attack on Idona and send the* dyani *at him alone if you must. After all, this little attack on Idona was only meant to send Diryan a message. Since Diryan has already received my message even before it was sent, we'll con-*

centrate our efforts on the second part of my plan. I would rather the Mage-general of Lamia captured and under my power, but if it's not to be so, then I want him destroyed."

"As you command, 'Highness,'" Kion replied firmly, taking Roderick's following silence as a dismissal.

Roderick turned in his chair to face the window where he had a clear view of some of his troops training below. He watched them critically for a few moments and then scowled at what he saw. *Fools, all of them,* he thought again with disgust as the men and youngsters continued to spar in their mock battles while others cheered or laughed at their efforts. *They believe this to be nothing more than sport. Perhaps it's time I make another example of just how high the stakes are for me.*

Chuckling to himself, Roderick rose lazily from his chair and slowly made his way down the narrow, dark corridors of his palace, suppressing a grin every time he passed a servant and saw the flash of absolute terror on their face. Every servant knew that when he walked the halls of his palace with such leisure, someone would die that day. He enjoyed watching them struggle to make themselves as invisible as possible.

After he had rounded a few corners, he wasn't surprised to find the corridors devoid of servants. No doubt they suddenly remembered that they were needed elsewhere when they heard his slow, calculated footsteps approaching.

When he finally reached the training grounds, Roderick merely stood at the end of the path that opened onto the field and stared out onto the field, purposely waiting for someone to notice his presence. He allowed his displeasure to be visible on his carefully calculated expression.

When one of the younger boys, a farm boy of about seventeen, finally spotted him and noticed his expression, his face suddenly drained of all its color. He dropped his sword, thus earning himself a hard rap on the side of his head by his opponent while a few snickered around him. A few of the men sparring around the downed boy stopped their sword-dancing and began to listlessly poke the boy with the points of their practice blades, laughing as the boy squirmed uncomfortably under their taunting and desperately gestured over to where Roderick stood.

"So boy, catch an eyeful of a wench o'er yonder did ye?" Roderick heard one of them sneer. "Let's just see who't be there hidin' in the bushes."

The laughter abruptly stopped as several eyes turned in Roderick's direction and froze in shock. The silence that followed was so profound that a dropped pin could have been heard striking the ground.

Containing his amusement with some effort,

Roderick strode dramatically into the practice grounds, every slow, deliberate step an agony to those who stared back at him in fear. He headed straight for the boy, whom he had instantly decided would be the object of his example. The boy was clumsy and distracted far too easily to be of any use to him in his army. Had he have been a mere twelve summers old, then the character flaw could have possibly been beaten out of him, but at around seventeen, Roderick believed that it was virtually too late to change him.

"Get up!" Roderick commanded menacingly to the frightened boy.

In his haste to obey, the boy tripped over his own legs, and with a wail of anguish, he fell flat onto his face before he could stop himself. Roderick reached down angrily and grabbed the boy roughly by his tunic, yanking him to his feet. The boy was trembling badly in his fear, and from the way he bit his lip and the pinched look of his face, it was painfully clear that he was struggling not to cry. This only made Roderick cast the boy away from him in disgust, and even before he hit the ground, his body was suddenly engulfed in a burst of green mage-flames.

The boy released a shriek that was almost inhuman and flailed his body wildly in a futile attempt to douse the flames that slowly ate away at his body as if he was merely a piece of timber. Within a few depths, his screams died down, and when the flames finally vanished, all that was left of the boy was a small smear of blackened ashes.

Roderick then glared out onto the group of fighters and said in a completely calm voice that made them wince, "Should anyone else displease me again, then your fate will be worse a hundred fold than the boy's. Mark my words, when I'm done with you, you'll wish I *had* cast the mage-flames upon you instead."

Satisfied that his point had been made, Roderick turned on his heel and arrogantly walked back to his palace that seemed, not surprisingly, as empty as it had when he had left it.

***

The stench of blood and burning bodies made Aidric wrinkle his nose in disgust as the acrid smell reached his nostrils, a constant reminder of the horrors before him and the horrors that surely were still to come. What seemed like a sea of bodies littered the ground before him—Lamian, Na'aran, and Mihran soldiers in equal numbers, lost to either the *dyani's* razor sharp fangs, magical attacks, or the end of an enemy blade.

Aidric clenched his jaw in both despair and anger as he wearily channeled the power of the Mage-field through his body to fuel the wind storm he had called up to dispel the *dyani* swarm. No matter how quickly he eliminated the hellish creatures, sending them back to the first hell from which they had been Summoned, twice as many seemed to immediately replace those that had fallen.

Where in the six hells is that damned mage finding so many dyani? he thought frantically as he became more aware of his tiring body with every passing depth. *There could not possibly be this many even in Ter-ob!*

For the hundredth time that night, he wished that Na'ar had a Mage-field. The strain that his mind was under in drawing the power from the Lamian Mage-field over hundreds of spans to himself and then channeling the power through his body was beginning to take its toll on him. He knew that he wouldn't be able to hold off the swarm for much longer—two sand-marks at the maximum if he was lucky.

However, during the last few sand-marks, it seemed to him that most of the swarm was concentrated at him personally than on Idona, itself. The more he thought about it, the more the Mihran soldiers appeared to be merely an annoying distraction to something that he was sure was yet to come.

The twins fought with the Lamian army, weaving their magic into a musical barrier that kept the *dyani* at bay while several mages concentrated on destroying them. He needed their assistance desperately, but he dared not tear them away from their current task. Without that musical barrier, the other mages would soon be overwhelmed by the swarm. No—somehow he had to come up with a way to eliminate the mage controlling them. However, Roderick's mage was giving him no opportunity to do just that by bombarding him with an ungodly amount of those hellspawn.

This is a trap, his mind screamed to him. *Somehow Roderick knew we had discovered his plans. His attempt to take Idona is at most, half-hearted. That isn't like him. He wanted us here.*

The longer he chewed on those thoughts, the more he was certain they had indeed fallen prey to one of Roderick's traps. The dark-mage wanted them to come here, and he had a pretty good idea why.

He's after me specifically, Aidric thought flatly. *The bastard's making good on his last threat to me. He knew I would come. How could I not? The bloody demon hasn't even the courage to face me himself. Instead, he sends his minions to murder the innocent just to draw my attention!*

Aidric could feel the anger building within him, fueling his hatred for Lamia's long-time enemy. He could feel the power within him increasing with his rising fury until he shook with the intensity of it. His body began to glow more brilliantly with the added energy of his anger until he was nothing more than a being of pulsating light.

The *dyani* swarm immediately stopped their attack, and they edged back, swirling amongst each other in chaotic patterns that reflected their agitation. The *dyani* swarm that had been attacking the village quickly lost interest in their human targets when they caught sight of Aidric's glowing form. They immediately joined the swarm that cautiously circled Aidric, hungry for the power of hate that emanated from him but not able to approach because of his shields and the light of the Mage-field's energy.

Enveloped with more power than he usually could channel safely, Aidric knew that he had to cast the power away quickly or the magical energies would soon consume him. He was already beginning to feel transparent, as if he was indeed a being of light and air.

Aided with the energy of his fury, he would be able to cast a spell that he seldom had enough power to attempt. He was going to cast the spell of implosion onto the swarm, causing the magical energies all around the beasts to collapse into a point of singularity, thus crushing the entire swarm within the blink of an eye. Whatever, if anything, was lucky enough to escape the pull of the energy would instead be obliterated in the proceeding explosion when the singularity reverted.

"Keldan! Aren!" he sent to the twins, grateful that their natural bond to one another allowed him to thought-speak them together without having to broad-send. All he needed now was for one of Roderick's mages who was a stronger thought-speaker than he to catch wind of what he was about to do. *"I need your help! This attack is a trap, and I suspect it was intended for me and any other mage he could get his hands on. I'm about to rid us of this* dyani *swarm."*

"Seni help us all," Keldan sent back in alarm, *"Aidric, you aren't going to cast—"*

"I have no choice," Aidric said flatly. *"We ran out of options a long time ago. Warn my troops. Warn General Caith. Make damned certain that every one of them is tightly shielded with as many shields as possible! The backlash of the explosion—"*

Aidric had no need to finish. He still had nightmares because of the last time he had cast the implosion spell. No one but Seni, Himself, could predict the force of the final explosion. Sometimes it covered a radius of a few hundred handspans—and sometimes it was a few hundred *spans*.

Last time it had been a hundred spans.

"I don't need to tell either of you how worthless the spell

will leave me. Keldan, I place command of the magical troops in your hands. The moment the dyani *are obliterated, concentrate your efforts on destroying Roderick's mages—if any survive the Reversal. Relay my message to the other mages. General Caith's men will take care of any Mihran troops still standing. I doubt there will be any."*

"We're on it," came the mingled, uneasy, reply. *"Seni's luck to us all."*

Anger and light thundering throughout the channels in his body, Aidric cast the power before him to encircle the *dyani* in a shield of magic that could not be penetrated.

The moment the shield was in place, Aidric shouted his incantation up into the darkened sky as if shouting his defiance, *"Di akanai ta lansou ti reist ta aena solvian!"* I command thou life and light combine and fold!

The moment the ancient words roared from his throat, the circle of power collapsed within itself in a flash of blinding, sapphire light and vanished into a point Aidric could not see, stretching thin what was material of the *dyani* swarm until the hellspawn fell into the abyss of the singularity. In almost the same instant, an explosion of power sounded out into the half-beat of silence after the *dyani* disappeared. Aidric instinctually shielded his eyes with an arm and closed them tightly the instant the world became a blinding inferno of white light.

Aidric felt himself collapse onto his knees hard as the backlash of power engulfed him, ripping mercilessly into his many shields, destroying the outermost as easily as the swipe of a snowcat's great claws shredding a piece of *sholkie* cloth. A deafening, high-pitched roar flooded his ears painfully. He couldn't even hear himself scream. He had *become* the light—

Silence.

The silence was so sudden and profound that it too, like the roar before it, was painful to his ears. Aidric's hands were firmly pressed over his ears. He hadn't realized that he had raised them.

Slowly, he lowered them until his arms hung loosely at his side, tentatively raised his head, and opened tear-blurred eyes. The sight that greeted him was his bloodstained hands. He felt weak and oddly transparent as though the night air was flowing directly through his body. Blood began to trickle from his nose at an alarming rate. He wiped at the warm fluid bemusedly as if he was merely swatting at an annoying insect.

Aidric grimaced as he tried to refocus his eyes in the surrounding darkness after staring into the brilliance of the power he had contained, afraid of what he was about to see. Numbly, he saw that he stood a few handspans from the outer edges of a deep crater.

The earth surrounding the point of singularity he had created had been destroyed down to the layer of bedrock deep below.

Through a haze of shock, Aidric realized that only the weakest energy from the blast had reached him. He knew with utmost certainty that it was the only reason he was still alive. Even still, the plant life around him had been scorched down to the dark earth. Only a small patch of grass and tiny wildflowers where he stood had been spared by virtue of his shields. The blast had miraculously only reached a radius of about a couple hundred handspans. The destruction hadn't even reached the battlefield.

He would have wept had he been able, but the shock had stilled his emotions. Seni had indeed been watching over his children tonight.

Aidric was vaguely aware of the mage battle that was waging on around him and that a couple of the shields he had placed around himself earlier to ward off the *dyani* were still soundly in place. The clang of metal on metal rang out into the night, and he heard the resonance of distant melodies that signaled that the twins were performing bardic magic. However, all of that seemed so far away now.

He had to rise. His duty was not yet finished. Aidric swayed dizzily as he tried to climb to his feet again, driven with the intent to aid his comrades in

the battle, and to his chagrin, he pitched forward onto his knees once again.

Aidius, I'm worse off than I had anticipated, he
thought irritably, grunting in pain. *Damn it! I do* not
*need this right now! Just concentrate you fool! It's the shock—
concentrate on dispersing it out of your body—*

"Aidric! Look out! Behind you!" he suddenly heard
Allison's mind-voice shout frantically within his
mind.

Aidric didn't have time to wonder how she had
managed to reach him at such a great distance because almost in the same beat as his weakened body
reflexively rose into action, his magical defenses
screamed out *"danger!"* into every nerve in his body.

He gathered what power he had left within himself, too weak to draw from the Mage-field, whirled
around, and released it as a dagger of concentrated
power without waiting to see who or what it was that
he faced.

CHAPTER TWENTY-TWO

A llison woke to the sensation that someone had given her an electrical shock. Her body convulsed painfully, trapped within a tightly enclosed barrier. A cry was wrenched from her throat. She instinctively clutched the blankets spread over her tightly in her fists, her hands feeling as though they moved through the resistance of water, until the spasms in her muscles ceased.

Wide-eyed, she stared at all the strange faces surrounding her bed and swallowed fearfully.

"What—who—" she began before the memory of what she had just witnessed came flooding back to her. "Aidric!" she shrieked and immediately tried to rise from her bed.

To her surprise, Allison found that none of her limbs seemed to be obeying her. *The paralysis spell*, she thought absently, her mind still hazy from sleep and panic. *But who? And why?* It was a moment before her befuddled mind registered the significance of the small crowd gathered in her room.

"Let me up!" she demanded as she struggled against the invisible bounds. "I have to warn him!"

"Allison, please—stop fighting us!" she heard a familiar voice plead, tense with exertion.

That voice was as effective as a hard slap to the face, and Allison finally came fully awake, stopping her struggles against the invisible bonds set on her body.

"Raya?" she asked hesitantly, blinking her eyes in confusion. "What's going on? Why did someone cast the paralysis spell over me?"

The young girl moved into her field of vision, and Allison gasped when she saw her appearance. Raya's face was drawn and haggard, her forehead glistening with sweat. She glanced around at the rest of those present in the room and felt the blood leave her face when she saw them in similar conditions as Raya.

"You were caught in the throes of a Foresight dream," Raya explained wearily. "At least we *think* it was a Foresight dream."

"*Think*? You're not sure?" Allison asked incredulously.

"No," Raya replied unhappily. "Nothing like this has ever happened. We couldn't wake you. I came in here to check on you, and your entire body was glowing with Mage-field energy. I don't know why none of us sensed the power. When I tried to touch you to wake you, the energy struck out at me and bloody well flung me across the entire room! That should have *never* happened. No one should be able to wield the power of the Mage-field without first Bonding your life-energies to it! Yet, I swear on everything that I hold sacred that the power you used was drawn from our own Mage-field!"

For the first time, Raya looked at her in fear, and that fear was like a knife in her heart. Allison despairingly closed her eyes so she no longer had to look at the fear on the face of her friend, a fear that only too clearly reminded her of the monster that she was in the eyes of these people. She viciously clamped down on the tears that swelled in her eyes, denying herself even that release in which she could find a bit of solace.

My God—what the hell have I become?

"The others," Allison said quietly without emotion, still keeping her eyes shut to the world, "they thought I would kill you—that's why they cast the paralysis spell over me."

Only then did she open her eyes to look at Raya

and was puzzled when she saw Raya's expression contorted with conflicting emotions. The silence in the room was profound—you could have heard a feather brush the floor—and the air was so saturated with tension that it left a foul taste in the back of her mouth.

"Is that what you think of us—of me?" Raya finally demanded as her face finally settled on a look of dismay. "That you believe us to fear that which is only a shadow of ourselves? If that were true, Milady Allison, then we would have done much more to you than restrain you with a paralysis spell!"

"Then why so many mages?" Allison asked, meeting her gaze evenly. "Why so many if they didn't believe that your life was in danger? I *saw* the fear in everyone's eyes, Raya. I saw it in *yours*! Couldn't you, alone, have cast this spell over me?"

Allison was surprised when a male voice answered her, not Raya's, a voice that she recognized from the celebration. "It's true that it was Raya who summoned us here," Maldon noted as he boldly moved up to her bedside, "but we came not for the danger that you posed to her, but to the danger you posed to yourself. And why so many? Well, to be frank, it took the combined powers of us all to cast a paralysis spell that was powerful enough not to be broken by all the energy you had accumulated in your body. We feared that you would start gesturing and weaving this magic into reckless spells in your sleep. You even managed to break our spell for a few moments after we jolted you awake! I could hardly believe my own eyes when I saw you clutch your blankets!"

Maldon stared down at her gravely. "You would have killed yourself for certain, if not by your reckless spells, then by the Mage-field energies consuming your body. Aidric charged us with your safety, as did the king, until the Mage-general returns. I, for one, would rather eat my dagger, point first, than allow anything to happen to you and have to face Aidric's wrath!"

At the mention of Aidric's name, Allison suddenly remembered the bone-chilling dreams she had been having before she was literally jolted awake. She abruptly tried to sit up in her agitation and to her chagrin, remembered that she couldn't move anything below her neck.

Her agitation must have been obvious on her face because Raya suddenly frowned down at her and asked, "Allison, what is it? Are you starting to see another—"

"My dream," Allison interrupted, swallowing nervously as she eyed all the strange and vaguely familiar faces around her. "You said that it was a Foresight dream. Does that mean that it's going to happen?"

"Possibly," Raya said carefully. "Sometimes the dreams are sent to us by Seni as merely a warning of one of the things that *could* happen. It depends on our actions. By the way you were carrying on earlier, I gather this dream involved Aidric?"

Allison nodded. "It did, and if there's even a remote chance that it'll happen, then we need to warn him! Please let me up!"

Raya glanced over at Maldon, who nodded slightly, before they both moved closer to the bed and waved their hands over her body. A split-second later, she felt the familiar pins and needles sensation sweep throughout her limbs as they came alive. Allison sat up gingerly with a grateful smile for them, and rubbed her arms to get the circulation going again.

"Thanks," Allison said as she started to get out of the bed. "I hate being under that spell. It makes me feel so helpless."

"And where do you think you're going?" Raya said sternly. "The healers say you still aren't well, and after channeling so much energy just now, you should feel as though a herd of crazed *antar* just trampled you."

"I feel fine," Allison insisted. "Really I—" Suddenly the room turned upside down and sideways at the same time and the next thing she knew, Maldon was laying her head back down onto the pillow.

"You see?" Raya said with a chuckle. "Damned if you are as headstrong as Aidric! He could be bleeding out of his eyes and still insist that he's fine!"

"But I *have* to tell you about my dream," Allison protested weakly.

Maldon sighed and said to Raya, "We might as well hear her out. I have a feeling that she won't rest unless she recounts it."

"Oh, very well," Raya grumbled as she turned to the three other mages in the room. "If you wish, you may leave us now. I'll keep Maldon here to assist me should she suddenly fall into another fit. I'm sure he'll be enough."

Was it her imagination, or did the other mages seem relieved to finally be allowed to leave?

After Raya and Maldon settled themselves into a couple of chairs near her bedside, Raya said, "All right, Allison, we're listening."

"I saw him on an open field," Allison began, frowning as her head began to pound insistently as she thought back to the dream. She did her best to ignore the pain. "I could see the shadow of mountains in the distance. There were bodies everywhere, soldiers dying, and those—creatures I saw earlier."

"*Dyani,*" Maldon said flatly.

Allison nodded and continued, "It was awful. People were being slaughtered right before my eyes. I could see Aren and Keldan and a few other mages keeping those—those *things* from swarming into a village I could just barely see in the distance.

"Aidric was off alone, fending off an even larger swarm. There was a sudden flash of both blue and white light, and for a few moments, I couldn't see anything. When the light cleared, I could see another strange man just barely visible in the distance behind Aidric. Somehow I *knew* that he was a mage and that Roderick had sent him.

"The mage's thoughts were flowing into my mind. The whole attack on Idona was a trap. It seemed that Roderick wanted King Diryan to send as many mages as possible to Idona's aid. He planned to either capture or slaughter all the mages as part of an even larger plan I couldn't see, but his main target was Aidric. That mage planned to strike at Aidric from behind with a poisoned dagger. Aidric was on his knees, dazed by that earlier explosion of light, I think. I knew he didn't know that the mage was there. I shouted a warning to him even though I knew he couldn't hear me, but then Aidric instantly turned around ready to strike as if he *did* hear me—"

Raya and Maldon exchanged glances and then

fixed their eyes on her so intently that she began to shift uncomfortably in her bed.

"What?" Allison asked finally when the silence and scrutiny became unbearable.

"What you described," Raya began slowly, "thought-speaking within a Foresight dream—it just isn't possible. The dream is a telling of a possible future. There is no possible way for the dreamer to affect what's being shown to them—at least it has never been possible before."

"What in the name of God does that mean?" Allison demanded.

"We're not sure," Raya replied uneasily. "This is out of my depth of understanding."

"As mine," Maldon said with a sigh. "This is a question that needs to be posed to the Providencen priests. After all, they should be the foremost authorities on the Golden Mage, and perhaps this is a power that only you possess. The Providencen priests are very secretive, and there may be some information they have chosen not to reveal about you. However, we can do nothing until Aidric returns. You are, after all, his ward and under his protection. As such, we must seek his permission first."

"His *permission*?" Allison asked incredulously, feeling her old anger surge within her. "Don't I have a say in this?"

"Not when it involves your abilities," Maldon replied firmly. "You are his ward, his apprentice. It's the law, milady."

Allison felt she should be outraged by such a backwards law, but strangely, she was a bit relieved that she wouldn't have to face making those types of decisions. She knew next to nothing about her new-found abilities, so any decision she made concerning them might not be the wisest one. So why did she still feel so annoyed?

She nodded, accepting it for now, and then asked, "When do you think he'll return?"

"It's most difficult to say," Maldon replied thoughtfully. "He could return tomorrow, tonight, in a few quarter-moons, or even a few moons. It just depends on how bad the situation is in Idona." He eyed her strangely. "Or if your dream comes to pass. Yet, I'm not at all certain that your dream *was* a Fore-sight dream. Is there anything else you can tell us about your dream? Was there anything that you felt was strange besides the obvious?"

Allison shrugged uneasily and replied, "I don't know. I know next to nothing about all these abili-ties, but——" She paused, and glanced uncertainly at both of them.

I don't want to remember...

"Yes?" Maldon prompted.

"I could—I could smell the b-blood," she stammered, shivering at the memory and feeling herself grow pale. "I could also smell the b-burning bodies. The stench was so terrible that I felt like retching. Even now as I think about it, I can still remember the smell."

Maldon's thoughtful expression grew troubled at her revelation. Raya appeared bewildered, and Allison didn't like either one of their reactions. *What have I done this time?* she thought miserably. *Will this nightmare ever end?*

"All we can do is wait for Aidric," Maldon said after a few moments of silence. "I'm at a loss to explain this."

"As am I," Raya put in quietly. "I only hope that Aidric won't be as baffled as we."

***

A terrible scream reached Aidric's ears before his vision cleared enough from the bright flash of light that followed when his dagger of power found its mark for him to see who or what he had hit. A charred and bloody body lay just a couple of strides from where he stood, a hole the size of two of his fists clearly visible in his chest as the result of his body not being prepared to withstand such an attack.

Even weak as he was, the force of energy Aidric had thrown had been more than enough to do its job.

Aidric tried to rise to his feet but immediately fell back down onto his knees as a wave of blackness threatened to overcome his mind. He squeezed his eyes shut for a moment in an attempt to drive away the darkness, while sounds of shouting from the battle that still continued around him echoed from the distance—a battle he knew he was too weak to give further aid to

After his head cleared a bit, he slowly opened his eyes and stared dully at the corpse who was most likely the mage who had been controlling the *dyani* swarm. He immediately saw that the mage clutched a dagger in his right hand. *A spelled dagger*, he thought grimly as he reached for it.

His hand instantly froze over the offending object as he saw the faintly green sheen coating the blade and realized that it was saturated with *kalie*, the only poison in Seni's World that the healers could not counteract. *He would have killed me unless—*

"She called to me," he whispered wondrously, staring down at the poisoned dagger with a sinking feeling in his stomach. "By Aidius, she *knew!*"

"Who called to you?" a voice asked behind him.

"She—Allison," Aidric replied quietly, recognizing Keldan's voice and not bothering to turn around.

"Allison?" Keldan questioned in surprise.

"She that was not a direct witness to this horror here," Aidric went on as if he didn't hear the bard. "She warned me of this mage's attack before I sensed him coming. She called to me in my mind with a warning she could not possibly have known to give."

Before Keldan could reply, Aidric shook himself out of the light trance he had fallen into and seemed to notice Keldan for the first time.

"Keldan! The battle!" he cried as he whirled his head around to look up at the bardic-mage. "Has it finally ended? Are Roderick's troops defeated?"

"Yes, yes, everything's more or less ended," Keldan replied absently, shifting his feet restlessly as if something excited him. "Most of the enemy fled in terror when you cast the implosion spell. When the troops still remaining saw their mage fall, they turned tail and fled like the cowards they are. Our troops gave chase for a while, but when it became clear that they were retreating for good, we stopped our pursuit. We had prisoners enough. But never mind about that. What is this about the Golden Mage reaching you with a warning of danger?"

"Just as I said," Aidric said with a puzzled frown as he accepted the hand that Keldan held out and slowly hoisted himself onto his feet again. Fresh blood began to trickle from his nose, and he wiped at it irritably. Keldan eyed him worriedly, but Aidric waved his concern away. It was nothing that a few days rest would not cure.

"She warned me of danger she couldn't have possibly known of unless she was here." He swayed as a new wave of weakness washed over him and leaned heavily on Keldan's shoulder for support before continuing, "In my weakened state after I cast the implosion spell, that fool mage sneaked up behind me, intending to take a swipe at me with that poisoned dagger, but before he reached me, I heard Allison shout a warning in my mind. Because of that warning, I was able to ready an attack and strike him down before he could mark me. If it wasn't for her warning, then you would have been presenting my corpse to Diryan when you returned to Lamia."

Aidric sagged against his friend, feeling more exhausted than he ever had in all his years. "By the Thrones above, Kel, what in the six hells does this mean?"

"The Prophecy of the Six," Keldan replied gravely as he helped Aidric walk over to where his brother was helping Selwyn and the healers with the wounded. "Seni, help us all, the Prophecy of the Six."

CHAPTER TWENTY-THREE

S itting in King Diryan's Council Room, Aidric tried to remain passive as General Caith reported on the situation in Idona, although inside, he was bursting with impatience to speak privately with the king—and to see Allison. It had taken those who had returned six days to reach Lamia again since the twins had put their foot down when he told them he wanted to build another portal to return. He had been tempted to order them to succumb to his wishes, but he knew, Mage-general or not, they still would not have obeyed his orders when they knew he was too weak to do any spellcasting.

The battle had also been extremely trying on his mage troops, and he would have died first before he allowed any of *them* capable of performing the portal spell to build the portal for him. Besides, no other mage could have transported so many people at once as he had. Therefore, they had commissioned horses from the very grateful Na'arans and had ridden home. A quarter of the army and a half dozen mages had remained behind to guard against any further attacks from Mihr in the coming quarter-moons.

Damned if Caith loves to drone on and on about his battles, Aidric thought irritably. *I am almost tempted to pull rank and silence him!*

"—though I regret, Your Majesty, that we weren't able to supply you with prisoners this time," General Caith was saying as Aidric brooded secretly.

"Oh?" Diryan inquired with a raised eyebrow. "Why is that?"

Looking uncomfortable, Caith cleared his throat before answering, "My troops *were* able to capture several of Roderick's men throughout the course of the battle, but as each was led away to be taken to our camp, they just suddenly started to convulse and then fall to the ground dead."

"A death spell, Your Majesty," Aidric broke in, feeling a little sorry for Caith despite his earlier annoyance and deciding to come to his aid, "cast over his troops to prevent them from betraying him should they be captured or become defectors. I had thought Roderick was not capable of casting such a spell, but we all know that he has been dabbling in the Dark Powers. This new turn of events doesn't really surprise me. These men are nothing to him, sheep."

"Wonderful," Diryan muttered darkly. "So that path of gaining information is now closed to us. We shall just have to find another to replace it. General Caith, I charge you with the responsibility."

"Yes, Your Majesty," the Arms-general replied firmly, looking eager for the challenge.

Aidric finally caught Diryan's eye as the king turned his gaze from Caith to address his Council. Wordlessly, he made his need known to speak with him as soon as possible. Diryan gave him a slight nod, and Aidric relaxed considerably. The king, no doubt, had sensed his urgency, and Aidric knew he would keep his monologue to the Council short.

"Roderick grows bolder in his attempts to influence me to surrender Lamia to him," Diryan began. "From what both the Mage-general and Arms-general have reported today, this little attack on Idona was only a taste of what we are to expect from him in the near future. I fear that soon the time will come when I'm forced to declare open war on Mihr."

Everyone began to mutter to themselves at once, and a few of Diryan's advisors nodded as they expected him to say as much. They all knew that war was eminent, but how soon warfare would break out was the question uppermost on everyone's mind.

And I know what all of them are thinking, Aidric thought with a worried frown as he cast his gaze over all the faces circling the table. *They believe that this is the war that Allison will play her biggest role in, and the question of whether she is our savior or our destroyer will be answered— and I don't in the least like what their expressions are insinuating.*

As if reading their minds, Diryan added, "I can't tell you when this war will take place, only that I feel it will begin sometime in the next two years. Roderick's impatience in his quest for more power won't allot for any longer than that. Until then, we must increase our efforts in protecting our allies and keeping Roderick's troops in Mihr where they belong. Now, I'm certain the Mage-general and the Arms-general are very weary from their journey and wish to rest, so I shall adjourn until tomorrow at nine sandmarks past the first morning-mark to discuss further strategies and also," he looked pointedly at Aidric, "the Golden Mage."

Aidric lingered behind as the king's advisors and General Caith filed out of the room. "Nice speech," he said casually when the last person was gone from sight. "I bet they'll all be sleeping soundly tonight because of it."

The king chuckled and said, "I was going to welcome you back, but now I'm not so certain I should. You would do best to leave that kind of sarcasm at the door."

Aidric smirked. "The truth does sometimes sting, I'm afraid."

"Especially coming from your mouth," Diryan replied with a wry grin as he slapped Aidric heartily on the back. "Now come lad. Let us go to my study since I have a feeling that what you want to discuss with me must once again be done away from prying ears."

Aidric sighed, all traces of his earlier humor gone from his expression. "I have only been back a little over a sand-mark with news of at least one problem resolved, only to bring you the news of another arising."

"The girl?" he guessed as they both walked out of the Council Room and towards the stairs leading to Diryan's private chambers.

"Who else?" Aidric answered wearily.

"Then you have spoken with Maldon Felan, I presume?"

Aidric stopped dead in his tracks. "No, I *haven't*. I came straight to the Council Room to report. What's happened?" *Damn Roderick! I should have never had to leave her!*

"It's better that we wait until we are in my chambers before we discuss the matter further," the king said, and Aidric nodded, though inside he was bursting with impatience.

Once safely inside Diryan's study, Aidric wasted no time in spell-silencing the room against the all-too-eager prying ears of the servants. Diryan motioned for him to sit down as he, himself, took a seat. He poured wine into a couple of goblets and offered one to Aidric.

"I have a feeling we'll need this," the king said with a wry smile as Aidric gratefully accepted his cup.

"Tell me of Maldon," Aidric said after taking a couple of sips of wine.

"The morning after you left for Idona, Maldon came running to me with the most incredible story. Apparently, Allison had been caught in a Foresight dream and couldn't be awakened. While in her sleep, she drew power from the Mage-field, and Raya called for help since she was afraid that Allison would begin to recklessly cast spells in her sleep. Maldon and a few other mages came to her aid and cast the paralysis spell onto her. From what he told me, I understand that it took the combined efforts of all the mages just to cast that simple spell on her and hold it."

"But—but that isn't possible!" Aidric cried in disbelief. "She hasn't yet *Bonded* with the Mage-field!"

"I know," Diryan said worriedly, "but that isn't even the half of it. Maldon and Raya seem to believe that she was not having a Foresight dream at all, but something—else. In the dream, she claimed to have been witnessing the battle in Idona, and apparently you reacted to her voice when she yelled out a warning of danger to you—Aidric, what is it?"

Seni, Seni, it is *true,* Aidric thought, utter staggered. *It's just as I've feared. She has the ability described in that old spellbook, the ability only the Natian Six are said to possess!*

"*Aidric!*" he heard Diryan shout, tearing him away from his troubling thoughts.

"She has it," Aidric said urgently. At Diryan's blank stare he explained, "The power to *Soulwalk*—by the Thrones above, Diryan, she has it!"

"What!" Diryan boomed. "You are saying that you did actually *hear* her give warning to you in Idona?" He groaned when Aidric nodded. "My dear Seni, if she possesses the ability of Soulwalking, then that means—"

Aidric nodded reluctantly and said gravely, "Yes, the Prophecy of the Six. I did indeed hear her give warning to me, and that warning saved me from the end of a poisoned dagger when otherwise I would've been killed."

"Wait, wait," the king interrupted in exasperation. "You failed to mention any of this in your report earlier."

Aidric shrugged, undaunted by Diryan's accusative expression, and continued, "I saw no reason that your councilors should know about that uncanny situation. Think, Diryan. If I would have raised my suspicions that Allison possesses the power to Soulwalk in that Council Room, it would have accomplished nothing other than creating chaos that we just do *not* need at the moment. You know as well as I that fear does disturbing things to a rational mind."

"But the Prophecy of the Golden Mage never mentioned anything about the Golden Mage possessing the ability to Soulwalk!"

"Didn't it?" Aidric countered and then quoted, "'This mage will possess power such as no man has possessed...' It says it. You just have to read between the lines."

"I see your point," Diryan said with a sigh. "Why now? And why, oh why, me? Why did this have to happen during my reign?"

"Seni knows," Aidric replied, rubbing his temple. *Damn, I feel a headache coming on*— "The Prophecy of the Six is mainly the reason I wanted to speak to you in private. I wanted to ask your permission to take

Allison to see the Providencen priests. They know more about the Golden Mage lore than we do—I suspect a *lot* more than they are willing to admit—and perhaps they'll be able to shed some light on whether or not this is the age that the Prophecy of the Six will be fulfilled."

"You have my permission, of course," Diryan said, "but when are you planning to leave for this journey?"

"The sooner the better, "Aidric said firmly. "Tomorrow morning, if it's at all possible."

"I agree, but whether or not it's possible depends upon the girl."

"Why?" Aidric asked in alarm.

Diryan shifted in his chair nervously and answered, "It's because I ordered the healers to keep her sedated with—with *tangel.*" He held up a hand before Aidric could begin to protest, and explained, "Believe me, lad, I had no choice *but* to order it. After that morning when she drew all that power from the Mage-field, she became deathly ill—the healers said from channeling more power than her body was able to withstand. Then, to make matters worse, along with the illness, she began to have nightmares. From what Raya has been able to wring out of her, they were visions of war and death, but she refuses to elaborate any further. I ordered that she be given *tan-*

gel before she cracked."

"It's a wonder that she hasn't been driven mad already, given everything she's been through." Aidric abruptly sprung up from his chair and declared, "I must go to her at once. It's important that I rouse her from her stupor and prepare for the journey. The sooner we speak to the Providencen priests, the sooner I can begin instructing her."

Before Aidric could raise a hand to dismiss his silence spell, the king rested a hand on his shoulder. His eyes rapidly cycled through a stream of emotions that Aidric couldn't quite decipher before they finally hardened.

"Aidric, I'm well aware that your feelings for this maiden run more deeply than those of a teacher to his charge. I just want to warn you to be very careful, lad."

Not bothering to deny it, Aidric met the king gaze for gaze and asked slowly, "Then you— disapprove of what I wish to do?"

Diryan eyes softened, and he sighed as he squeezed Aidric's shoulder reassuringly before he said, "No lad, I do *not* disapprove of you pairing with the girl. I know how lonely you've been feeling of late, and I believe the maiden will be good for raising your spirits. I only want you to be careful, Aidric. *Both* of you are very special individuals, and you must never forget that."

"I know," Aidric said somberly. "I wish I could forget, but we all can't have everything we wish for, can we?"

"No, lad," Diryan agreed with a sad smile. "We cannot."

***

I'm still dreaming, Allison reasoned when she had felt a warm hand gently brushing a lock of hair from her forehead and had opened her eyes to see Aidric smiling down at her. *At least the nightmares are gone.*

"Come on, little cat, wake up," he coaxed gently. "I do believe you've slept long enough to last you a lifetime."

Blinking stupidly at him, she whispered, "Are you really back, or am I dreaming?"

He chuckled. "I most certainly hope you are *not* dreaming! I'm too exhausted to still be sitting on the back of a horse!"

Allison started to sit up, then blushed a fierce scarlet when she realized that she didn't have a stitch on. She quickly pulled the blankets up to her neck, and croaked, "Where are my clothes?"

"You had a fever, so the healers undressed you to try to lessen your body temperature," Aidric explained hastily as he reached over to grab a robe from the chair next to her bed. He handed it to her and said, "You shouldn't try to get out of bed just yet, but if you're uncomfortable, put this on. While you do that, I'll go and fetch you food and drink. You've been long without real subsidence."

Then before she could blink he was gone. With some difficulty, Allison managed to shrug on the robe. She felt so weak, and her muscles screamed with stiffness and soreness as if she had overdone a workout.

How long have I been asleep? she thought, remembering Aidric's earlier comment. *Surely I shouldn't be this weak and hungry even after I was sick.*

As she was stubbornly trying to drag herself out of bed to at least sit in the chair, Aidric returned with a tray heaped with food and a bottle of wine.

"I told you that you shouldn't be out of bed," he scolded. He set down the tray onto the chair and turned to glare down at her in disapproval. "Recovering from magical shock is no small matter. You could make yourself more ill, and right now we can't have that because you and I'll be taking a journey tomorrow morning if you are well enough."

Feeling guilty, Allison obeyed with a word of argument and settled herself back against the headboard. "Where are we going?" she asked as she eyed the food on the chair hungrily.

"I'll tell you later," he said firmly, following her eyes. "For now, you need to eat. Let's see if we can get some color back in your cheeks first."

He presented her with the tray, and Allison automatically reached for a piece of meat before she suddenly remembered that she still didn't know from what animal it had come from.

"Aidric," she said somewhat hesitantly, "I don't mean to be picky, but what kind of meat is this?"

He seemed to find her question extremely amusing, although he was trying very hard not to show it. Allison could distinctly see the laughter in his eyes even though his voice was neutral when he answered, "It's *ang*, derived from our main supply of livestock. I suppose you might not be familiar with our types of livestock. The animal is called an *antar*, and it's as large as a horse and has a white hide. Do you know what a horse—oh, good. I assure you that it's quite safe to eat. Our people have been feasting on its meat for centuries, and none of us have died from it yet!"

"You're making fun of me!" she accused, blushing in embarrassment.

"I'm sorry," Aidric said with a smile, looking not at all sorry. "I shouldn't, I know, since you are a stranger in our world. I promise to behave henceforth. Now, before you ask, the rest of the meat is mutton and venison, and they are derived—"

"I know where it comes from," Allison interrupted sharply. "We have deer and sheep on Earth, but as long as we're playing this Name That Food game, what's this?" She pointed at a piece of fruit that looked to be a cross between a peach and an apple. It was similar to a peach in its fuzzy texture and softness, but it was larger, shaped like an apple, and blood red.

"A *mitis*," Aidric said. "Very sweet and quite delicious. I recommend that you try it. Our best wines are made out of the juices of *mita*."

Allison daintily picked up a piece of *ang*, and with a look of uncertainty, she tore a small piece off and popped it into her mouth. To her surprise, it was quite good. It tasted very much like beef, but with a much richer flavor, as if it had been seasoned with a variety of exotic spices. Well aware that Aidric's eyes were on her, she began to eat more of it, pausing only to take a few sips of the wine he offered her and wondering if they used silverware at all since he hadn't offered her any.

She even tried the *mitis*, which was every bit as sweet as Aidric claimed it to be, with a mingled "greeny" flavor that reminded her of pine forests. It didn't taste even distinctively like any fruit she had ever eaten.

After a few moments of silence, Allison looked over at Aidric and said shyly, "I was afraid you wouldn't come back."

"What and miss the opportunity of a lifetime to instruct a living legend? Never!" he said with a lop-sided grin. She made a face at him, and he laughed and then said soberly, "Seriously though, if it hadn't been for your warning, I might not have returned with my life."

He was watching her closely.

"So, it wasn't just a dream, was it?" Allison said flatly, putting down the piece of bread she had been nibbling on. She had suddenly lost her appetite. "My God, Aidric, I *hate* being able to see the future! It scares me! Can't you just—turn it off somehow?"

Sighing, Aidric knelt down beside her bed, took her hands in his, and said, "I'm afraid I can't, little cat. Foresight is a gift given to you by Seni, and there are only two ways you can rid yourself of it. You must either damage your brain beyond that which the healers can repair, or Seni, Himself, must take the gift away. I can't shield it either because apparently, yours is an ability so powerful that it breaks through even *my* shields. Besides, even if I could, do you think something as trivial as a mortal's magical shield could obstruct what Seni wishes you to Foresee?

"Even when you're trained, you cannot prevent the images from coming to you. I share your Foresight ability, though obviously not as strong as yours, and I never know when I'll be overcome with a vision. Although it, at times, is troublesome, Foresight is very useful, and over the years, it has saved many lives."

"Like yours," Allison said with a nod.

"Ah, but what happened between us was *not* Foresight," Aidric explained with what appeared to Allison to be a touch of fear. "You weren't seeing the future but the *present*."

"But—but—" she sputtered, taken aback. "How can that be? Besides, I was asleep!"

"Asleep, awake, it doesn't matter," he said. "Our mage powers work when we are in either state of consciousness. However, yours is a power that no mortal has ever possessed in recorded history—the power of Soulwalking. I don't expect you to understand what that means when I, myself, don't fully comprehend it. That's why we are leaving tomorrow morning to see the Order of the Providence, for they know more about the Golden Mage than anyone. I don't know how to instruct you on how to control your power to Soulwalk, but I suspect they do."

He stopped, his expression suddenly turning both hesitant and distant, as though he had abruptly forgotten that she was even there and his mind was a million miles away mulling over a matter that greatly troubled him. *More bad news for me, I'm sure*, Allison thought bitterly.

"There's more," Aidric finally said a couple of minutes later.

"Isn't there always?" she noted resignedly.

Aidric nodded, his expression sympathetic. "I'm beginning to have my suspicions that something greater than your coming here is stirring in the wind, and it has me extremely worried. There is a prophecy, told over millennia probably, a prophecy that may or may not involve you."

"I don't understand—" Allison began before a *look* from Aidric made her fall silent again.

"You will in time," he assured her, "but for now, I can tell you this. The Prophecy of the Six is the foretelling of a possible ending of mankind, of a time when all six hells of Ter-ob, the dark plane, are aligned with the plane in which our world resides, and a mage has the power to Summon all the demons of each hell to overrun Seni's lands, demons with the power to Summon the dark god, Arioch, to our world, a being with the power to destroy Seni, Himself. I'm beginning to suspect, as do the twins, that the time of alignment is near and will occur sometime during our lifetime. This will be one of the things, among others, that I wish to discuss with the Providencen priests."

"You don't think that I'll be the mage who—" Allison said, her eyes widening with horror.

"No!" Aidric interrupted fiercely. "I *don't*, but if everything is as I fear it to be, then you'll be a *part* of it—as shall I and the twins."

Allison shivered at his tone, wondering for the thousandth time what she had ever done in a past life to deserve the fate in this one that had landed her right smack in the middle of this convoluted mess. *I almost wish that I was back home getting religion beat into me every day by Will!* Allison thought and then abruptly paused, startled by a realization. *Wait—I'm not supposed to remember anything about that bastard at all! I must've broken through those mental shields Aidric put in my head. Crap! What if I—*

"We'll leave by portal, of course," Aidric said, breaking her out of her panicky thoughts. "We can't possibly afford to delay your training any longer than necessary."

"A *portal?*" she all but squeaked. "Once was enough for me, thank you. The one that brought me here made me feel like I was experiencing death. That's something I don't care to experience again until my time comes."

"I assure you it'll be different this time," he insisted. "The first time you weren't aware that what you were experiencing was a journey through a portal. Besides, you aren't well enough to travel ahorse. It's a long and perilous journey. The Seers' abode lies high in the Calamon Mountains at the edge of our northeastern border. It's extremely difficult to reach by horse, thus we would have to walk several spans on foot along steep, icy paths to reach it. It would take us a half-moon at the very least to reach our destination, so you must agree that a portal is more sensible."

"Yes," Allison said reluctantly. "I admit that as terrible and weak as I feel right now, a half-moon trip riding and hiking up mountains doesn't sound like too much fun. There's also the little problem that I've never ridden a horse in my life."

"Truly?" Aidric said, surprised. "If you didn't ride horses, then how did you get around?"

"On my feet," she replied with a smile, "or I drove what we call in my world a 'car.' The best I can describe it is that it's sort of like a carriage, but instead of being pulled by horses, it's powered by a system of mechanical devices and fuel." At his puzzled look, she added with a shrug, "That's the best I can explain it. Your language lacks all the terms I would need for a more thorough job, and I really don't know the exact mechanics of how they work, either."

Looking thoughtful, Aidric muttered a few strange words under his breath, and Allison gasped when an object appeared in his hand from literally thin air. She was equally surprised to see, on closer inspection, that it was her wristwatch.

"How did you do that?" she asked, her eyes wide with wonder.

"Magic," he said simply with a shrug. "I'll teach you how it's done later. For now, can you tell me what exactly this is? Is this a 'mechanical device' as you say this 'car' contains?"

"Not exactly," Allison replied. "It's called a 'watch,' and we use it to tell time."

"And the bars within don't move with magical energy?" Aidric asked skeptically.

"I told you that we don't have real magic in my world. It's a form of energy that makes it run, but not magic. I suppose that it's useless to me here, so if you want to keep it, you can. King Diryan mentioned that the clothes of that French man who appeared in this world are in the archives of that kingdom. Since the clothes I came in seemed to have disappeared, I wouldn't doubt that someone took them to Lamia's archives. You might as well have the watch, too, for future generations to gawk at."

"It's really a quite clever idea," he said, more to himself than to her as he continued to frown down at it with a perplexed expression. "I'll give this to our mage-smith to study. Perhaps he will be able to devise a magical counterpart to it. It would be very useful, I think."

Aidric muttered another set of strange words and the watch banished just as quickly as it had appeared. Then he rose rather stiffly from his kneeling position and said, "I don't want to tire you, Allison, so I'll take my leave. I still have much to do before our journey tomorrow. I'll leave you to your meal, and then I want you to get some rest. A healer will arrive later on to examine you and to determine if you are well enough to go. I'll send Raya in shortly to keep you company, for I fear I'll return in only enough time to wish you pleasant dreams. From what I've heard, you'll need it."

Then before Allison could say another word, he was gone.

CHAPTER TWENTY-FOUR

D ressed in her apprentice uniform, Allison dubi-
ously eyed the portal Aidric had constructed
only moments earlier in the center of his sitting room
and sighed. How she wished that Raya was there to
lend her cheerful support, but no one was present to
see them off.

King Diryan had wanted to keep the whole trip
as quiet as possible to prevent unnecessary specula-
tion and panic. Only a handful of people knew they
were even going—Maldon, Raya, Selwyn, and the
twins—but they were all off on various assignments.
Diryan, of course, was presently occupied at the
Council meeting he had called the previous day.

I swore to myself that I would never go through one of

these things again, Allison thought irritably as she gathered up the pack Aidric had assembled for her and mentally began to prepare herself for the dreaded journey. *Now, here I am, seven days later and fixing to deliberately go through another one. God, I can't even keep my promises to myself!*

"Ready?" Aidric asked with a tired smile.

"No, but do I have a choice?" Allison replied wryly.

"Yes, we can always walk," he teased. "However, I prefer this method because right now I feel as though a herd of *antar* just trampled me."

"Are you going to be all right?" Allison asked him worriedly, thoughts of her own discomfort instantly forgotten as she eyed him critically. He *did* appear to be paler, although it was hard to see since his skin was already so pale. "Shouldn't we wait awhile and let you rest a bit before going through?"

Aidric shook his head. "I'll be fine. When you build your first portal, then you'll understand how I feel. The weariness in my body will vanish once it's had enough time to recuperate from the shock of channeling so much energy through it. We'll have plenty of time to rest once we reach the Seers' abode. Now come. Despite what you may believe, I can't hold this thing open forever!"

"Oh! Right...sorry," Allison said as she took a

hesitant step towards the shimmering, multicolored oval light and then stopped. She could feel her knees begin to shake with nerves as she turned to him and pleaded, "Can we please go in together? I know that I sound like a whining brat, but I—I don't think I can face going in there alone again."

"Of course," Aidric said gently and reached out to take her hand. "Now, hold on to your skirts!"

Then before she could begin to feel nervous again, he suddenly pulled her into the brightness and then there was only chaos. He was right. This time was not as frightening since she knew what to expect and especially since she could distinctly feel Aidric's presence, acting as her personal anchor, almost within her very being. It was warm, strange, and exhilarating all at once.

Her first time traveling within a portal had felt like an eternity. This time it seemed only seconds had passed before Allison was suddenly falling into Aidric's arms. She shivered as an icy wind immediately tore through the thin material of her dress.

"You need to work on your landing a bit more, little cat," Aidric said with a chuckle. "You almost earned yourself a face full of snow!"

"Snow?" Allison asked stupidly, clinging tightly onto Aidric's shirt and trying to find her bearings again.

For the first time, she really saw her surroundings and sucked in a sharp breath. True to his word, they now stood deep within a mountain range. Mounds and mounds of snow lay all around them, and not a single green thing was visible anywhere. Gray rock protruded here and there above the snow, but other than that, there was no color present anywhere. In this snowy landscape, they seemed to be the only life around.

It was no wonder that Aidric had insisted that she wear one of his cloaks. She now gathered it more closely around her body and shivered harder when an icy draft nevertheless found its way underneath again.

When she turned to look behind her, she gasped. An enormous, steep staircase carved out of the mountainside rose up before them. It stretched up until she could no longer see it as the clouds swallowed the mountain's peak. The stairs, themselves, seemed to sparkle with a golden light. *It almost appears to be—holy*, she thought, stunned.

"Beautiful, isn't it?" Aidric commented, noting her expression. "Yet, it's only an illusion. The staircase doesn't rise so high. Although the Providencen priests would like any visitors to think that this is the staircase to the Thrones, it's far from it. I suppose if I were to live out my life in this cold desolation, then I would construct something such as this just to amuse myself."

Shaking herself out of her reverie with some difficulty, Allison said, "It looks so out of place here. I mean, that golden light is the only color I see around here. Why is everything so dead? Are we so high in altitude that *nothing* can grow here? I don't feel lightheaded at all!"

"We are at the base of Death's Peak. Although we aren't as high as you may believe, it's still far too cold for anything to survive here. This peak was named well. We should probably go inside before our shoes start to freeze onto the path. They are expecting us."

Allison gazed one last time at the mystical "staircase to heaven" and wondered aloud as Aidric took her arm, "If this is only an illusion, then where is the entrance?"

"It's only partly an illusion," he said. "Come, and you'll see."

Puzzled, she allowed him to lead her towards the ethereal staircase, and then to her surprise, carefully up the stone steps. She started to say something but then changed her mind.

I give up trying to figure this world out, she thought in exasperation.

About halfway up, just when Allison was about to believe that the stairs *would* go on forever, Aidric suddenly stepped forward and walked through what had seemed like solid steps. She felt a slight tingling on her skin when she passed through the illusion. The bitter cold and snowy landscape were instantaneously replaced by the mouth of a monstrous cave and glorious warmth.

The cave was alive with sounds and color, a shocking contrast to the dreariness outside. The sound of water dripping echoed throughout the cave, as well as the gentle slapping of what was likely a stream against the rocks somewhere in the distance. Green and blue mage-flames illuminated the cave from suspended lanterns and torches along the walls of the cave. Shadows from the flames flickered about, giving the impression that many people were lurking behind every rock formation. Allison shuddered at the uncanny effect and instinctively moved closer to Aidric.

"A bunch of priests live in a place like this?" she asked in disbelief, her voice sounding hollow and appallingly amplified.

"Yes and no," Aidric replied with amusement. "This is merely the—visitor's chamber, if you will. No soul knows the exact location to the entrance to their abode. All I know is that it lies somewhere deep within the mazes of this cave."

"Then what do we do now?"

"We wait," he replied simply. "Our presence will be sensed by a member of the order and a guide sent. A confusion spell will be cast over us so that no matter how hard we try, we'll never find the true way on our own again. As I said, they are a very secretive order, and this is done merely as a precaution."

"We have long been expecting your arrival, Mage-general Aidric Stanisnik," a deep voice suddenly said behind them, causing Allison to start badly, yet Aidric seemed unperturbed by their visitor's abrupt appearance.

They quickly turned as one to face the owner of the voice, a tall, middle-aged man halfway concealed in the shadows, his dark hair just beginning to gray at the temples, dressed in an assortment of elegant silver and white robes lined with every precious jewel imaginable. At his neck hung a large, circular gold medallion that seemed to glow faintly with power. It was divided by deeply-etched lines into five equal sections, each containing its own strange symbol.

Allison shamelessly stared at this ominous figure, both in fascination and fear. Never had she seen a person look so—well, powerful. His steely green eyes matched hers gaze for gaze, forcing her to immediately look away nervously.

Aidric gave a slight nod of respect towards the priest and said, "Yes, I suspect you have, Seer Etain.

Seer Penrith most likely has told you much, and as usual, found it pertinent to tell us nothing."

Allison's eyes widened at the unmistakable sarcasm in Aidric's voice. She glanced up at the priest. *He's brave. I could never stare into those eyes and talk to him that way. I hope he wasn't insulted.* However, not only did Seer Etain not seem to mind the comment, it appeared as if he found it rather amusing.

Seer Etain smiled slightly and replied, "Indeed. I'm certain Brother Penrith had his reasons. Many of us have Foreseen your coming here to seek answers, and perhaps he did as well and thought it best to allow fate to run its course."

The Seer turned his attention once again to Allison, who struggled not to cringe under that intense gaze. Etain's eyes seemed to carry the knowledge of many secrets about her, which she found very unsettling.

"I see you have brought the Golden Mage to us at last," he said. "Never had I thought that I would live to see the day when legends were born."

"Her name is Allison," Aidric offered neutrally, although she knew that it bothered him for people to call her the "Golden Mage."

"Yes, yes, we have been hearing her name whispered among us over the years from knowledge gained by the study of ancient scrolls and by dreams," Etain said, "but I shall not delve into such matters with you here and now. It is for Master Kiryl to decide what will be revealed to you here today. Come. We have food and drink waiting, and after you have broken your fast, I shall take you to see Master Kiryl."

Aidric's neutral expression melted into surprise, making Allison even tenser. Seer Etain's offer of breakfast was the first thing that had made sense ever since they had set out this morning, so Aidric's unexpected reaction caused a multitude of alarm bells to start screeching in her head.

In the next second, Allison had her answer, and it had nothing to do with breakfast.

"Master Kiryl will speak to us, *himself?*" Aidric asked incredulously. "I have never heard of a single instance where he has spoken to an outsider face-to-face."

"The matter at hand warrants his and *only his* attention," Etain explained rather impatiently. "For this, he has made an exception. Now come."

Before they set off, Seer Etain placed a hand on both of their foreheads and instructed them to close their eyes. A split-second after her lids were closed, Allison felt a sharp jab in her head, unpleasant but not painful. When she opened her eyes again, she was surprised to see that nothing around her had changed.

"The spell causes you to forget the path you have taken after you walk it," Aidric said, answering her unspoken question. "The spell will lift only when we have returned to this spot."

Allison nodded and followed Etain without a word as he led them deeper into the cave. The farther they were within the cave, the closer the trickling of water seemed to be. Before long they came to a small stream of surprisingly clear water, which they crossed using a series of large, flat stones that had been placed in the water as a rudimentary bridge.

Allison could see small, white fish and what looked to be fish similar in appearance to trout swimming in the stream. Her mind told her that at this altitude and climate—not to mention in a freaking *cave*—it should be impossible to find a stream full of fish, especially trout, but she promptly told her mind to shut up as she hurried after the two men, afraid that she would fall behind and be lost forever in this maze of creepy caverns.

Before long they came to a huge door in the face of one of the cavern walls made entirely out of silver with more of those strange symbols she had seen on the Seer's medallion etched into it. Allison stared at the door in fascination, wondering what those strange symbols meant—then blinked in confusion when she suddenly found herself in a small chamber, seated on a wooden bench alongside Aidric.

What the—

"W-What just happened?" she croaked, glancing around wildly.

How had she gotten here? She had barely taken a couple of steps after Seer Etain!

The room, aside from the bench, was completely bare, instantly giving her the impression that it was some sort of jail cell. A thousand probabilities of why they had been put in the room flashed across her mind, none of them pleasant.

"The Seer's spell," Aidric said, reaching over to give her hand a reassuring squeeze. "You no longer remember anything from the moment we left the cave's entrance to the moment we were seated here. Etain has gone to fetch us our meal and will return shortly."

"I'll never get used to all of this magic craziness," Allison grumbled. "I *hate* knowing that someone can just make me forget a huge chunk of my life whenever it pleases them."

Aidric patted her arm sympathetically and said, "You'll grow accustomed to it more after I begin your lessons. I know it all seems so frightening and strange to you—it is so for all apprentices—but once you are in control of your abilities, this anxiety will pass, I promise."

"Why do you even put up with me?" Allison blurted out.

Aidric tilted his head at her with a look of mild confusion. "Why shouldn't I?"

"I've been nothing but trouble to you from the moment I set foot in your kingdom. You look ready to fall over with exhaustion, and yet, you bring me all the way up here when I'm sure you have more important things to take care of. Why would you want to take on another problem?"

"Come now," he chided gently, "you speak of yourself as though you were merely an object to be dealt with. When I found you, you were alone, frightened, and a mystery. I chose under my own free will to protect and teach you. What kind of man would I be had I just left you to struggle through the chaos of a new world without guidance?"

That was an opening if she ever saw one. Did she dare?

"Is that—is that the only reason why you took responsibility for me?" she whispered, afraid to hear the answer, but knowing she had to ask.

Aidric stared at her, his eyes questioning, though his shoulders had suddenly stiffened, betraying an underlying—suspicion? Understanding? However, before he could answer, the door suddenly swung open, and Seer Etain and another priest entered, carrying trays of food and drink. Aidric quickly turned his attention to them, looking a little relieved, and Allison silently cursed their timing.

"You must eat with haste," Seer Etain commanded, his tone a bit distracted. "Master Kiryl is most anxious to speak with you, Mage-general."

The Seer was frowning, his forehead wrinkled with worry, as he addressed them.

Something's happened, Allison mused as she half-heartily began to eat the food the priest had brought. She had long ago lost her appetite, but she ate anyway out of politeness. These strange priests were the last people she wanted to offend. She watched the priests self-consciously out of the corner of her eye, feeling their eyes burning into her.

Although they tried to remain passive, she could tell they were on edge and longed to be somewhere else. *Is it me that has them so worried, or does it maybe have something to do with that prophecy Aidric mentioned earlier?*

"*Perhaps we should go to Master Kiryl now,*" Allison suddenly heard Aidric say in her mind, almost causing her to cry out in surprise.

Damn him! I wish he would stop doing that!

"*Etain and Anvil are rather anxious to know what truth their master is to reveal to us,*" he continued, oblivious to her irritated thoughts, "*and they must wait until after our meeting as is their custom. I'm afraid they will drive themselves mad here with the anticipation."*

"I agree," she replied, shoving her tray away with relief.

Aidric rose, motioning for her to do the same. Etain and Anvil blinked at them in surprise, clearly expecting them to take far longer with their meal.

"The food is excellent," Aidric said, "but I really do not wish to keep Master Kiryl waiting. I know how unusual, how *rare*, it is that he would speak directly to those who come here to seek answers. Thus, we shall finish our meal after we have spoken to the Master."

"As you wish," Etain replied, clearly relieved and not bothering to try to hide it. "Brother Anvil will take you to the Master's chambers."

Aidric bowed towards Etain's companion in acknowledgment, and Allison followed his example awkwardly, bowing deeply before she remembered that women should curtsy. She blushed a deep scarlet and prayed that she hadn't embarrassed Aidric with her screw-up as much as she had embarrassed herself.

She sighed inwardly with relief as she followed Aidric's lead behind Seer Anvil, noting that Aidric didn't seem to have noticed her blunder. At least outwardly he gave no sign of noticing until she heard a soft voice brush across her mind, *"Don't blush so brightly, little cat. It doesn't suit you. A bow, a curtsy, what's the difference?"*

His words only caused her to blush more profusely, and Allison could hear his laughter echoing in the back of her mind although he never even cracked a smile.

"Stop reading my thoughts," she grumbled.

"Why bother to read your thoughts when they are clearly being expressed on your face for all to see?" he sent back innocently.

She chose not to honor that comment with a response, instead, turning her eyes from a face that mocked her with its passiveness when she knew that he was anything but, to her surroundings. Despite the grandeur of the place's outside appearance, the inside was surprisingly plain. The dwelling was completely devoid of anything personal—no decorations, paintings, or any trinkets.

The walls lay bare, merely the uneven surface of the cave, carved to their desire. The floors were oddly marble, however. To Allison, it seemed the only hint of human habitation in what was otherwise a natural, desolate place that was a more fitting home to a family of bats than an order of holy men.

Seer Anvil silently led them down a maze of narrow corridors. Shadows flickered along the walls from the lanterns that were magically suspended from the ceiling. The whole place had an uncanny feeling of foreboding that made her shiver. That feeling of dread strengthened the farther they trekked down the seemingly endless corridors. As her apprehension grew, Allison feared that she was not just letting the dire atmosphere of the place affect her imagination, but that she was on the brink of another Foresight attack.

"Aidric—I feel—" she began anxiously.

"I know," he interrupted. *"I feel it also. Whatever it is that Master Kiryl will reveal to us will not only greatly affect Lamia, but all of Seni's World."*

"How do you know?"

"You forget, I share your Foresight ability, only I have been trained to use it effectively and not allow it to control me as it controls you."

"What else do you see?"

Aidric turned his head slightly to glance down at her. The look he gave her was disconcerting, almost haunted. *"Many things—horrible visions that I suspect you have also seen."* Before she could get over her surprise, he added, *"Diryan has told me of your nightmares—ah, but we are here. We'll speak of this matter another time."*

No doubt they would.

Before them stood a great door of the purest gold that looked out of sorts in the dullness of the natural corridor. More of those strange symbols were carved into its surface, set in a pattern that suggested that it was part of an incantation or message of some sort.

"What do those symbols mean?" Allison asked, peering at the door curiously.

"They are words of Ti'ar, the language of magic used in all spells. What is written on the door is a spell to ward off all that is negative. No soul with evil intent can pass beyond this door."

"Will I have to learn this language, or can that Linguist put it into my mind like he did yours?" she asked.

"I'm afraid that you must learn this language on your own. Zenas doesn't have knowledge of Ti'ar because any who are not mages are forbidden the language."

She was about to ask another question when a strange voice abruptly cut into her thoughts, "Master Kiryl will see you now."

She started, then realized that it was Seer Anvil who had spoken. His voice was raspy as if with disuse, and she realized that it was the first time she had heard him speak.

What a desolate lot these priests are, she thought sadly.

The door groaned and screeched as Anvil slowly swung it open, signaling that it more than likely was not opened often. They were immediately greeted by darkness, and a faint, musty odor invaded her nostrils. Vaguely, Allison could make out the dim, green glow of a mage-flame barely visible in the far gloom. The darkness seemed to feed hungrily on that single light source as if it was alive, causing her to eye the room warily. She was thankful that she would not be going into that room alone.

Sensing her apprehension, Aidric firmly took her arm as they entered the impending gloom, for support or to prevent her from fleeing, she wasn't sure. Allison jumped when the door slammed shut behind them with a boom, leaving them to the darkness and the man who lay somewhere beyond. Silently, they headed towards the illumination. Allison hoped that Aidric knew where he was going. For all she knew, the room might be just another maze of corridors. She shivered to think of being lost forever in that hungering darkness—

"Easy, little cat," Aidric sent before that sudden thought could begin to feed her rising panic. *"There is nothing to fear here. There is only the dark and us."*

Despite his reassuring words, Allison clung nearer to him until they reached the light. She saw that they were now in yet another narrow corridor, but unlike the others, this one was relatively short. Another dimly lit room stood at the end, and in the center of the room, seated cross-legged on an assortment of cushions and surrounded by a dozen or so mage-flame lit candles, was the infamous Master Kiryl.

CHAPTER TWENTY-FIVE

T hese people sure love to be dramatic, Allison thought as she followed Aidric's lead to stand before the intimidating figure, this time remembering to curtsy and not bow.

In the blue illumination of the candles, Master Kiryl appeared otherworldly, as if he wasn't mortal but a god, himself. He gazed up at them serenely with the bluest eyes she had ever seen. They seemed to glow with their own inner light rather than being the uncanny result of reflected candlelight.

The Seer looked to be middle-aged, mid-forties maybe, though his entire manner seemed to suggest that he was far older in experience. Raven hair so far untouched by gray hung long and full to fall down in swirls around his knees.

He was dressed in a simple, unadorned silver robe that gave no indication of his high status among the order. The flickering of the flames played off eerily with the sheen of the *sholkie* material, causing the garment to appear to be slightly glowing.

About his neck hung the same medallion Allison had seen the other priests wearing. She couldn't help but think that compared to this man, Seer Etain was about as intimidating as a newborn baby. Even sitting down, he seemed to loom over her menacingly.

With a graceful wave of his hand, the Seer motioned for them to be seated onto the two *sholkie* cushions before him. Allison sank down onto hers gratefully, certain her wobbling knees would have given out on her soon.

"I have long awaited your coming," Master Kiryl began, his voice heavy with a strange accent that made it difficult for her to understand his words. His eyes flitted between Aidric and her so that she was not sure if he meant her or both of them. "Even as a child, when I was but a novice here, did I Foresee this meeting. I know the questions you have brought to us, as well you know why it is I who must give answer to them."

"Yes," Aidric said simply.

"Her arrival in our world was felt by all here," he

said, fixing his eyes onto her so intensely that Allison did not dare look away. "As I, myself, felt the tremendous increase in magical energy by her arrival, Seni blessed me with many visions of the near future. It is of those visions that we must speak of in order for your questions to be answered."

Aidric stiffened. "Then my fears are true," he ventured. "The Prophecy of the Six is to be fulfilled in this generation."

"Yes, the Prophecy of the Six," Kiryl replied calmly. "The coming of the Golden Mage was but one of two of the last stones cast into the lake of fate, and now the ripples it has caused have triggered that which Seni has forewarned. The cataclysm has indeed begun, and how it will end depends upon the path she is to follow now. Of that path, Seni has chosen not to reveal to me. It is for her, alone, to choose."

"As fate would have it, I have charged myself with her guidance," Aidric said. "Yet, of the special abilities she possesses, I know so little that it might as well be nothing at all. You, the foremost authority on the Golden Mage, I seek to know more of these abilities in order to properly instruct her. Nowhere in the Prophecy of the Golden Mage did it mention that she was to possess the ability to Soulwalk—the power which only the Natian Six are said to wield. The prophecy merely hints towards unknown abilities, thus we were unprepared for its manifestation. Tell me, Master Kiryl, do you have knowledge of the power of Soulwalking that exceeds what I know?"

Master Kiryl was silent for a long while before he answered, so long that Allison had begun to fear he wouldn't.

"Long ago," he began slowly, staring off into the darkness beyond them as though he was seeing those ages past, "when Seni's World was but one great, united kingdom, the kingdom of Natia, Seni entrusted a book to a young Seer named Aesir, the same Seer who is the originator of the Prophecy of the Golden Mage."

Allison turned to Aidric and saw surprise in his eyes. Had he not known this? It seemed strange to Allison that he didn't, since it was a prophecy that everyone in Lamia seemed to truly fear.

Master Kiryl also noted Aidric's expression with a nod and continued, "Yes, I trust you have always believed that the origin of that particular prophecy was lost in time or never revealed. It is what we of the Order of the Providence have led you to believe through the ages for reasons only our ancestors know.

"Now, this book contained all the special spells and their instruction of a legendary mage whom was yet to be named. It is written that this revelation drove Aesir mad. It is not clear all that Seni chose to reveal to him, but some say that he also held the knowledge of the war that ultimately destroyed the peace in Natia and the Prophecy of the Six, though it was never proven. Apparently, he had not been strong enough to bear the burden of knowing all mankind's future calamities, and thus, had failed in his duty as Seni's vessel.

"It is said that Aesir raved for days, ultimately lost in his madness. Fearing that he would harm others as well as himself, his brother Seers confined him within a mage barrier. Yet, he somehow broke free and disappeared, the book along with him, never to be seen again. He did, however, leave behind a scroll containing the verse we now know of as the Prophecy of the Golden Mage. He had written it before his visions drove his sanity away.

"There in that book lies the answer to all the questions you have of the power she wields. In all the millennia that have passed, the book has never been found, yet visions I have had have shown that the book still exists—where, I cannot even begin to guess."

"So it's hopeless to know exactly what she is capable of doing?" Aidric asked flatly.

"Not entirely," Kiryl replied. "In our archives,

our ancestors left documents which recount some of the ravings of Seer Aesir. One such document speaks of his ravings concerning the book, which he had allowed none to see. He spoke of offensive spells of such great destructiveness that it drove fear into the hearts of the Natians, who had yet to experience war or the sight of great magicks. It speaks of spells that had the power to break open the earth and to draw flaming boulders from the Thrones. It also speaks of an amazing ability which allows a mage to move freely throughout the world in spirit form. This ability, of course, is Soulwalking. Alas, the spellbook is lost, else the spell could have been a most powerful weapon in your struggle against the Mihran king, Roderick."

"Wait a mi-depth!" Allison burst out. "Are you saying that I have the power to make my spirit to travel *outside my body*? We actually do have *souls*?"

Her question seemed to disturb Aidric, though he only raised an eyebrow to show his displeasure. If Master Kiryl was also bothered, his expression gave no indication.

"Have you no spiritual beliefs, child?" the Seer asked, fixing her with those eyes that mirrored the flames around him.

"Of course I do," Allison said in a small voice. "It's just that I—I'm not as—sure about the existence of my god as you people seem to be about yours. I believe, but sometimes I do have my doubts."

Although he accepted her answer with a nod, his eyes were openly disapproving. "Indeed, we *do* have souls, child," Master Kiryl said firmly. "I know not of your deity, but I assure you that Seni does exist as surely as we now sit in this room."

Allison stared down at her hands, feeling somewhat ashamed by her words. She felt that she had offended him, but what really bothered her was that Aidric looked even more upset by her words. "I didn't mean to be—if I offended you, then I'm really sorry. I have a bad habit of saying things I shouldn't."

"You are not of our world and could not possibly share our beliefs," the Seer reasoned. "Thus, I took no offense of your words. Tell me, why is it that you find it so difficult to accept the ability to Soulwalk when you have already used it once before?"

Allison's head shot up, and she stared at him in sudden fear. The thought of having that kind of freaky ability frightened her, and she had hoped to keep what she had done earlier from him lest he suggest that she try to do it again. Apparently Kiryl had other plans.

"H-How do you know I've u-used it before?"

she stammered.

"That is of no importance," he replied offhandedly. "What *is* important is that you *have* used this ability, and you must continue to use it."

"But—but—I don't know how I did it!" Allison cried. "I was *sleeping*, and I thought that it was a dream. When I called out to Aidric with my warning, I had no idea that he actually heard me!"

"Then you must learn," Kiryl said sternly, ignoring the hysteria in her voice. "It is prudent that you discover the power you hold within—this I have Foreseen, for you are indeed the third sign Seni has sent us in warning that the melding of the two worlds is near. It is our duty to protect all Seni has wrought, and our failure means the destruction of all mankind."

"Please," Allison pleaded, her eyes beginning to swell with tears, "I don't understand any of this."

Aidric took ahold of her right hand and squeezed it reassuringly, but even that seemed to comfort her little after hearing Kiryl speak of her "duty" in matters that she didn't understand. *This is madness*, she thought frantically. *The end of the world—prophecies—magic—it's all madness!*

"Child, know you not of the Prophecy of the Six?" she heard Kiryl ask, distant as if he had spoken from a memory.

Her mouth was suddenly dry, and when she answered him, it was all Allison could do just to get the words past the huge lump in her throat. "I know some, Master Kiryl, but only the little that Aidric tried to explain to me. I didn't understand any of it then, either."

"Then we shall ease your confusion," he said. "Know you any of the history of the kingdom of Natia and what befell it?"

"No."

"Then we shall begin there."

The Seer folded his hands and laid them onto his lap as if the story he was about to tell was a long one. He stared deeply into her eyes for a long while, maybe trying to read what lay hidden within, until Allison cast them down nervously.

"You flee from the truth," he commented after a few seconds of uncomfortable silence. Her hands suddenly became very fascinating. "However, truth is what you seek, thus the chaos that I sense within your soul. Listen well, Allison McNeal, for within the words I shall speak, you will find the answers your soul hungers for."

Allison raised her eyes and blinked at him stupidly, more confused now than ever. *Truths—what truths? And, did I even tell him my name...*

"When Natia was the sole kingdom under the

Thrones," Kiryl began, "mankind lived peacefully, and war was a word which had never crossed their lips. This kingdom stretched far across the lands, its populous numbering greater than anything you could imagine. However peace, as we all know, cannot last among mortals, especially in a kingdom so great.

"As it happened, twin sons, Reznik and Rhan, were born to the king, possessing unusually powerful mage abilities. Both brothers were ambitious and held greed for power within their hearts. They grew up rivals, and when their father was killed while on the hunt under suspicious circumstances, though it was never proven that his sons were responsible, the battle began for the throne.

"Understand that this was a time before the existence of Mage-fields. Now, you may ask where then did mages draw their power from? Every living thing consists of energy, thus constantly expelling energy. It is from this residual energy in the air that a mage drew from. Mind you, none were more powerful than the weakest of present-day mages, so you may well imagine the stir the birth of the twins caused. Power such as they were capable of wielding was simply not seen, thus they were greatly feared, more so when their father died.

"Factions quickly developed within the kingdom, those who sided with Reznik and those with his brother, eventually dragging Natia into a civil war. Thus, the kingdom split into three nations—Marzina, Masia, and Jadwiga. Reznik held power over Marzina and Rhan over Masia, driving their personal forces against each other, a savage slaughter of men who knew nothing of fighting for a throne which each thought was rightfully his and his alone.

"Then there were those of Jadwiga, who chose to side with none, horrified by what had become of their peaceful kingdom and wanting nothing of war. For a year, they hid in their homes in fear as the swords clanged and the very world seemed to rock on its foundation as the twins cast spell after spell against each other. Many innocent lives were lost in the chaos, in battles, or from starvation, for many feared to leave their homes. This war threatened to destroy all of civilization."

Kiryl paused in his tale and looked pointedly at Aidric. Aidric stared back, unmoving, unblinking, and for the life of her, Allison could not figure out how he could maintain such a steady composure in the presence of this priest.

"This," Kiryl continued, "which I am to speak of henceforth, not even you, Mage-general, have knowledge of."

"Why does that not surprise me," Aidric replied dryly. "Today I'm learning that there is indeed much your order has chosen to keep hidden from the whole of mankind."

"All for good purpose, young one, I assure you," Kiryl said undauntedly, choosing to ignore Aidric's accusative tone. "Now, to my tale—finally, in desperation, those who sought peace sent six men into the wilderness far beyond the borders of the three nations, away from the madness that was spreading like a plague hungry for flesh to devour, to meditate and plead to Seni to deliver them from their torment. When the six men returned after a half-moon, the Jadwigans were shocked to discover that they had undergone a tremendous change. Seni had answered their prayers, but not as they had expected.

"This world, Seni created solely for mankind to dwell upon alone beyond the celestial thrones of His divine kingdom with very little intervention from Him. Why? It is simply beyond a mortal's comprehension. Our ancient ancestors simply did not know that Seni left the fate and affairs of mankind completely to mankind. They had thought Seni to strike the twins dead. Instead, these men became His weapon, returning no longer mortal and wielding the powers of Seni, Himself.

"Together, they confronted the twins and gave them an ultimatum—either they cease their fighting and rule peacefully together, or by the will of Seni, they would be destroyed. The brothers laughed at their warning, for they did not know that the hand of Seni had touched their confronters' souls, and refused to yield. Hate and greed had been a resident in their hearts for far too long for them to forget their differences and make right their wrongs. Instead, they turned their power onto the six men to rid themselves of what they believed to be merely a nuisance so that they may return to their power struggle.

"As you may well imagine, Reznik and Rhan were shocked to discover that their magic had no effect on the men. In a panic, they attempted to flee, but they were easily caught and imprisoned within a circle of magic so powerful it could not be penetrated. This circle drained them of their life-force and created the first Mage-field of their life energy.

"The Jadwigans, having witnessed this unnatural battle, cowered in terror in the presence of these men who had been their brothers, husbands, fathers, and sons only a few days earlier. They were like gods, themselves. The people fell to their knees in worship, but this dismayed the six. They explained to the people that they had not been made gods by Seni, but protectors of mankind. Seni had given them immortality and god-like powers—but at a price. They must live apart from all mankind, watching over them throughout the ages, and never would mortal eyes behold them again until mankind once again threatened to destroy itself.

"Before they departed, a prophecy was revealed to the people, one that told of the possible ending of mankind, triggered by the actions of a mage who harbored no love in his soul, only darkness much as the twins had. However, before this was to come to pass, Seni offered to give mankind a chance to save itself by uniting as one as Natia had once been to battle the evil this mage would set free in the world. His only aid would be the sending of five signs to warn that the time is at hand when the worlds of light and darkness are aligned on the same plane and demons from all six hells of Ter-ob may be Summoned simultaneously to walk our lands, demons with the power to Summon the ultimate dark god, Arioch, onto our plane whose goal is to destroy Seni, Himself.

"Now, four of these signs are first, the coming of mages which possess powers beyond those of any mage living under the Thrones, the other, the deciding factor of which fate will most likely befall us. The first three have already transpired. The first was the birth of twins who wielded the power of the bardic-mage. The second was the birth of a mage more powerful than had been seen in ages. The third was the coming of a mage of legends. As for the fourth sign," he looked pointedly at Allison, "the downfall of a great kingdom, it depends solely upon the Golden Mage. As I have said, I cannot Foresee the path she will take. Whichever kingdom falls, be it Lamia or Mihr, the success of preventing the destruction of mankind depends upon that fall. I need not voice which fate will bring mankind the more hope."

Don't put any pressure on me or anything, Allison thought bitterly.

"And the fifth sign?" Aidric whispered, so softly that Allison almost didn't hear him.

Master Kiryl smiled and answered, "Ah yes, the fourth warrior, a name unknown beyond the boundaries of our abode, and also the fifth sign. Have you not guessed by all I have revealed within my tale?" Before Aidric could nod or shake his head, Kiryl plowed on as if he had never asked the question. "The last sign is, of course, the return of the Natian Six, Seni's immortal weapons."

Aidric whistled softly. "It's no wonder your order has kept the last sign a secret. The Natian Six are beings that we know little about and through the ages have been taught to greatly fear because of what they represent. But tell me, Master Kiryl, why didn't you reveal this last sign to Keldan, Aren, or me sooner? Was it not necessary for *us* to know?"

"It was not the right time until now, impatient one," Kiryl answered matter-of-factly. "I do as Seni commands, and it was by His will that I should not reveal the knowledge of the fifth sign until he deemed it to be the proper time."

Allison barely heard the conversation between the two men. Her mind was instead on the names of the three nations that Natia had become, names that seemed vaguely familiar to her but couldn't imagine where she had heard of them before this. A sense of foreboding washed through her as she thought of the names, trying to put her finger on where she knew them from. The feeling screamed out to her that these were dangerous thoughts and a path that was best left unsought.

She immediately cleared her mind of those troubling thoughts to find that Kiryl was once again staring at her as if he had knowledge of every secret she harbored even in the dark corners of her soul.

He knows what I was thinking, she thought suddenly, feeling the hair behind her neck start to rise as she mutely returned the stare. *God help me, he knows something about me, some secret that maybe I don't even know myself, yet all he does is stare at me with that damned knowing look in his eyes. What is it? Do I dare ask him?*

So many secrets, so much she didn't understand about this world, about what she had become, even about Aidric who seemed to carry his own aura of mystery about him. Would there be an end to it all, or was she cursed to be the pawn in some preternatural game in which an alien god commanded her every move, for good or ill, for the rest of her life?

Prophecies, myths, legends—she had once been really interested in such things. Allison never thought that she would end up as one, and now as she stared into the eyes of Master Kiryl, she wondered why she had ever thought they were fun and exciting.

"Truths, child," Kiryl spoke suddenly. "Only when you find them will the turmoil within your soul cease to torment you. Aidric Stanisnik will guide you with his teachings, but it is ultimately *you* who will discover them and use them to choose which path fate has sent you to walk upon. I know your mind. You long to be released from that which you have been destined to decide, but it cannot be so. Seni has *chosen* you. Now go, and remember well what I have said today. Remember and learn what you must, for the time of decision is nearly upon us."

ABOUT THE AUTHOR

C.G. Garcia lives in a small West Texas town whose claim to fame is having the world's largest Rattlesnake Round-Up. She has a degree in computer science, but due to life's twisted sense of humor, ended up working in a pharmacy. A lifelong lover of all things fantasy, science fiction, paranormal and romance, she is also the author of the *Fractured Multiverse* urban fantasy/science fantasy series and the *Old Souls* epic fantasy series.

THE MAN WITHIN
THE TEMPLE
The Golden Mage Book Two

Depressed and overwhelmed by learning the true meaning of her destiny as the Golden Mage as well as the major part she, along with Aidric, Keldan, and Aren, will play as foretold within the Prophecy of the Six, Allison despairs of ever picking up the pieces of her shattered life. Then to add insult to injury, the Temple of Seni sends representatives to Lamia to collect her in order that she may swear oaths to Seni as is required by divine law. The party is led by Eban, a Domnae full of an infinite amount of ambition and utterly despised by Aidric for reasons he refuses to confide to anyone.

However, though suspicious of his motives, Eban's the least of her worries as going to the Temple means leaving the protection of Lamia's Shield with very little mage training under her belt at a time when hostilities with Mihr are at their highest, and rumors of a spy planted within the palace by Roderick have begun to arise.

The wheels of fate are turning ever so quickly, and Allison feels the threads of her life becoming helplessly and dangerously entangled within its spokes, even more so now as she is exposed to the politics of the Temple, itself.